Secret Seekers Society

and the

BEAST OF BLADENBORO

J.L. Hickey

Black Rose Writing | Texas

ISBN: 978-1-68433-067-6
PUBLISHED BY BLACK ROSE WRITING
www.blackrosewriting.com

Printed in the United States of America
Suggested Retail Price (SRP) $18.95

Secret Seekers Society and the Beast of Bladenboro is printed in Palatino Linotype

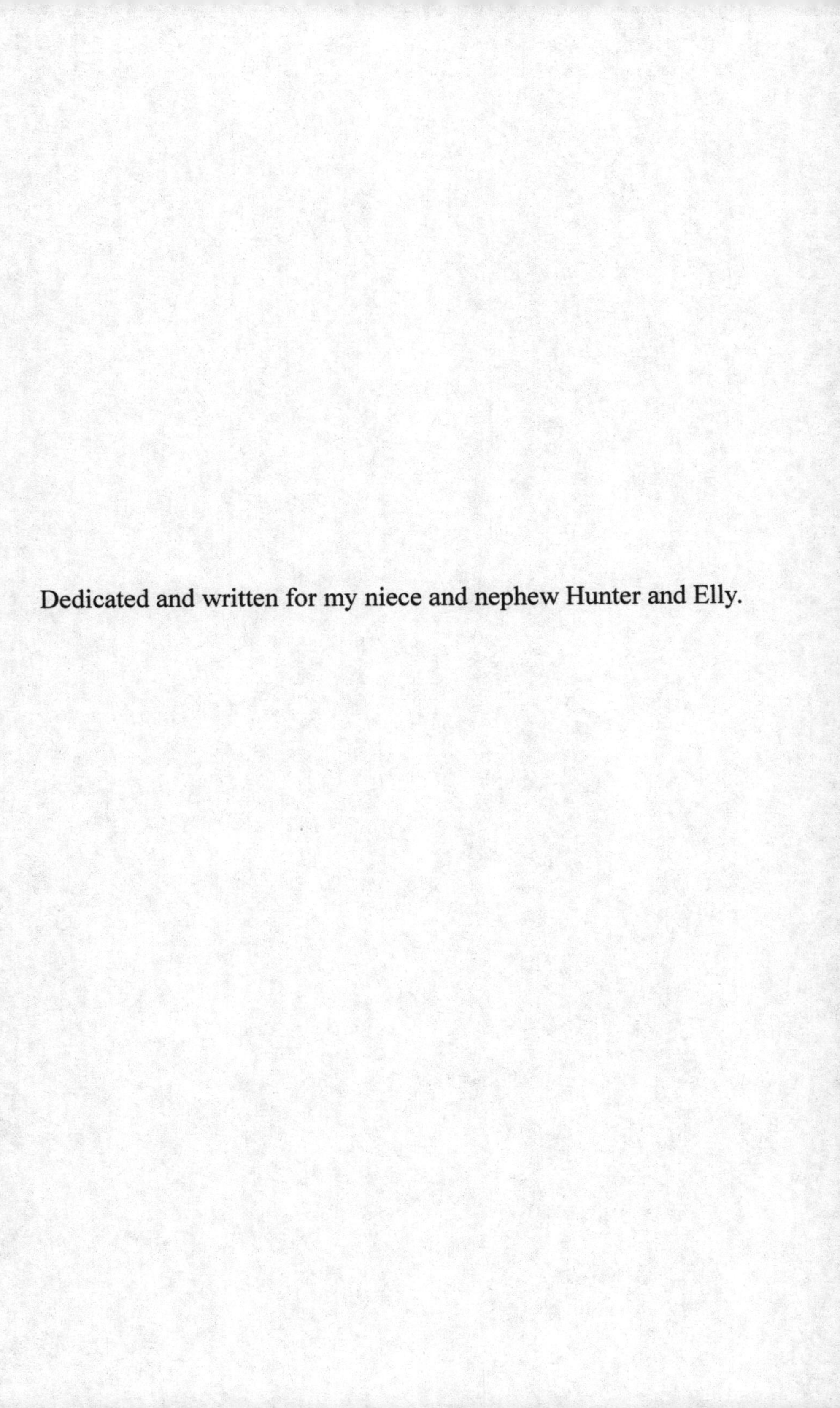

Dedicated and written for my niece and nephew Hunter and Elly.

Secret Seekers Society

and the

BEAST OF BLADENBORO

Chapter 1
A Mansion Full of Secrets

Hunter pushed his glasses tightly against his nose, a nervous habit he had picked up from his mother. He had sat in the back of the old musty taxicab for nearly three hours not muttering a single word to the wrinkle faced cabdriver who smelled of burnt cigarettes and coffee. Alongside him sat his younger sister, Elly Anne, who was equally as quiet, which in her case was a rare oddity. Elly had a fascination with attention, especially when she was at the center of it. Any normal day would see the two siblings arguing over who deserved more of the back seat, or who got to choose what radio station to listen to. It was very unfortunate for the children that from that moment on; there would not be any more *"normal days."*

The children were two years apart, Hunter the eldest of the two at thirteen years old. He was small for his age with a slender frame. He had messy dark brown hair with eyes a shade darker, a spitting image of his father. Elly was the polar opposite of her brother when it came to looks. She took after her mother with fair skin and auburn red hair, with a few sparse freckles spread across her face.

The taxicab wound its way through a nasty storm down a muddy country road. Hunter peered out the passenger side lost in a daze of melancholy, as raindrops the size of quarters fell onto the windows. Lightning streaked through the dark sky, briefly illuminating the overcast roadway, the thunder making Elly jump in her seat. She never was one to like storms.

The ominous weather was fitting for the siblings' current mood. Hunter and Elly welcomed the raging storm; if anything, it was a small distraction from the current dark reality that summed up their lives.

"Well," the cab driver tried to break the awkward silence, "…not sure where it is you two are going. The directions they gave me sure aren't taking us down the beaten path. I don't think there's a paved road for miles 'round these parts."

Hunter didn't reply, he preferred the silence. Elly also ignored him, quietly humming an old tune her mother used to sing her to sleep, making it apparent she wasn't interested in any type of conversation with the strange man. It had been a long drive already, the only thing keeping the cabdriver awake was his trusty mug filled to the brim with coffee.

"Most kids I know never want to shut up." The man chuckled to himself, taking a cautious sip. "I have two kids of my own about your ages. They go on about everything. You kids haven't said squat in over three hours."

"Our parents are dead." Elly explained, doing her best to void herself of all emotion.

"Er… oh…" The driver stammered, slightly choking on his coffee. "I'm sorry… I didn't know."

"So, now we're being sent off to some stranger we've never met, to our *new* family," Elly rolled her eyes.

"Well…" The driver mumbled. A sudden flash of lightning illuminated the dreary sky once again, a thunderous boom sent vibrations through the dusty old cab. The driver jumped in his seat, spilling his coffee all over his lap.

"Damn it!" the steaming hot coffee soaked into his jeans. "Great…"

"Shut up, Elly," Hunter shifted his body away from hers towards the window. His eyes swelled up with tears as he stared blankly at the passing forest.

"It's the truth," she shot back. "They're dead! Deal with it."

"Well, how about some music, aye?" the driver tried to calm the mood. His chubby fingers quickly turned the radio knob. He fiddled with the buttons until some old-fashioned music chimed in. The children went quiet, not muttering a word.

It was another hour down the muddy road when the taxicab crept up a rather steep hill. When they reached the top a large eerie-looking building came into view. Hunter's eyes widened at its immense size.

"Elly, what is that?" Hunter's mouth fell open.

"It looks like a creepy castle," she replied.

"That, children," the driver answered, also a bit taken aback by the building, "I'd wager is our destination."

The structure sat in the midst of the dark forest, alone with no signs of civilization around for miles. It appeared that the muddy road leading off the main interstate, hours back, was its only entrance. The rest of the building's grounds were covered in thick, impenetrable foliage. The main complex stood seven stories high with elegant stained-glass designs windows on every level of the building. It was definitely old, from their vantage point, the Exterior of the building look decrepit, worn down.

It was bigger than any building the children had ever seen, even larger than the local hospital where Hunter had stayed two summers ago when he broke his arm playing street ball. The estate didn't house only the mansion. There was an entire estate with numerous sub-buildings placed throughout the grounds. There was a vibrant greenhouse that looked abandoned from the outside, but peering through its glass structure would show it was beaming full of flora inside. From the outside looking in the entire estate looked abandoned, overrun with weeds and vegetation. Even the main building had let Mother Nature run its course; long vines twisted, curling all the way up to the seventh-story windows. Large patches of vegetation had overgrown the mansion's approach; the naked autumn trees decorated the massive lawn with their fallen autumn leaves.

"We're living in an abandoned castle?" Hunter asked. "Who's going to take care of us?"

"Well, I don't know about it being abandoned," said the driver. "But I assure you whatever that building is, it aint a castle. I bet you, it's some old rundown mental institution. Ya know, back in the late sixties, they'd send crazy old coots and serial killers to these types of out-in-the-middle-of-nowhere places," he went on with excitement. "About three hours' drive south of the interstate, there's that famous penitentiary that's haunted. Yep…" the driver went on despite the fear in the children's eyes, "…bunch of crazy stuff happened in those old buildings back then. I'd put my life savings on it, this building has some dark history. Electric therapy, lobotomy, they did crazy things to those people. I guarantee it!"

The taxi finally came to a slow stop at the end of the winding path. A large stone fence surrounded the estate's land, blocking them from driving any closer to the mansion. It wasn't much of a fence in the traditional sense; it was more of a huge, thick stone wall that stood fifteen feet high with razor wire running along the top of it. This was the only entrance into the estate's grounds. A large iron cast gate blocked off the group's entry into the compound. Alongside the entrance sat two giant gargoyles perched atop ten-foot-tall monoliths. Etched from granite, the winged creatures looked like they came from the gates of hell, with sparkling bright ruby-red eyes that shot a sense of fear into the children's hearts. They looked all too real, as if during the moonlit nights they magically turned to real, living, breathing gargoyles.

"Yep," the driver shifted his taxi into park, "this here's the place." He looked back over the driver's seat with a smile.

"Seriously?" Elly responded in disbelief, her lip curled in anger.

"A mental hospital?" Hunter questioned.

The wrinkle faced driver stepped out of the taxicab directly into a large mud puddle. He groaned, cursing under his breath, the cold water soaking through his shoes. He slammed his door shut with a deafening thud that rattled the entire cab, and walked around to the rear of the vehicle and popped the trunk open. He then gathered the children's things together and tossed them onto the roadside.

"There is no way he's serious," Elly shot a frightened look at Hunter.

"I don't think anyone even lives here. He must be pulling a prank on us," he replied.

"Well, it's not funny," she added. "I'm not getting out of this car."

The driver opened the back door, letting the cold damp air hit the kids' faces; it stung their cheeks for a split second. Their bags sat out in the rainy driveway awaiting them. The driver smiled, holding out his hands to help the kids out. Hunter brushed the man's friendly gesture aside and stepped out, tightening his long scarf around his neck. Elly frowned at the man, crossed her arms defiantly looking the other way.

"Come on now, you can't stay in my cab." He had a stern look on his face that didn't sit well with Elly. She let out an annoyed sigh as the man helped her out of the back of the musty cab.

"It's gettin' close to winter, at least the snow held off. I'd hate to make that drive back on this dirt road in the middle of a blizzard." The man slammed the car door.

"What do we do now? There's no one here." Hunter picked up his two large suitcases, not knowing what to do next. He didn't feel comfortable waiting in the freezing rain outside of a scary looking castle.

"I miss Mom and Dad." Elly's eyes watered. "I want to go home…"

"I don't need this," the driver moaned, feeling inherently bad that he was angry at having to take care of the two lonely children. "I don't get paid enough as it is; I don't want to sit around and babysit you two," he murmured under his breath, knowing he didn't have the heart to actually leave the children out in the rain alone in the midst of a forest.

"Hello? Anyone around?" the cabdriver yelled. "Hey! Anybody?" Turning to the kids he shook his head.

"You can't leave us out here… right?" Elly protested.

"I'm not that cold hearted, kid," he shot back. "I'll stick it out for a little while, but if no one comes soon, I'll have to drive you back and charge you double."

Hunter groaned, dropping his luggage onto the muddy earth. He took a seat on a large stone in front of one of the gargoyle monoliths. At least the rain had subsided to a slight drizzle he thought to himself.

"Did they tell you kids who you were meeting up here?"

"Our godparent," Hunter replied, tossing a stone into a nearby puddle.

"Professor Calenstine," Elly added. "We've never met him."

The three of them waited silently for some sort of sign, anything at all, that told them the creepy mansion was inhabited by someone… anyone. They spoke no words, emitting random sighs of annoyance. A half-hour passed before the wrinkle faced cabdriver was about to give up and drive the children back.

The loud thundering noise of a helicopter broke the silence of the forest. The kids stood up from their stony seats to see a jet-black helicopter hovering over them. It was quite low to the ground; so low that all the wet leaves littering the ground around their feet blew forcefully from beneath them. The cabdriver held onto his musty old hat as the helicopter made its way over the large stone fence, landing near the large mansion.

"Well, it's about time," the driver yelled over the loudness of the rotor blades. Even being a little way off, the noise of the helicopter was still quite deafening.

"I have never seen one up close before," Hunter said. "Cool!"

"Who's getting out of it?" Elly and Hunter both pressed their faces in between the iron bars of the gate with excitement.

Three well-dressed men in black suits came out of the helicopter first, distinguishing between the three was impossible for the children at that distance, they seemed to be faceless suits. The three men didn't rush off; instead, they waited as a fourth elderly man was lowered from the aircraft's side door in a wheelchair. The elderly man had a small dog resting on his lap, covered by a blanket to protect it from the fierce cold. One of the men pushed the wheelchair away from the landing pad towards the house. The other two men helped a woman down from the helicopter before rejoining the pilot, swiftly lifting off once again. The helicopter flew off into the distance, its loud rotor blades slowly fading off into the horizon.

By this time, the suited men had maneuvered the old man, and his dog, into the comfort of the giant mansion. The woman hurried her way towards the children.

"I wonder if that's the professor," Elly said.

"Maybe," Hunter replied, but it wasn't who he had pictured as his godparent. He thought of a man his father's age, strong with big shoulders, not some woman.

"She has red hair like me!" Elly smiled brightly as the woman drew nearer, allowing the children to make out her appearance. She was in her mid-fifties with a round friendly face that beamed a friendly smile towards them. She was still a few yards away from the iron gate, but the children could already tell that she seemed quite happy to see them. She had a full figure but walked with prominence in every step. She wore a bright green overcoat and a pointy hat with a wide circular brim. Hunter thought she looked like a colorful witch, albeit a friendly one.

"Children!" she yelled now only a yard away from the gate. "I am so very sorry for the wait! I do hope it wasn't too long?" She smiled as she pulled a large rusty key from the bulky turquoise purse dangling at her side. The children had never seen such a key, a solid foot in length, when she inserted it the iron gate made a loud mechanical churning noise. "You can never be too safe, am I right?" She grunted softly for a brief moment as she put her weight into swinging the gate open.

"Oh heavens," she panted. "I forget how heavy this blasted thing is; we don't use it much you see."

"Well it's about time, lady," the driver said, tipping his hat to her. "I was about to drive off with them; we've been out here in this murky weather for a long time."

"Well, thank you, kind sir." She handed the man a few folded up bills, waving him off, barely paying attention to him. "That will be all."

"Nice to meet you too," he grumbled, pocketing the cash. He cursed under his breath once again, making his way back to the cab. His tires kicked out some rocks as he sped off down the road.

"You must be Elly?" The lady gave an elaborate bow.

Elly smiled at the gesture.

"This is my brother, Hunter," Elly replied.

"I have heard much about you both. I'm very pleased to meet you." She waved her hand towards the mansion. "Oh, where are my manners? My name is Patricia Ellingbee."

"You're not Professor Calenstine?" Hunter asked.

"Oh, heavens no, I am merely the caretaker of our lovely mansion." She stopped for a second during their long walk towards the entrance. "Welcome to the Belmonte Estate!"

"It's kind of scary," Hunter frowned as they passed by a large eerie oak tree that seemed to be alive.

"Yes, we get that a lot," Ms. Ellingbee chuckled. "Our estate is not without its wonderment, for those who know we exist that is, and I assure you, that's not many." She winked at the children.

"This is really weird," Hunter whispered to Elly, making sure he spoke low enough that the friendly Ms. Ellingbee couldn't hear.

"At least she's nice," Elly whispered back.

"It's a bit of a walk from the entranceway, I know. The estate is rather large."

"Is the giant castle where we'll be staying?" Elly asked.

"Oh yes, Belmonte Manor: constructed in 1886 with renovations ongoing for the last century. We're constantly upgrading; a lovely and warm place it is. I think you will like it."

"Does Professor Calenstine live here?" Hunter added.

"You could say that," she replied. They finally made their way up to the large stone steps that led to the giant main doors of the mansion. "You will meet your godfather soon enough, but until then, I have been given the honor of getting both of you set up and comfortable with your new living quarters. The room we have saved for you is quite spacious, and I am sure you will find it very accommodating."

Elly stood before the giant doors in bewilderment; she felt like an ant peering up at the towering threshold. The large oak doors were over twenty feet tall, made of thick wood and dense iron. Hunter joined her in the amazement, his mouth fell open, staring at the peculiar sight. They were no average doors, beautifully decorated with elaborate designs etched meticulously into the oak. There were pictures of wild animals, some Hunter could recognize, wolves, gorillas, although both animals were strangely standing upright, bipedally. There were other animals that were a bit more mysterious to him, like the half-man half-horse figure guarding a chest, or the large animal with the body of a bat and the head of goat wielding a trident. Both doors were covered in these mysterious designs, every single inch of them.

"We don't use the front door often, a bit tricky these buggers are; they feel like they weigh a ton too." She felt around the left-hand door until her hand covered up one of the many designs; this particular one was of a five-pointed star that stood about waist high from the ground.

"You'll come to learn all sorts of secrets here," said Ms. Ellingbee. Each of her fingers now covered one of the points of the star. She pressed it with the palm of her hand, the star sunk deep into the door. Hunter thought it was like some sort of secret switch. She turned the sunken star design to the left. Hunter was amazed, a smaller door hidden inside of a giant door.

"Here we go, a bit easier to open and close when the door doesn't weigh a couple of hundred tons." Ms. Ellingbee held the door open for the two siblings.

They entered a large room completely void of any light with the exception of a small amount of sun creeping in from the entrance. That little speckle of light quickly vanished as Ms. Ellingbee closed the smaller door tightly behind her. The children now stood surrounded in darkness, their hearts racing a mile a minute.

"Sorry, madam!" a friendly woman's voice echoed from deep inside the room. "We went lights out. I need to flip the master switch still."

There was a loud click, followed by a strong electrical buzzing. The main corridor of the mansion's first floor flickered briefly, allowing the children short glimpse of its mysterious decor. "Needs to warm up a bit, stay put," said the cheerful voice. A few seconds later the bright lights all came buzzing to life, burning Hunter's eyes temporarily.

"There we go, children. Is that better?" Ms. Ellingbee asked.

Hunter didn't answer, he found himself at a loss for words. The room was magnificent, like nothing he'd ever seen in his life, fully decorated with strange, bizarre things. Immediately he was drawn to the northern wall, where a collection of mounted animal heads were displayed brightly upon their crests. Hunter expected to see regular game on display, like an elk, or the snarling head of a grizzly bear, maybe something more exotic like a lion. These had to be fake, some sort of faux decorative animal heads for show, far too strange to be anything else. There were a dozen or mysterious heads, the first one Hunter noticed was a reptile head with thick dark skin, it's mouth filled with sharp teeth, which wouldn't be any cause for concern, except for the fact that it was the same size as the saber-tooth tiger's head that sat next to it. There was also what appeared to be the head of a Big Foot sitting in the center of them all. The head was enormous, larger than any of the other strange creatures alongside it. The face was snarling, its mouth wide open, it's lips pulled back, showcasing its teeth, its brown beady eyes staring at Hunter like it was ready to rip his head off with one bite. Hunter didn't feel comfortable looking at the display. In fact, it frightened him. Even if they were decorations, they were extremely realistic.

The monstrous heads shouldn't have surprised Hunter, nothing the children had seen outside or inside the mansion was anywhere near ordinary. Hunter and Elly didn't move from the mighty entrance, still too taken aback at the overpowering sight of the inner castle. To the left and right of the children were two staircases, both winding upwards, connecting to create a fancy balcony that housed a few elegant couches, tables, and the doors to a large elevator. In front of the children, a few dozen feet into the mansion was a very large desk where a woman sat, presumably the woman who had powered on the lights. The desk itself was enormous; fitting for the simple fact that everything the children had seen thus far on the estate was massive in stature.

Hunter poked Elly with his elbow, motioning towards the

mysterious mounted heads, but she had already been caught up in her own amazement, next to the dual staircases stood two life-sized unicorns. Much like Hunter and the weird mounted heads, she knew they couldn't be real unicorns; she assumed someone had created them from stuffed horses, expressing some sort of artistic creation. Everyone knew unicorns didn't exist. Despite that fact, their beauty was still unmatched by any living animal she had ever seen. She felt a momentary sense of happiness looking at them, for a brief moment she forgot about the troubles that plagued their young lives.

Elly could only guess that whoever had spent the time changing the horse's bodies into the unicorns must have spent years perfecting the craft. Even though they were surely the results of a clever taxidermist, Elly felt she could see the unicorns prancing about the woods outside the estate's protective gates, their coats shining brightly against the setting sun. The unicorn on the left was much like the traditional unicorns she had read about in many fairy tales as a child. It had a beautiful solid-white coat with a long thick golden-white horn resting midway on its forehead. The opposing unicorn was much different though, with a lighter shade of yellow for its coat, and a smaller, pure white horn. This was Elly's favorite of the two.

"Children, meet Margot Merrymen," Ms. Ellingbee led the way towards the desk.

"Hi, kids," Margot said, smiling. "I'm so excited to finally meet you both!"

"Hello," They replied in unison, paying half of their attention to Margot. Instead, their attention was still drawn to the mansion's weird decor.

Margot was a younger woman in her early twenties. Youthful in mind and spirit, she was always full of energy. She had shoulder length black hair, fair skin, and capturing her youthfulness was a piercing on her lower lip. Margot was also quite keen on fashion, wearing a dark bohemian sweater, black leggings with tall black boots. Elly loved her outfit, especially the black boots, which were decorated with a big bow. Even though Elly was only eleven, she too had a love for fashion. Her mother had sat in bed and read fashion magazines with her until she fell asleep. She dreamed of one day becoming a designer for a European clothing line.

"I see you're quite interested in our décor," Margot walked out from behind the desk meeting the children with energetic hugs.

"You have your mother's red hair," she said to Elly. "And you, Hunter, you have those dark brown eyes like your dad!"

"You knew our parents?" Elly asked.

"I sure did." Her bright smile faded a little. "We knew them well, and miss them dearly."

"Ms. Margot, we will discuss that later," Ms. Ellingbee interjected in hopes of not dwelling on the sad subject.

"Yes, sorry, kids. I apologize." She pointed towards the mounted animal heads that Hunter had been eyeing. "My favorite one is the lycanthrope."

"The what?" Hunter replied.

"The lycanthrope, you probably know it as a werewolf." She walked over to the werewolf's mounted head. It sat on the bottom row below the Big Foot. Margot ran her fingers across the creature's grizzly teeth, "I know it's sort of cliché with the current popularity of werewolves and vampires running rampant here in the states, but I've always had a special place in my heart for them. They make for great love stories," she said with a laugh.

"Those aren't real, right?" Hunter added, a bit baffled by the conversation.

"I don't know, you tell me," Margot added slyly. "Are you a believer?" she asked.

"In what?" Hunter replied.

"Of the unknown, of course," Ms. Ellingbee joined in. "Of fairy tales, legendary creatures, magical items, and of course all those wondrous little things in between." She smiled.

"Oh…" Hunter paused for a moment, thinking of the question.

"I do!" Elly jumped in, her eyes wide with excitement. "Those unicorns are real, right? They're so pretty; I want to ride one someday."

"They're not real, stupid. They're fakes, just like the mounted heads," Hunter shot back at Elly. "Remember, Dad had that stuffed thunderbird with the creepy eyes. That thing was bigger than us both!"

"Yeah, I remember!" she shot back angrily. "—And I'm not stupid! I get better grades than you."

"Well, Dad said he bought it when he went on one of his trips overseas; he said there are a lot of people who make these things and sell them, they're fakes, all fakes."

"Well now, kids, no need to argue," Margot interrupted. "Elly, its okay to believe in extraordinary things. I do."

"As did your parents," Ms. Ellingbee added.

"See, Hunter?" Elly looked at her older brother with disdain. "I can believe if I want. Mom and Dad did."

"Whatever." Hunter crossed his arms in annoyance.

"What do you do here, Margot?" Elly asked.

"Margot is one of our caretakers here at the Belmonte Estate," Ms. Ellingbee answered. "She has a very important job because our humble little abode is much more than a place where we live."

"You both live here?" Hunter asked.

"Yes, we do. It's quite a large place. There are many of us who call this place home. You'll meet everyone soon enough," Margot replied. "We also get a lot of visitors who come and go for different reasons too, so I'm the one who keeps everything running smoothly, managing the books, answering the phones, keeping an eye out for intruders. It's fair to say I love my job!"

"Are their rooms ready?" Ms. Ellingbee asked. "It's been a long day for the kids, they need some rest."

"Of course," Margot answered. "Would you like me to show them now?"

"Please," Ms. Ellingbee answered. "I've arrived myself, and there's still quite a bit to put into order before our other guests arrive. The big day is coming soon; you know how excited I get."

"Other guests?" Hunter asked, not really directing the comment at anyone. He was more quizzical than anything.

"Yes, Professor Claudio Calenstine is expecting quite a few people to be coming through this next week; it's exciting times here at the Belmonte Estate. But, please, don't worry yourselves over the other guests. In a few days, after things quiet down, we'll see about introducing you two to the professor. Until then, Margot and I will be taking care of you both."

"Okay," Elly replied.

"Then it's settled. Margot," Ms. Ellingbee smiled as she looked over to her, "please escort our new family members to their room."

"My pleasure," said Margot. "Follow me please, children."

The children followed Margot up the eastern staircase towards the balcony sitting above the mansion's entranceway. The terrace wasn't all that large. It did provide a small resting area with a couple of dark leather armchairs that sat next to the balcony ledge, overlooking the main entranceway. Behind the resting area sat the main elevator for the mansion, which Margot had already called for. If one didn't care for elevators, both the eastern and western staircases continued upwards all the way to the seventh floor.

"How big is this place anyway?" Elly asked.

"Well, we have seven floors here in the main building, not including the numerous sublevels of the mansion. Each level reserved for something, infirmary, library, and the likes. The second floor has our guestrooms, that's where you'll be staying."

"It's still creepy. I don't like it here," Hunter said uneasily.

"Well, it isn't the most traditional place for children, I know. Some of the stuffed animal mounts can be a bit scary. I know I was scared at first. But you get used to all the weirdness, I promise," Margot added.

"I'm not scared," Elly added. "I think they're cool."

"Now, remember, children, room 206 is yours, you only get the one key, so make sure you don't lose it, okay?"

"Okay!" Elly answered.

Margot took the key off her large key ring, which rattled with every step she took. There must have been over two hundred different keys attached to it, but it took her no time to find the correct one unlocking their room.

"Well, we hope you like it," said Margot. "To the left over there past the bed, you'll see the bathroom door. You get your own shower and washroom, so you don't have to worry about running around at night and getting lost."

The room was fairly large for the children's needs. They felt a bit anxious standing in the well-furnished quarters. Hunter guessed it was the size of their old family room, which was exciting because it was the biggest room in their house. There were two beds on separate sides of the room. There was nothing fancy about them at all, but they looked cozy enough. The kids stood on a colorful floor rug, decorated with an army of medieval knights storming a large castle that covered the majority of the hardwood floor. It would be perfect for keeping the children's feet warm at night when the flooring got cold. A big bay window overlooked the front courtyard of the grounds, although Hunter found it eerie that the window was barred from the outside. Across from the window was a wall filled with a library of fine leather-bound books. Elly immediately ran over to them filled with anticipation.

"Look at all these books," Elly smiled.

"Oh yes, Ms. Ellingbee remembered your mother said you loved reading, so we had that built into the room last week when we found out you would both be coming here to stay with us. We hoped it might make the transition a little easier on you."

"There's no television?" Hunter fell onto his bed with a frown.

"Well, no," Margot answered. "We don't get much reception out here. We're kind of far from any cities so not too much makes its way out here. I feel your pain; my cell phone hardly ever gets service."

"What do we do for fun then?" Hunter asked.

"Read, write, do what you would normally do." She could tell Hunter wasn't amused. "We have to ask that for this first week, you stay in your room unless we come get you."

"What? You're locking us in here? What did we do?" Hunter asked, visibly upset.

"I'm sorry. I promise it's no type of punishment." Margot sat down next to Hunter to put her arm around him, but he shrugged it off moving away from her embrace. "Look," she added with a bit of sternness, "not everywhere on the estate is safe for children, or even for adults, for that matter. We need to keep you safe. The professor promised your parents if anything ever happened, he would take care of you both. It's temporary until we can sort some things out."

"What about our school? Do we get to go back? All of our friends are there," Elly asked.

"I'm afraid not," Margot answered, struggling to be the bearer of bad news. "You'll be home schooled here, though."

"What?" Hunter's face grew red. "That's not fair! How am I going to see my friends?"

"Look… I know this will be a tough transition." Margot stood up with an evident frown across her face. "Our heart goes out to you both, but it's up to us now to fulfill your parents' wishes. I'd better hold on to this key until you settle in a bit. Please, make yourselves at home," Margot took the key back from Elly, sliding it back onto her large key ring.

Margot walked over to the bedroom door stopping towards to offer the children one last gentle smile. Elly sat on her bed with a book open, giving Margot a disheartened look. Hunter stood with his back turned, peering out the bay window with his arms defiantly folded across his chest, hiding his angry tears from both the girls. Margot solemnly closed the door, locking it firmly behind her.

"Hunter?" Elly spoke up.

"What?" he murmured back.

"There's a bunch of cool books about monsters. That's cool, right?" she asked.

"We're trapped in this room, Elly," Hunter shot back. "It's like we're prisoners or something. They can't do that to us, they can't lock kids up in a room. It's not right."

"Maybe they're protecting us from something. They seemed really nice. They know Mom and Dad too."

"They 'knew' Mom and Dad," Hunter corrected. "And we don't even get to go back to school, or say goodbye to all our friends. We're stuck in this creepy old place forever."

The thought of never seeing her friends again made Elly angry as well. These new living arrangements were proving to be more hurtful and confusing for the children than they could have ever anticipated. Elly had already lost her parents, now the thought of losing all her friends frightened her even more.

"What are we going to do?" she asked Hunter.

"Nothing, we have to wait," he added.

"For what?"

"For the right time, then we break out of here. I don't care if they seem nice, something isn't right about this place, I want to know what it is."

Chapter 2
Mysteries Abound

The children sat in the room for hours before anything eventful transpired. Elly didn't mind terribly, she found herself spellbound by one of the thick, leather-bound books she had pulled from the small library. Unfortunately, Elly had found the book to be a bit troublesome to read, struggling with more than a few of the words she had never seen before, it was absorbing nonetheless, keeping her mind of more troubling matters.

This particular book was entitled "Professor Claudio Calenstine's Memoirs of Weird and Wonderful Things," which turned out to be a journal chronicling a young man's route around the world exploring myths and mysterious. The author wrote in detail about strange creatures and items he had come across. Elly found the artwork in the book to be quite pleasurable, although she figured it was a fictional story about mysterious legendary creatures and hidden treasures, she couldn't help but wonder if any of it was true.

Hunter, on the other hand, sat idly by, peering out through the bay window at the massive courtyard. He hadn't said much since Margot had left them, ignoring the few times Elly had tried sharing something interesting she had found in the book. He struggled with the sudden feeling of abandonment. Hunter had always been a lively child, albeit a bit shy when it came to unfamiliar social activities, but he was always energetic and imaginative around the house. Since the loss of his parents, he had become a different child altogether, reclusive, quiet, hot-tempered. It was easy to tell that Hunter had quickly become a shell of the fun-loving, smiling young man he once was.

"Hunter, look there's a picture of that werewolf thing Margot told us about in this book." Elly got excited, running over to her big brother's side to show him.

"It's all fake, Elly. I've seen plenty of movies about werewolves. They're not real, neither is that stupid book," said Hunter, blowing off her enthusiasm.

"Whatever, I was trying to help," Elly ignored him, returning to her book.

"Don't bother," Hunter told her.

"Fine," she added. "I won't talk to you then."

"Fine with me!" he shot back.

Hunter didn't truly understand why he was so angry with his little sister. He had no idea how to manage the tornado of emotions running rampant through his mind, he was completely at their mercy.

Despite the lavish view from the bay window, it added no excitement to Hunter's afternoon. If anything, it left him feeling very discouraged. The window looked out over the main courtyard, through which they had been escorted by Ms. Ellingbee when they first arrived. In the far distance, he could see the small pathway that led up to the immense iron gate, even the big eerie oak tree near the entrance. From this vantage point, Hunter thought the iron gate didn't look all that enormous and awe inspiring like it had earlier when he first gazed up at it.

He looked around the landscape for anything noteworthy, something that potentially could aid them in an escape attempt, but mostly he found the thickness of the surrounding forest very daunting. Hunter couldn't see much of the estate from the window, nothing looked too promising.

The dense woodland that grew around the large stone walls completely encircled the property as far as his eyes could see. Hunter found the forest strange, leaving him with a sick feeling in the pit of his stomach. It didn't look, nor feel to him like an average forest. He had been out in the woods before with his father camping; he had always loved the summer months when his dad would take him out for a few weekends, the two of them living off the land. No, he knew this was vastly different from any other forest he had been in. These woods seemed alive… like one massive breathing organism, completely aware of its surroundings. At first, he had felt silly thinking this way, but while they had waited outside in the cold with the taxi driver, he could have sworn that the trees were watching them, that they had eyes hidden deep in their trunks. This made Hunter nervous, but he didn't mention it at the time due to the fear of sounding childish. No, all this talk of creatures and werewolves was nonsense; he knew his imagination was getting the better of him.

Now, as he stared through the barred window, the forest worried him for a different reason altogether. He had thought of escaping, running away back home. If they could manage to escape… somehow scale the surrounding stone walls, or maybe steal the large key and sneak out through the iron gate. It was the next step in the escape plan that had Hunter worried the most. He didn't think he and his sister would be able to cope with the inherent dangers that may lay in wait in the mysterious forest. He knew very little about navigating in the wilds. He remembered there was the small stony road that the taxi had followed to get them to the mansion, but the drive along that small path had taken over two hours. Hunter had no idea how long that would take two children on foot. What if the people living in the mansion set out looking for them after they escaped? The road would surely be the first place they would look. It wouldn't be safe; they would need to keep hidden to evade detection.

"Attention children!" the familiar voice of Ms. Ellingbee shot through a large speaker that, until now, had remained unnoticed. "We do apologize for the wait, but dinner will be brought up within the hour."

"Great, we can't even leave this room to eat. We really are prisoners," Hunter groaned.

"I do have some good news to deliver. Your Uncle Joseph is on the line, I have him patched through so you can speak to him over the speaker. Give me a second to connect."

"Uncle Joey!" Elly jumped down from the bed.

After a few seconds of silence, there was a beep connecting their uncle through to them.

"Hey, guys, can you hear me?" Uncle Joe asked over the speaker.

"Uncle Joey, can you hear us?" Elly asked back with excitement.

"I sure can!" he responded. "How are you guys holding up over there?"

"Hunter's upset, but I'm doing okay. They gave me lots of books to read," Elly answered.

"Hunter, what's wrong, buddy?"

"They have us locked up in here like criminals," answered Hunter. "They locked the door and they even have bars on the windows. The place is scary too. I hate it here."

"Well… there are some adjustments we're working on. be patient for me, okay, guys? Things will get better soon, I promise."

"Why can't we come live with you?" Hunter asked.

"I'd love for you guys to live with me, but now's not the right time. I can't afford much for myself, let alone provide for you guys."

"We don't care, we hate it here," Hunter said again.

"Your parents wished for you guys to be raised there under Professor Calenstine's care if something ever happened to them. They knew what they were doing, so trust in their judgment. I'm sure you're in good hands."

"I doubt they even really knew Mom and Dad, and we haven't even met this professor guy, yet," Hunter argued back.

"Margot and Miss Patricia are both nice though," Elly added, trying to ease the situation.

"Well, I have met Professor Claudio Calenstine before. He's a very bright man, he knows what's best for you both. You know… I was invited to the mansion once when I was little!"

"Really?" Elly asked.

"Yes, do they still have the unicorns when you walk in? They were my favorite when I was your age. There are a lot of neat things in the mansion, guys, and it holds a lot of very important things too. So please, understand that it's very vital for you to listen to Professor Calenstine and his staff. When the time's right, they'll let you in on some of their secrets. Until then, behave and be courteous."

"Secrets?" Hunter asked.

"Yes, but not until the time is right, and you've proved you're trustworthy. It isn't something anyone can take in overnight, but little by little, you will learn. I mean it though, your parents would want you to be respectful, listen, and take your home-schooling seriously."

"This is so unfair!" Hunter yelled, unable to hold his tears back any longer. "I want my mom and dad back. I want to go home, I hate you all…" Hunter ran to his bed pulling his covers over his head.

"Hunter, it breaks my heart. I loved taking care of you guys when your parents left on their trips. It's a terrible thing that happened. Our family will never be the same. I do have some good news though. I'm braving my fear of flying to come up and spend some time with you guys very soon. I won't let you be alone during this time, I promise."

"Really?" Hunter wiped away the tears from his face, sticking his head out from under his covers.

"I swear it. You know, it's been like ten years since I've been back to the mansion. Despite all the terrible things that have happened, returning there makes me happy. I'm excited to see you both." Uncle Joe added before hanging up, "I have to go now guys, stay strong, and listen to your new family. I'll see you soon… Hunter, take care of your little sister."

The connection clicked off leaving only the lonely sound of a dial tone before Ms. Patricia came back on.

"I'm sorry, children. I know this is hard for you right now. Ms. Margot and I will do our best to comfort you during this time. In approximately an hour, I shall bring up your supper."

The phone call from their uncle, who had been as much a parent to them as their mother and father, watching them for months at a time when their parents left on their business trips, had left the children feeling hopeful. Hunter knew deep down that their parents and his uncle wouldn't leave them in the hands of strangers. He decided to put his guard down a bit, make the best of the situation.

Hunter picked out one of the multitude of books, taking a seat next to his sister, who remained on the bed reading Professor

Calenstine's journal. Hunter thought Elly seemed fine despite everything the two of them had endured in the last two weeks. She sat quietly, feet swinging back and forth, turning the pages, humming a song her mother used to hum to her when she was younger. Hunter opened his book, "Secret Societies and Mysterious Figures of the U.S.A." He didn't do much reading but randomly thumbed through the pages, trying to reconnect with his sister, who he felt bad for yelling at earlier.

"Sorry, Elly…" He kept his eyes on his book. He never liked apologizing to anyone, especially Elly, who oftentimes got him in trouble and rarely apologized for it.

When his uncle had asked him to take care of her, it had echoed loudly in his head. Things weren't the same anymore. He was a bit too young to know exactly how much they had changed at the time, but his instincts told him that he had to take care of his little sister more than ever before. He wasn't angry about it, despite the sibling rivalry; his sister and uncle were all that was left of his family. He wanted to make sure he could protect them. The only anger Hunter felt was from the loss of his parents, the inability to keep them safe himself. He felt abandoned, struggling with the whirlwind of emotions.

"Why are you sorry?" Elly stopped reading.

Hunter didn't reply. He tried his best to mask his watering eyes. Elly saw his pain, which was more than enough to start her crying as well. She hugged her older brother, not letting go until a loud knock interrupted them.

"Children?" Margot's voice asked, followed by a loud click from the lock mechanism inside the bedroom door. Margot popped her head in with a sympathetic smile. She carried in a large tray filled with numerous plates of food. It didn't take long for the wonderful smell to hit the children's nose, causing Elly's stomach to rumble, she hadn't realized how hungry she was.

To the children's surprise, behind her was a man wearing a black suit with a dark red tie and a thick Teflon vest with bright yellow letters saying "MFPA."

The man didn't say a single word, nor make eye contact with the children. He stood in the doorway, guarding the room, his eyes attentive. Hunter made the assumption that he was there in case he and Elly made an attempt to run. The man was bald, but rather young, in his late thirties, very fit, intimidating.

"Don't mind my friend over there," Margot said, acknowledging the children's worrisome stare. "He's just doing his job. Not much with words, but he does have a friendly smile."

"Doing his job of keeping us locked up in here?" Hunter asked.

"Yes and no…" Margot answered truthfully. "I wish I was at liberty to explain a bit more of the predicament we're in." She made her way over to the children's small dining table, which sat in the corner of the room alongside the bay window.

"Why can't you?" Elly grabbed a seat.

"Well," Margot began, dishing up two plates with rosemary mashed potatoes, a huge pile of honey-glazed carrots, and chunks of thick-cut salty ham steaks. "Let's say he's more of a protector for us than a guardsman."

"Protecting us from what?" Hunter took a bite of his cured ham. It was sweet and salty, the honey glaze of the carrots mixed wonderfully with the meat.

"Well, that's the part I can't say," she added. "No worry, you're both safe as can be in here, which is why we can't have you roaming around. Do enjoy your meal." She nodded leaving children behind.

"The food is good," Elly crammed a mouthful of mashed potatoes into her mouth, leaving all her table manners behind.

"We need to find a way out of here." Hunter pushed his plate to the side.

"Why? I'm not running away into those scary woods. I'd rather stay locked up here. Plus," Elly added, talking between mouthfuls of food, "I still think everyone here is nice, even if they are keeping us locked up. Like Uncle Joey said, Mom and Dad wouldn't give us to anyone mean."

"Maybe not on purpose," Hunter added. "But I'm not talking about escaping at the moment. If they won't tell us why they're keeping us locked up, then I say we go exploring, find out for ourselves."

"That sounds scary, I don't want to do that, you're nuts." Elly answered.

"Look!" Hunter ran over to the bay window. Something had caught his eye.

"What is it? I'm eating," Elly was interested in picking over Hunter's leftovers.

"Seriously, come look, now!" he shouted.

Elly reluctantly abided.

Outside stood Patricia Ellingbee with the older man in the wheelchair that they had seen earlier. There was a second, younger man with them that they didn't recognize. The chill of the night air had brought with it a small snowfall, which normally would be quite a beautiful sight from the bay window if it wasn't for the argument ensuing below.

The children could only hear the murmurs of the yelling, but their body language told them that the younger man was quite angry.

The man had a thick head of black hair; his face was scarred terribly from his eyebrow all the way down to his cheekbone. He looked livid, tensely waving his hand in fury towards the older man, who sat very calmly in his wheelchair. The man with the scarred face was dressed in an all-black outfit. His attire reminded Hunter of a SWAT team member he had seen on a cable television show. He wore thick black boots with black cargo pants tucked into them. His long-sleeved shirt was covered by a Teflon vest with the letters MFPA in bright yellow letters across it, exactly like the guard that Margot had brought with her. Across his shoulder was a leather strap that held a large gun.

"Why is that guy is so angry?" Elly asked.

"What does the MFPA stand for?" Hunter answered, ignoring his sister's question.

"Never heard of it, what about the old man in the wheelchair, who is he anyway?" Elly added.

There came a loud bang from downstairs that made them both jump, something had hit the floor hard and smashed. They could tell the arguing party outside had also heard it because their heads darted towards the mansion doors. Then a very loud growl echoed throughout the mansion walls, followed by an even louder scream. Hunter ran over to Elly to help her up off the floor. She was visibly shaking from the fear of the loud piercing howl.

The man with the scar cocked his rifle and entered the mansion. Patricia followed suit, pushing the elder man in the wheelchair back into the warmth of the mansion.

"Hunter, what in the world was that?" Elly cried! She was terrified, her cheeks now stained with salty tears.

"Err… I don't know, Elly," Hunter cupped his hand up to his ear placing the side of his head against the door to see if he could hear anything else.

"Get away from the door, Hunter," Elly begged. Her knees trembled; she hid under her bed, curling tightly into a ball.

"You heard them. They said we were safe in here. Maybe that animal is running around inside the mansion. That must be what they're so afraid of," Hunter answered.

"What do you think it is? That growl was loud." Elly's voice shuddered.

"This mansion is huge. Who knows what it is. Maybe a stray dog or something," Hunter added. "Or a bear… I bet the woods are loaded with bears." Hunter had never really seen any wild animals, unless you counted the summer his parents took the children to the local zoo. The most he had ever come across, camping with his father, were a couple of wild deer.

Things settled down a little after the eerie growl. Elly relaxed, leaving her hiding spot behind, she was able to get lost once again in one of her books. Hunter, however, had a different plan in mind. He wandered about the room, looking for any way he may be able to sneak out.

A few hours passed before Margot came knocking on their bedroom door, followed quickly by the well-dressed guard they had met earlier that day. Once again, he stood silently by, keeping watch out in the hallway. The kids could tell right away that Margot wasn't her normal cheerful self, she seemed anxious. The children decided not to ask about the incident, nor did Margot give any information as to why she was so edgy. Instead, she quickly gathered the dishes and made her way to the door.

"I'm sorry, children, but it's late," Margot said, "and it's been a very stressful day for us all. Sweet dreams."

"Goodnight," Hunter said as he unpacked his pajamas from his suitcase to ready himself for bed.

"Will we see you tomorrow?" Elly asked.

"Of course, you will," Margot said, forcing a smile. She then turned off the lights locking the door behind her.

Sleep didn't come quickly for either of the children, but it did come eventually. There was a full moon that night, and it rested high in the sky with very few clouds to mask its brightness. This allowed for the perfect amount of natural moonlight to creep into the children's bedroom, which aided them both in sleep. Neither of the children felt comfortable sleeping in the complete darkness of their new home. There was too much going on for them to be at peace with any of their surroundings.

It seemed to be a peaceful night until Hunter was awoken from a deep sleep. There was a loud rumbling coming from in the corner of their room. Hunter had always been a light sleeper, unlike Elly who could sleep through an earthquake. He sat up from his bed, rubbing the sleepiness away from his eyes. He inspected where he had heard the strange noise, tiptoeing so as to not startle his little sister in case she woke up. The noise came from high in the wall, almost at the ceiling, on the opposite side of the room from where their beds sat.

Hunter pinpointed where the mysterious sound had originated from, but he couldn't figure out what it was; now it sounded like the thing was moving. He followed the strange shuffling noise, from within the wall, for a few feet until he came upon one of the large heater vents. These heater vents were one of the few modern elements of the children's room.

Through the grated vents, Hunter finally saw something move, but it was dark, making it difficult to see what he was looking at. He could barely make out the sound of something softly breathing. Something wasn't right; he backed away, tripping over one of the wooden chairs from the dining table. He fell over it, causing a loud crash, but Elly didn't stir, whatever in te vent sure did.

Hunter froze in terror. Whatever was inside the vent had made a violent jolt from the noise.. He stirred something awake… two bright green eyes reflected from the shadows of the shaft. A sudden sense of panic stiffened every muscle in Hunter's body. The bright eyes stared at him momentarily before darting out of sight. The creature scrambled through the vents, within seconds, the noise faded off into silence.

Hunter gasped for air; something big was lurking about this creepy old mansion's ventilation system. For the first time since arriving, Hunter believed Margot and Ms. Ellingbee *were* actually trying to keep them safe. He sat in the corner of the room for the rest of the night as far away from the vents as possible, his knees tucked up to his chin.

Hunter felt fear creeping over his body, the crippling pain of depression took a strong hold. He missed the safety of his home, his parents, his once normal thirteen-year-old existence. It took hours, until he was able to fall asleep in the corner, rolled up into a ball.

He dreamed that night of those glowing green eyes.

Chapter 3
The First Escape

The next few nights were uneventful with no loud noises, no growls, and thankfully no green reflective eyes lurking in the vents. The children had been outright bored for the majority of the time. There was only so much for a kid to do being stuck in a room, twenty-four hours a day. However, after the incidents from their first night, Hunter and Elly were less defensive towards Ms. Ellingbee and Margot about their confinement. They also found themselves opening up to Margot the most. They saw her more often, she brought them their meals and randomly checked up on them throughout the day, catering to their needs.

Last night, she had even stayed up late with them playing board games, which Elly had won despite Hunter's proclamation of her abusing certain rules. Margot's friendly demeanor wasn't for show; she really was a sweet young woman who wanted nothing more than to make the children feel at home. Hunter had mentioned the glowing eyes he had seen to Elly and Margot, only to have the motion dismissed as an overactive imagination.

The children assumed Ms. Ellingbee was a busy person, as she hardly ever made her way down to their room. She only spoke to them over the speaker when something important was announced. As for Professor Claudio Calenstine, their actual godfather, they still hadn't met him let alone spoken to him. Margot said that the professor was a very busy man, that he was booked up with meetings and important matters to be addressed within the Estate. Hunter surmised that a rabid green-eyed animal running around his ventilation system was probably a big nuisance.

The children had been at the mansion now for three nights, stuck that entirety of time in their room. They weren't even allowed to wander around the hallway, or get some fresh air out in the courtyard. Despite the fact that they were provided with pretty much anything they wanted, Hunter grew bored, the curiosity of what secrets lurked within the mansion only grew greater as the days went on. Elly, however, was quite happy spending the majority of her day reading all the wonderful books they had given her.

Hunter seemed to have more mischievous notions on his mind. After a few days of preparation, he had a brilliant escape planned. If all fell into place later that night, he would be sneaking about the mansion halls in no time.

"Aren't you scared the monster will get you?" Elly asked. She wanted nothing to do with the plan.

"I told you that you weren't coming anyway. It's too dangerous for little girls," Hunter retorted, sick of his sister's constant meddling. "You'd better not blow it tonight either. I'm counting on you to help me sneak out."

The door locking mechanism clicked, which meant that Margot was checking up on them. Elly jumped down from her bed with excitement.

"Hello, children," Margot made her entrance. The bald well-dressed man stood silently behind her with his back turned to the room, not uttering a single word. Margot had a long leash in her hand, leading a large dog that did more waddling than actual walking into the room. It looked and moved like a giant oversized puppy. The kid's eyes both lit up with amazement.

They were never allowed to own a dog at home, their mother had been allergic, and no amount of begging or pleading had won their parents over.

Margot's furry companion was no ordinary dog, it was huge, making even the larger of dog breeds seem small in comparison. It moved more like a puppy than a mature dog. It was downright clumsy, curious over everything it saw, wagging its tail a mile a minute. Its fur was long and shaggy, it had a unique color to its coat, a shade of dark green. A color neither Hunter nor Elly had ever seen on a dog. The massive pup stumbled over to Elly, eagerly licking her face with its bulky wet tongue.

"I'd like you to meet Trayer. He's our newest addition to the Belmonte family, and we all thought it might be nice if you kids could help us watch over him," Margot said.

"He's huge!" Elly laughed, giving the tremendous dog a huge bear hug. "He's a puppy?"

"Only eight weeks old," Margot responded.

"Is he mean?" Hunter asked, a bit more hesitant. He had always wanted a dog, but he had envisioned something a bit more lap friendly, a Chihuahua perhaps.

"Not at all. He's a pup, he loves attention."

"What kind of dog is he?" Hunter asked, hesitantly petting the large animal's head.

"Well, it's a rare breed…" Margot paused for a minute, thinking of how to answer the question. "I'm certain you've never heard of it before. It's actually from Scotland, sadly, the breed is almost extinct."

"Oh no… that's so sad," Elly frowned.

"Well, yes… it's quite sad actually," Margot answered. "We're fairly sure he's the last one alive in the entire world… and with no female to mate with, well…"

"We promise to take good care of him!" Elly smiled.

"It's much bigger than any dog I have ever seen, you sure he is just a puppy?" asked Hunter, worried about what taking care of such a large dog actually entailed.

"Well, Trayer's breed is called a Cusith. It's an enormous canine breed, when he's an adult, he'll be the size of a large calf."

"Seriously?" Hunter's eyes widened with concern.

"Hey, I read about the Cusith in one of those monster books." Elly's eyebrows rose. "The book said they were mean, like a dog version of a Grim Reaper. They snatched people, dragging them to hell…"

"Yes. Unfortunately, many books describe them as such. I assure you they are wrong. They are no demon dogs," Margot laughed, "Just look at this face, you think he'd hurt anyone?" She scratched his wet nose.

"What do you mean 'Grim Reaper'?" Hunter pulled his hand away.

"Well, I applaud you for reading those books," Margot winked at Elly. "However, the legend and the truth are vastly different. You see, people fear what they don't know, those legends are based on fear. Even in the wild the Cusith were very isolated spending most of their time in hiding. It was extremely rare for anyone to ever set eyes on one, but every once in a great while, someone would. They'd stumble unknowingly into the presence of a large dog-like animal, which can look terrifying if you didn't know any better. So, the legend was born out of fear and a lack of understanding. Truth be told, they are extremely smart and loyal animals. He'll make a perfect friend for you both. He lost his mother; the litter she had was too much for her. She was quite old… she didn't make it. He was the only pup to make it through the first week without their mother to nurse them. We'd hoped the litter would keep his species going…"

"What about the dad?" asked Elly.

"We lost him from old age a month before the litter was born…" Margot frowned.

"He's like us, Hunter," Elly added, giving Trayer an even bigger hug than before.

"What do you mean?"

"He lost his mom and daddy too. He needs our love."

"Yeah, I guess you're right."

Trayer pounced playfully on Hunter, licking his face.

"Well, I'll come up to help you feed and water him every day, and you can leave it up to me to take him out. We don't want a dog his size to make any messes in your room, trust me. I had to housebreak him, and he's still learning a bit."

"Eeeew!" Elly laughed.

"Well then, I'll leave you three alone until its dinner time."

"Okay!" said the kids in unison.

Trayer was a playful pup, despite his size he was very gentle. Elly and Trayer quickly developed a strong bond. Wherever she went, Trayer followed, it wasn't long before Elly had Trayer sitting, lying, and staying on command. Not too bad for a so-called "monster" she thought.

Hunter joined her in the excitement for their new furry companion, but his elaborate escape plan easily outweighed the new pet. It was a waiting game, he had to sit back until Margot and the guard returned to make sure they were ready for bed. Hunter and Elly had been locked up in their room for long enough, and although Margot insisted the lockdown should be over by the end of the week, the children assumed she was merely trying to ease their frustration by giving them false hope.

The hours flew by for Elly, who spent every waking minute with Trayer, teaching the eager pup as much as she possibly could. She even found an interesting book about training large canine breeds, wasting no time reading it aloud to Trayer, who had stretched out peacefully alongside her. They both cuddled up cozily on the bed. The mammoth pup rested his enormous head on her lap, snoring away. Elly didn't even mind the little bit of warm drool that pooled on her thigh as he slept, she welcomed the companionship.

"Margot should be coming back any minute." Hunter walked over to Elly with a mischievous smile, a tad nervous about his plan coming together.

"You're not still planning on sneaking out, are you?"

"You bet I am." He pulled a wadded-up piece of paper from his pocket, showing it off to Elly with pride.

"How in the heck is a crumpled piece of paper going to help you break out of here?"

"Well, at first I wasn't sure how to draw attention away from me getting to the door, but now with Trayer and your help, it will be easy," Hunter explained.

"What do you mean?"

"You're going to show Margot and the bald guy the new trick you taught Trayer." Hunter smiled devilishly.

"What… to sit and lie down?"

"No, to play fetch," Hunter corrected her.

"But, Hunter…" Elly looked confused. "Trayer doesn't know how to play fetch, he runs away from me with the ball in his mouth."

"Exactly! When you throw the ball, toss it out the bedroom door into the hallway. He'll run out of the room to fetch it, they'll have to chase after him."

"Why?" Elly still didn't see how a crumpled sheet of paper would get him out of the room.

"Because it will cause a distraction, then I can sneak over to the door, where the deadbolt locks into the doorframe. See? I tuck this wad of paper into the notch where the latch would normally lock into it, and boom! An hour later, I'll be out of this cruddy room and into the mansion's halls exploring all its secrets!"

"I still don't see how the paper will unlock the door." Elly was confused.

"Well, when Margot goes to lock it, normally the deadbolt would fit perfectly into the hole in the doorframe. With the paper crammed in there, it should only partially lock. Margot won't know the difference because the key will still turn, then I can use this." Hunter took out his wallet and pulled out a plastic card. "My library card!" Hunter waited for a response, eyes wide with excitement at his plan.

"Your library card?" Elly didn't seem impressed.

"Yeah, see, I use it to slide in between the door and the frame and wiggle it between the lock and the wad of paper. Then I push the lock back into the door, presto-change-o, unlocked door. Get it?"

"Err… I don't think that's going work." Elly was unconvinced of his plan.

"Sure, it will." Hunter frowned, expecting more positive reinforcement from his little sister. "I mean, I saw it on a movie once," he added.

"Well, I'll only help because I think it will fail," Elly told him.

"Whatever," Hunter shot back. The footsteps approached their room. "Get ready!" Hunter shouted.

"Okay, fine." Elly grabbed the ball, tossing it up and down in her hand. Trayer jumped from his peaceful nap, tail wagging frantically in excitement.

"How's Trayer doing, guys?" Margot poked her head into the room. "Looks like someone's having fun."

"We love him! He's a big baby," Elly answered. "I've been teaching him new tricks all day. He's a quick learner."

"Cusiths are very intelligent animals. That's why it's so rare to ever see one in the wild, excellent hiders."

"I've taught him to sit, stay, and roll over."

"Didn't you teach him how to fetch too?" Hunter nudged her with his elbow.

She nodded with a dirty look.

"Want to see?" Elly asked Margot, hoping she would say no.

"Of course, I do," Margot answered, but Hunter had already seen the hesitation in his sister's eyes.

"Let me throw it." Hunter grabbed the ball from Elly's hands. Her face grew dark red, but she didn't interject. Hunter needed to get the bald guard and Margot out of the room if his plan was going to work.

"Here, boy," Hunter waved the ball around.

Trayer grew anxious, playfully growling, his eyes never left the ball. "Go get it!" Hunter tossed the ball at an angle so that it flew outside the door down the hallway. Trayer bolted out of the room, knocking Margot back against the door, while hitting the bald guard so hard he fell to one knee.

"Hunter!" Margot shot him a dirty look before bolting after Trayer. The guard didn't completely leave his post, but he did walk far enough down the hallway for Hunter to get to the threshold.

"Stupid, mutt," the guard cursed.

Hunter stuck his head out. "Sorry! He usually catches it right away!" Hunter wedged the paper into the notch.

"Very funny, Hunter." Margot returned moments later with the ball in hand, an over excited Trayer circling around her. She was not amused.

"Sorry, I thought he could fetch," Hunter overacted his own innocence.

"It's time for bed. Settle Trayer down. I'll bring your breakfast down in the morning," Margot did her best to hide the scowl on her face. "You should apologize to Agent Roberts for knocking him over. He's a guest here and is being nice enough to help us out while we're short staffed. You should treat him with respect, not let him get trampled by Trayer."

Agent Roberts? Hunter thought to himself. He had never given it a thought that the bald guard would have a name, let alone a title like "Agent."

"Sorry," Hunter placed the ball away into a dresser, Trayer whined in return.

"Hmmph," Agent Roberts curled his lip.

"Agent…?" Margot added, with a stern, motherly look.

"It was an accident," Agent Roberts nodded.

"They're trained to always be professional. Don't mind him," Margot answered for the Agent. "It was an accident, and it won't happen again, correct?"

"Yes, ma'am," Hunter answered.

"Good." Margot nodded with a smile. She flicked off the light leaving the children once again in the dark, with only the glow of the waning moon breaking through from the bay window.

Hunter waited eagerly for the next step in his plan. He hoped the key would turn far enough to trick Margot into thinking it was completely locked. It must have worked because they closed the door and made their way down the hall.

"Jackpot!" he grinned.

"When are you sneaking out?" Elly whispered back. She secretly wished his plan would fail. Even though she too grew tired of being locked up in the room, she trusted that Margot and Ms. Ellingbee were protecting them from the wandering creature, or perhaps something even worse.

"I'll wait a few hours until everyone is sleeping. That way I won't have to worry about running into anyone down there. I'll have the whole mansion to myself."

Hunter lay under his blankets, anxiously staring at the large grandfather clock across the room. There was no worry he would fall asleep waiting for the time to pass, he literally shook with anticipation. The eagerness was torture, every minute felt like ten, and every hour felt like a day.

"Elly?" Hunter whispered. She made no sound. *Good*, he thought, he wasn't looking forward to the inevitable argument that would erupt after demanding that his little sister stay put.

Hunter cautiously made his way out of bed, tiptoeing towards the door, being careful not to wake his sister. From his wallet, he pulled out his library card and slid it between the door and its frame. He slowly moved the card upward until he hit the bolt mechanism. He wiggled it until he felt it slip between the bolt and the threshold, he couldn't help but smile. Slipping the card into place meant the plan worked. Hunter pushed the card bending it against the lock mechanism, generating enough force to push the bolt back into the door. Hunter had finally freed himself from the room. For the first time since arriving he felt excitement surge through his body. He wasted no time, his journey was beginning.

The hallway was dark, with no source of light from either end despite the numerous light fixtures hanging from the ceilings. Hunter had only taken a few steps into the hallway when he doubted making his journey deeper into the mysterious mansion was such a good idea. As well as he had thought out the escape, he hadn't given any thought as to what he would need once he had gotten out. If only he had a flashlight...

Hunter remembered that the hallway outside their room was nothing more than a long corridor with numerous quarters for the mansion's guests, he figured he would pick a direction and stick to it. He assumed he would run into some stairs sooner or later, so he made his way deeper into the creepy, dark corridor, traveling to the right from his room. The hallway slowly curved, once Hunter made his way around the bend, the first specs of light came into view. There, in the near distance, he saw a small button emitting a glowing orange hue. He recognized the color from the main elevator ride that they had taken up to their room when they arrived.

A very distinct noise broke the eerie silence of the darkened hall.

A door had creaked open somewhere in the distance.

Hunter knew he had to make a move. He wasn't about to get caught already, he hadn't even made it past the hallway outside of his bedroom. Hunter cursed, he moved cautiously, hoping not to wake anyone. He must not have been quiet enough. *Stupid*, he thought to himself.

Hunter wasted no time, darting swiftly towards the elevator. The cool steel doors sat before him, he frantically hit the button to summon it. Nerves tied his stomach into knots, it felt like he had swallowed a bucket full of volcanic rocks. Blood rushed to his face, for a split second, he thought he might get sick to my stomach. The sound of footsteps crept up, closer and closer. He envisioned it now, whoever it was, was about to round the curve. They would see him, he would be caught, everything was over.

Come on you blasted elevator, c'mon! Hunter clenched his fists, cursing the contraption in his head.

The elevator door chimed opened, Hunter jumped in, he didn't have time to think, he needed to get off this floor as soon as possible, hitting the first button he saw. It happened to be marked SB-1 with the words 'Library' neatly typed next to it. The elevator doors closed and the soft calming sound of generic elevator music played. *That was close*, he thought. *A little too close.* Hunter let out a deep resounding sigh of relief, his nerves faded away, replaced with a pulsating sensation of adrenaline shooting through his body once again.

He had made it... He had really made it!

∽

What Hunter didn't realize was that the noise wasn't Margot, Ms. Ellingbee, or anyone else who lived in the mansion. It was his little sister. Elly had never gone to sleep. She had pretended to be sleeping while waiting for her older brother to make his escape. Once he snuck out, she waited a few minutes before taking her leave. She tiptoed out of their room, so as not to stir the snoring behemoth of a dog, Trayer.

Elly wasn't sure where to go at first. She stood in the darkened hallway fighting away the fear of being outside the protection of her bedroom while a monster was on the prowl. A small chime sounding like an elevator door opening came from down the hall. It must have been Hunter. Elly followed the noise, tip toing as fast as she could.

By the time Elly made her way to the elevator doors, Hunter had already disappeared. She hit the glowing orange button waiting for the lift to return. Now, Elly second-guessed herself, wondering why she thought it was a good idea to follow her nosey older brother in the first place. She was never one to care for the thrill of sneaking out or stirring up trouble. She would much rather be in bed sleeping, cuddled up with Trayer.

Then again, the thought of Hunter bragging about his adventure tomorrow morning would definitely make Elly steam up with jealousy. Hunter always was the one to have all the fun, and she wanted to prove to him that she could be as sneaky and rebellious as him. So, there she stood, waiting, palms sweating, for the elevator door to chime open.

She entered, looking carefully at the multitude of buttons glowing before her. There was a dozen or so, but the only one that really caught her attention said "SB-1 Library." Of course, Elly loved reading. It was a no-brainer for her to pick the mansion's grand library for her destination.

Elly was very thankful that Margot and Ms. Ellingbee had gone to all the trouble of stocking up their own personal library for the children. At first, Elly found the collection fairly interesting, but an eleven-year-old girl could only read so many informative texts about Big Foot's so-called cousin, the 'Yelping Yeti,' or the ancient and equally mystifying legend of the Fountain of Youth. She really wanted to grab a few books that identified a little more with her age group.

The lift descended into the bowels of the mansion causing Elly to feel rather nauseated from motion sickness. Elly always felt a little ill when she rode in elevators, she was like her mother, in that respect, and thus spent most of her life avoiding them as much as possible. The door chimed again, opening the doors to her destination.

Elly found herself standing alone, staring at most elegant and extraordinary library she had ever seen. She was completely awestruck by its grandeur. This was nothing like the library back home which up until this point, Elly had thought housed every book in the world. She couldn't have been more wrong. This library was easily triple the size of the one back home. The books stretched out in every direction with seemingly no end in sight. From the lowest shelves a few inches off the library's floor to the towering displays that literally touched the top of the domed ceiling dozens of feet up. The room was bursting with books. Elly thought it was the prettiest and most amazing room she had have ever seen.

Unfortunately for Elly, the impressive display was a bit unsettling; the library at this time of night was very dark with dreadfully little light to allow her to truly take in its splendor. The little light there was came from a few strategically placed dim wall mantles. Luckily, there was enough clarity to maneuver through the labyrinth of bookshelves and tables.

Elly skimmed through the countless books, eagerly exploring the aisles. Unfortunately, she found literally every book to be long-winded with wordy and confusing titles. There was nothing in the impressive collection for someone her age. She assumed all the books were ancient, half of them she couldn't even read because they had been written in different languages. Elly was flustered, wishing more than ever that she hadn't left the comfort of her cozy bed. She walked around the library for easily an hour to no avail, she couldn't find any books she was interested in. She decided that she had had enough action for the night, she was ready to head back to the elevator when she caught sight of Hunter from the corner of her eye.

"Hunter!" she whispered.

Hunter hadn't heard, but she heard something else....

A loud noise came from behind her, a rhythmic bumping somewhere in the darkness. Elly thought it was footsteps at first, only louder. She peeked around the corner of large bookshelves. And that's when she saw it through the shadows. She could barely make out the darkened silhouette; whatever it was had a bulky, colossal frame. It moved very stiff, like some sort of machine, jerky and kind of off balance, the thing towered in size.

Elly gasped, thinking of the monster Hunter had seen in the ventilation shaft. This figure was far too bulky to fit into any ventilation system, but if there was one monster lurking about, then why not two? Panicked began to settle in, her face flushing red. She was losing control of her body, trembling so bad that her knees were literally knocking together. She wanted to run away, scream for help, but she couldn't muster enough courage to turn away from the shadowy figure, she was frozen in fear...

There was a quick tug on her shoulder, she found herself being pulled underneath one of the study desks by Hunter.

"Quiet," he mouthed slowly not saying any actual words, signaling to her by pressing his index finger to his lips.

The menacing figure was a few aisles away, thankfully it hadn't reacted to their presence. Elly covered her eyes with her hands, Hunter watched wide-eyed as the figure stepped through the dim lighting, briefly illuminating the daunting figure in all its magnificence. Elly peered through her fingertips, her mouth fell open at the sight.

Neither of the children really understood what they were witnessing. The figure was quite tall, its head standing a foot or two above the already high bookshelves. The thing walked upright on stocky legs, making loud noises that echoed throughout the library's numerous aisles. The dim lighting reflected off its metallic frame.

"Is it some sort of armor?" Hunter whispered.

As the behemoth neared their hiding place, Hunter could hear the mechanical, gear grinding sounds, accompanying its every move. It definitely wasn't human, it must be some sort of android... Its eyes were a vivid cerulean blue, not strong enough to pierce through the entirety of the room's darkness, but enough to see it eerily glow upon closer inspection. Hunter only caught a brief look of its head from an awkward angle, it had no face, just the piercing blue eyes, and what Hunter could only describe as a V-shaped vent where its mouth should be.

The children waited a few minutes, allowing the android to pass before speaking.

"Was that a robot?" Hunter whispered.

"It was scary… I thought it was going to eat us," Elly answered.

"Don't be stupid," Hunter mocked. "Robots don't eat humans, they eat, you know, err… oil and gasoline, that sort of stuff," he guessed, trying to put his annoying sister at ease. "What are you doing down here anyway?" Hunter shot his sister a dirty look. "I told you to stay put."

"I wasn't going to stay in that room all alone," Elly shot back.

Their argument was short-lived. Another loud noise caught their attention. Hunter poked his head out towards the aisle in time to make out the outline of the robotic figure. It had made one of the bookshelves sink into the floor of the library, revealing some sort of secret passage. He watched closely as the figure slowly disappeared into the darkness of the hidden room. After it vanished into the secret opening, the passageway slowly closed once again, returning the bookshelf to its previous place in the wall.

"A secret room…" Hunter whispered to Elly with a wild smile.

"What?" Elly whispered back, unimpressed with the thought of a secret anything.

"Follow me!" he added.

Hunter wasted no time running towards the back of the giant library, his sister following quickly behind him, begging for him to slow down.

"This bookshelf." Hunter pointed at the spot in the wall where the android opened the passage.

"What about it?" Elly answered. "It looks like every other bookshelf."

"The robot opened some secret passage here, and we're going to follow it!"

"No, Hunter. C'mon, it's too late. Let's go back to bed," Elly protested.

"Go right ahead, but I'm going to find the passage, I'm going in," Hunter a felt around the books for any sort of lever or hidden button.

Hunter was more than elated with the idea of a secret room hidden in the mansion's library. He thought of all sorts of hidden treasure, gold medallions, long-lost scrolls, rubies... his imagination was running rampant. There was no way Hunter was turning back now, he was too close. Now, if he could find the blasted lever to open up the passage.

Chapter 4
Behind the Curtain

Hunter and Elly both searched for fifteen minutes finding nothing. They moved every book on every shelf hoping some sort of hidden latch would spring to life and unveil the passage. Yet, not one book seemed to house the secret entry. Hunter knew it was around here somewhere, but he was running out of ideas.

"We can't find it. Let's head back to our room before we get caught," Elly urged.

"No. I saw it with my own eyes. This bookshelf is the *key*, it's somewhere close by. It has to be!" Hunter frowned.

"Why do we want to follow that giant monster anyway?" quizzed Elly.

Hunter ignored the question, he was too focused. It had to be one of the books on the shelf. He had seen it in movies, pull out a book and release a hidden latch opening the door. Hunter didn't see anything else on the bookshelf that seemed to be out of place, frustration boil under his skin. He knew it was here somewhere.

That's when he noticed the stone gargoyle under the nearest light fixture. Much like the monoliths that sat outside the mansion, the gargoyle's head was eerily detailed. It had a pointy face with two small ears that sat atop its head. Its eyes were slim, disturbingly realistic, with high cheekbones and a furrowed brow. Hunter knew it was the object they had been searching for. Somehow, this ugly statue held the secret to the room, he could feel it.

He probed the gargoyle with his fingers feeling for any hidden knobs or buttons. He noticed the head itself could move in a circular motion. Eagerly, he turned the head clockwise until it clicked. A rumbling came from behind the bookshelf.

"I found it!" Hunter beamed. "I told you!"

"I don't want to go in there," Elly said, frowning.

The bookshelf noisily inched backwards into the wall. Elly watched the face of the bookshelf swing backwards into the darkened hallway then pulled up along by a series of ropes and pulleys.. "Then stay here and wait for me to come back." Hunter nudged his little sister aside, walking triumphantly into the darkened entrance. "It's pitch-black in here," he added. "Why the heck didn't I bring a flashlight?"

"I'm not waiting here by myself," Elly whined, reluctantly following her brother in.

Hunter searched around blindly until he found a steel railing. It was very cold, almost numbing his hand. The downward angle of the railing told Hunter it wasn't another hallway before him but rather a steep spiraling staircase that led into the depths of the mansion.

He made his way downward, being careful not to trip or miss a step. His sister followed suit, grabbing onto her brother's shoulder for support.

The air was thick, the deeper they went, the colder it got. They walked downward in complete darkness for what Elly thought was at least an hour, her legs started to cramp up, she was ready to stop and make Hunter rest with her when a small ray of light broke through the void.

"Look!" Hunter pointed.

Elly almost cried with relief.

They inched closer to the light, exposing two large doors that had been left partially open. Hunter reached over, edging them farther apart when Elly grabbed his arm.

"What if that thing's in there?" she warned.

"We'll check it out before we get too far in," he shot a whisper back. "Let me peek in to see if it's safe."

Hunter poked his head into the room, just enough to get a decent look around. His eyes lit up with fascination, he couldn't believe what he saw…

"What is it?" Elly asked.

Hunter didn't reply. He stood dumbstruck at the room before him. It was massive, filled with computers and what Hunter could only imagine was some sort of high-tech monitoring system. There wasn't much to the room aesthetically, no gothic décor of strange beheaded creatures mounted on the robust metallic walls. It was literally a giant machine-driven room, filled with nothing but mechanical wonders and gadgetry. This included the walls, which were nothing more than giant monitors, all of which currently read "System Offline." There were desks and numerous monitoring stations spread out across the room illuminating the place with blinking lights and random computerized noises. Everything he saw reminded him of a mad scientist's secret lair from the sci-fi movies his father would watch with him on lazy Sunday afternoons.

"Let me see!" Elly wedged her head underneath Hunter's. "Wow… it's kind of pretty," she added. "Like, Christmas lights."

"I don't see that thing. I think it's safe to look around a bit." Hunter stepped through the door.

The siblings split up, exploring the computer room. Hunter went straight to one of the many workstations. There were ten stations in all, each hub had a personal computer and a slew of other computerized gadgets Hunter had never seen before. He sat down in one of the leather chairs, where he stared blankly at a computer monitor. He didn't know much about computers or how they worked, but he would often sneak into his parents' study and wander the web, watching user-submitted videos of the latest and coolest video games being played. He wondered if he could sign in to the system.

Elly ignored the workstations altogether. Instead, she walked farther into the room where the large computerized walls turned into a small corridor. Elly wasn't quite sure what she was looking at, but the corridor was blocked off by a thin yellow veil of what looked like light. The closer she got, the brighter the veil became, until she realized it was some sort of energy field. She could hear the raw energy buzzing from it, but dared not touch it in fear of a getting shocked. Elly couldn't help but notice how this hidden underground room was such a stark opposite to the rest of the mansion's medieval and gothic nature.

The children stood, unbeknownst to them, at the epicenter of the most sophisticated computer system in the world.

The energy field that buzzed before Elly's eyes was in fact a state-of-the-art defense system that ran on electrical waves. This energy field could easily incapacitate anything that dared try to pass through it. Elly noticed a six-digit keypad to the right of the buzzing force field. This was a system keypad where one would swipe their identification card and input their security code to allow entrance into the safeguarded passageway.

Hunter sat at the desk looking for anything he might find interesting. It took him a moment to realize that this particular computer had no mouse or keyboard. He wasn't quite sure how to operate a computer without those necessary tools, he'd never seen one without them.

After a little rummaging he found a small latch hidden within the actual desktop itself. He slid the latch to the left and revealed what resembled a flat keyboard. Each key illuminated its designated character with a blue glow. The keyboard was glossy and smooth to the touch. It wasn't a keyboard in the traditional sense; it was more of a large touchpad. Hunter was used to laptops, both his parents owned one. They never left home without them, coming in quite handy for their work as anthropologists.

Hunter tapped a few of the buttons, attempting to type out his name, but to no avail. The monitor was still lifeless, a dark black abyss that only read "System Offline." Below the illuminated letters was a large outlined section in the same blue color. Hunter thought it may be like the mouse pad on his parents' laptops. He double-tapped the square and the monitor beamed to life.

"Awesome…" Hunter whispered to himself.

A screensaver appeared before his eyes. It bore a bright and vivid animated logo that slowly spun on an invisible axis. Hunter had seen the strange logo before. It took him a moment to pinpoint where exactly until he remembered he had seen it... He remembered it mostly being stamped on papers his parents would sometimes leave around the house. He remembered specifically asking his mother one morning what the logo was for. He wasn't sure why, but his mother had gotten strangely defensive and told him to go play outside, ignoring his question. Now it had shown up once again, here of all places. Hunter knew this was no coincidence.

The logo was quite strange, he was drawn to it. He inspected it carefully before touching anything else. It had a snake that sat in the middle of a circular crest. It struck Hunter as odd because the snakelike beast had two heads, one on each side of its body. Its long torso was shaped into a very distinctive letter "S" with the two heads almost meeting in the middle as if they were battling over its shared body. The crest that sat in the background behind the snake was split into quarters, separating the four other inner designs into sections.

On the top left, Hunter saw a picture that looked like a muscular ape of some kind. It stood upright in the picture with elongated arms. Directly to the right was another confusing image. This design was of a mysterious relic, a grand sword stuck slanted into a large rock, an image Hunter was familiar with, but he couldn't quite remember the legend that it derived from.

The bottom two designs were equally puzzling. Sitting diagonally from the ape creature was a second beast sticking a long slender neck out from a body of water. To Hunter, it looked like a sea-dwelling dinosaur. The fourth piece of the logo held another relic image. This appeared to be a lone circle holding within it a six-pointed star with six dots in-between each point.

Hunter didn't know much about the two artifacts represented on the logo. However, he had seen many television shows and online videos that had supposedly "caught" the other two beastlike images on tape. Hunter could only guess he was looking at a representation of Nessy, the infamous Loch Ness Monster, and Big Foot, the fabled bipedal ape. Hunter was still a bit perplexed by the logo, but he decided not to fixate on it any longer. He swiveled his finger in a circular motion on the touchpad, eliminating the screen saver. To his surprise, whoever was the last to use the computer hadn't logged off completely. Luckily, the mansion's networking email system was still operative, along with the last read email.

Master Benjamin Michael Jenson:

We are excited about you and your son, Alistair's, arrival tomorrow evening. It is of the utmost importance that you, please, promptly show Alistair to his room, number 112. He is not to depart from his quarters until further notice. We are under stringent orders from Professor Calenstine himself. Please report directly to the Ocelot Room for further updates on the current state of affairs. Here is what is known:

Five days prior to the scribing of this memorandum, a security breach occurred manipulating the Ocelot's inner cellblocks. It is unconfirmed where or how the breach occurred, but it is known that only one cell has been breached, Cell number 0012987. It housed subject number 1228, codename: The Beast of Bladenboro. There have been sightings of the Beast around the estate and a close encounter during the arrival of the Jakobs' lineage.

Reminder: Masters Kim and Geoffrey Jakobs' aircraft went down during their last assignment, and their children have been entrusted to the care of Claudio Calenstine and the Belmonte Estate, as per their parents' request.

We hope to integrate the children as soon as the rest of the lineages arrive for the 'Enlightenment.'

We look forward to your arrival.

Signing off,
Codename: Plato

Message sent: 17:23:13
Message received: 18:58:23

BEAST OF BLADENBORO

Plato,

You old rusted out toolbox… they still got you talking all matter-of-factly? I told Patty not to allow you onto the web to download your information anymore. Too many linguistic databases for you to learn from, stick to present-day standard English slang. You speak so stiff, you should incorporate more local jargon into your speech. People may warm up to you faster hahaha. Hmmm… Have you figured out humor yet?

Anyway, looks like Alistair and I will be walking into a mess. We've never had a breach like this. Wonder how that's even possible? Possibly an insider's job? Frightens me to think that.

I caught the news on Kim and her husband, Geoff. Very unexpected. I was very upset I couldn't make it to the funereal. Kim was a great Seeker, and Geoff wasn't that bad either for not going through the 'Enlightenment.' I wonder how Joe's doing?

The Beast of Bladenboro? We picked that cryptid up not even a month ago. Yussaf's team snagged that beast if I remember correctly, -ugly thing. Not good to have one of those fiends on the loose.

So, we'll arrive around five tomorrow. I'll settle Alistair up in our room the minute we step foot into the estate. He's ecstatic, he's never seen where his dad works, nor does he have any idea what the Jenson's do to pay our bills. Kid's full of questions.

Tell Patty to whip up that chicken penne pasta dish I love so much, we're going be hungry after this plane trip. Extra red peppers.

Later Gator,

Master Ben, I love that you still call us 'masters.'

Message sent: 20:19:55
Message received: 21:14:32

The information Hunter read left him with a sour sensation in his stomach. He hadn't expected to read about Elly and himself, or his parents' plane crash. Not to mention the escaped Beast of Bladenboro. That had to have been the creature he had seen the other night in the ventilation system. His brain was going a mile a minute trying to digest everything from the email. So many questions flooded his mind. Who were Plato and this Ben character? What was the 'Enlightenment' all about? Why had his mother been called a Seeker? What are cryptids? Too many questions swelled up in his head, his masterminded plan of escape had suddenly lost all of its fun.

How long had it been anyway? Hunter had lost track of time, a little over a week, two weeks maybe? He counted the sleepless nights in his head. It hadn't even been two full weeks since he had lost his parents in that dreadful plane crash. Sitting there in that strange room, reading that cryptic email, their death once again hit him out of nowhere. Adding to the realization of how absurd his life had become... he sat in that chair unable to control the tears welling in his eyes.

Elly hadn't caught up with Hunter yet, she was still far across the room happily roaming around until she came upon a large statue that seemed a bit out of place with the rest of the high-tech gadgetry that surrounded it.

This statue was huge, like everything else in the mansion, standing easily seven feet tall... Elly thought it was an ancient bronze statue of some sort. The figure had a rustic look, with a broad chest and solid husky legs. That's when she recognized it... it was identical to the mechanical robot they had seen earlier in the library. She stared up at its face; there were the two horizontal slits that had earlier been lit up with a blue light. The robot's eyes flickered to life, emitting the blue hue. Elly's heart sunk to her stomach.

"H-Hunter..." Elly stuttered. She tried to yell, but she could only manage a weak whimper.

The statue's eyes were now fully illuminated. Its mighty head looked down toward Elly. The machine's arm rose outward to grab Elly ran screaming as loud as she could.

Hunter stood up quickly from the workstation, wiping away the tears. He saw Elly from afar, running towards him. He couldn't figure out what was wrong, but the terrified look on her face was all he needed to see.

"Elly, be quiet!" he said in the loudest whisper he could muster.

The towering robot turned the corner giving chase. Its' cool blue eyes bounced methodically with every menacing step, its arms outstretched, trying to grab her.

The children were both terrified now. They darted through the double doors that entered into the stairwell, slamming the doors behind them. Hunter took off his shirt and tied it as tight as he could around the two doorknobs with the hope that it would prevent the giant robot from opening the door.

"Good thinking!" said Elly, now staring up at the spiraling staircase, a bit dismayed at its height.

"Don't stare at them, run!" Hunter yelled.

Hunter pushed his sister to pick up her momentum; they ran with all their might, never looking back. By midway through their flight up the stairs, both their legs throbbed in pain, but the mix of fear and adrenaline pushed them onward to the top. By the time they made it, both children collapsed with exhaustion on the library floor.

"Did it follow us?" Elly gasped for air.

"Let's not wait to find out." Hunter swallowed hard, his mouth now dry. "What was that thing anyway?" He wiped the sweat from his brow.

Hunter stood back up, peering into the darkened library, now more than ever he wanted to get back into his room, to lie comfortably in the warmth of his bed, far away from secret rooms and large creepy robots. It wasn't his legs that burned either, it was his head swirling in pain, overflowing with questions that weighed heavily on his mind. It was too much for him to comprehend.

"Hunter, what's on your chest?" Elly pointed to a small red dot.

Hunter looked down, but before he could see anything, a click of a flashlight turned on, a bright light shined into the children's eyes blinding them.

"Halt!" the deep voice of a man bellowed across the room. "State your name and lineage!"

The children, once again stricken with panic, had no idea what to say or even what a lineage was...

Chapter 5
Hot Water

The bright light blinded the children; they couldn't see the tall man with the scars on his face pointing his large rifle at them.

"M-My name is Hunter..." he somehow managed to choke out.

Elly hid behind her big brother shaking in fear.

"Are you the Jakobs' kids?" The man lowered the blinding light completely. Hunter recognized the man with jet-black hair and the menacing scar across his face from the argument with the old man in the wheelchair outside his bedroom window during their first night at the mansion. Nothing about the man was friendly; the large rifle with the laser scope he currently had pointing at the children didn't help the matter.

"Yes, sir..." Hunter replied.

"You're supposed to be locked in your room until we get this mess straightened out," the man yelled, walking over to the kids with fury in his eyes. "You're in big trouble!"

"S-sorry." Hunter's apology was drowned out by the sound of one of the bookcases suddenly smashing to the floor, setting off what sounded like an explosion a few feet away from them.

"What was that?" Elly shrieked.

"Shut up!" the scar-faced man ordered. He turned towards the noise shining the rifle's floodlight onto the overturned bookcase. It fell face down with books sprawled all over the floor in a heap.

"I tracked the beast into the library. It's in here with us." the man explained. His eyes darted across the large stretch of the library trying to see anything else that may be out of the ordinary.

"No…" Elly frowned.

"You kids stay close," the man demanded. "I could have bagged him already if you two hadn't disobeyed orders!" He pushed the children forward cautiously, safeguarding them from any potential threats. They slowly made their way towards the opposite side of the library where the elevator doors awaited their freedom. Hunter and Elly could hear something lurking about the shadows as they got closer, but they felt a sense of safety now that they had the scar-faced man there to protect them.

They weaved in between the maze of bookshelves, moving slowly and quietly, stopping every so often for the scar-faced man to shine his bright light towards a potentially threatening noise.

"Stay by me, I'll get you to safety," whispered the man.

"I'm scared…" Elly said, starting to panic. The mysterious noise around them seemed to get louder and more prominent. Something was definitely out there stalking them.

"How much farther…" Elly jumped, a vicious growl bellowed from nearby, it was so loud it shot a piercing ringing through the children's ears, deafening them momentarily. Before they could react to the noise, the large blur of a catlike creature leaped in front of them. The beastly figure crashed into the scar-faced man's chest, making a sickening thud upon contact. The man let out a low shriek of pain, the wind having been knocked out of him. He gasped for air, prone on his back, clutching his chest in pain.

"Run!" Hunter yelled as he and Elly hid behind a bookcase from the beast's preying eyes. This was the Beast of Bladenboro, the creature lurking about the ventilation system in their room. Hunter now understood why Ms. Ellingbee and Margot wanted to keep them safely locked away. This creature was terrifying. The snarls flooded the library halls as the children fled not daring to peer back and witness the menacing attack.

"Hide!" the scar-faced man yelled out, he struggled with the feline creature on top of him, doing his best to fend off the attack.

The children found safety underneath one of the large study desks a few yards back from the scuffle. They watched in horror, fearful for the scar-faced man's life as he fought with the creature in the dark halls of the library. The creature now sat atop of him, mauling him with its sharp claws. Elly's eyes filled with tears; never in her eleven years had she seen such violence.

The beast was roughly the size of the panthers Elly and Hunter had seen two summers ago during their visit to the zoo. Yet strangely enough, it had dark purple fur around the majority of its body, with a small white patch on its underbelly. The creature appeared to have a large patch of leathery scales on its back, naked of any hair. Its frame was quite muscular, its feline face hissed, showing off its grotesque teeth as it tried to take the life of the scar-faced man. It thrashed repeatedly with its razor-sharp claws.

The beast had the man's rifle locked between its mighty jaws, attempting to chew through it to get to the man's neck. The man used every ounce of strength to stay away from the monster's deadly jaws. His eyes locked with the beast's large, soulless, green eyes, doing everything in his power to keep calm. The fiend drooled dripping onto the man's face, eager for its meal. He quickly jerked his hips to the right, causing the beast to lose balance, briefly stopping its attack. The movement caused the man's index finger to pull the trigger of the rifle, a loud gunshot echoed throughout the library. He quickly took the opening to crawl off his back, getting to one knee, his rifle perfectly targeting the fiend's neck. A perfect shot.

The accidental shot had frightened the beast, it had fallen onto its side. Before the man could shoot, the feline jumped upright onto its four legs, its hair standing upright on its neck. It was evident now, as Hunter peered on, that what he had thought was a patch of scales on the beast's back was actually a set of large, leathery bat-like wings that stretched out magnificently. It jumped high into the air to flee, soaring off into the far corner of the library. The man regained his composure, able to get off a quick shot which barely missed the creature's head.

"Son of a…" the man cursed loudly. He began reloading the rifle to try to get off another shot.

The beast wasted no time managing to pry open one of the ventilation shafts high above the library floor. It fled hastily from the battle, quickly disappearing into the safety of the vents, retreating into the heart of the mansion's darkest areas once again.

"Damn it!" the man yelled, dusting himself off. His clothes tattered by the beasts' claws. Blood dripped from his wounds, pooling by his thick-soled boots. "You kids okay?" His injuries didn't seem to faze him.

"Yea, we're fine," Hunter answered. Now that it was safe he left the hiding spot under the study desk. "Elly? Where are you?" He looked around, unable to find his sister.

"Oh, no…" The man raced over, throwing one of the library desks on its side causing a loud thud as it hit the ground. Hunter saw his sister... she laid motionless under the desk, a small dart stuck in her shoulder.

"Elly!" Hunter gasped, a crippling sensation of fear striking his body.

The man pulled the dart out of her shoulder, tossing it to the floor. "Hurry, boy, we need to get her to a room!" He slung Elly over his shoulder and ran towards the elevator.

Hunter shook in fear doing his best to follow suit. Was his sister dead? She lay motionless in the man's arms. He really was all alone now…. no parents, no sister, his life was completely empty. He had no words, no real emotions, he felt like a body void of life. The emotional pain overtook his body with every step.

"Hit the button for the lift!" the man's hoarse voice demanded. He pulled a two-way radio from his thick black leather belt. "Patricia, we have a 211 on our hands. The female Jakobs! Medical attention is needed. Over." He released his finger from the button on the radio.

"Dominick?" Patricia's voice blared over the radio. "Are you serious?"

In the midst of everything, Hunter realized he didn't even know the name of the man who had saved his life, the man who was rushed despite all his injures to save his sisters. Dominick was the name of the man with the long scar across his face, the man who had single-handedly fought off that creature to save them.

"This is not a drill," Dominick replied. "She's been hit by one of my darts. Get there, NOW!" he ordered.

The elevator ride was the longest thirty seconds of Hunter's life, standing next to the Dominick holding his little sister in his muscular arms. Hunter felt helpless, staring at his sister's motionless face. It was all his fault. *She is never going to wake up...* Again, the dreary word popped up in his head, *alone*. He thought of how fickle the word was. It was used every day for so many reasons, but now such a simple term haunted his thoughts more than anything in the world. Hunter couldn't stand, his knees wobbled, his hands shook, the elevator's doors dinged and opened.

"C'mon, kid," Dominick urged. "She should be okay; the dart's a heavy dose tranquilizer. She's a small one, so let's hope she doesn't overdose..."

"Overdose?" Hunter swallowed hard.

"Err... she's gonna sleep it off." Dominick wasn't used to talking to children. He didn't want to scare Hunter any more than he could tell he already was. "Patricia will take care of her. Now hurry!"

The two rushed around the small curve in the long hallway. The children's room was now in their view. The door was already open, the light from the room illuminated the hall. Dominick ran into the room at full speed, trying his best to not rock Elly too much in his arms.

"Heavens, no..." Patricia jumped up from the bed, her face beat red from fear. She had tried to stay calm but was failing miserably.

"We were attacked by the beast. My gun discharged during the struggle. Somehow she got hit." Dominick explained.

Margot shot up from the other bed, where she sat with Trayer, whose canine instincts knew something was amiss. Margot helped Dominick gently lay Elly down on the bed. Ms. Ellingbee put a towel on Elly's head which quickly became soaked in sweat.

"Hunter!" Patricia Ellingbee yelled. "How on Earth did this happen?"

"We... I... err..." Hunter's head hung low, his face now flushed with emotions and tears. He took a deep breath and continued, "I wanted to see the mansion... I snuck out, and she followed me. I told her to stay, and now she's dead… just like my parents… everyone is dead!" His low, sulking voice grew to an abrupt shout of anger. Hunter was far too young to understand and deal with the travesties that seemed to be mounting up on his young shoulders, anger was his only control. He ran out of the room, back into the hallway, away from the others.

"Margot," Ms. Ellingbee said, but she didn't have to. Margot was already running after him.

"She'll be okay, right?" Dominick asked. "I mean, I was escorting them back here when that bastard came out of nowhere and attacked me. It was an accident I swear, I jolted, and somehow it went off," Dominick explained.

"Shush, quiet, dear," Ms. Ellingbee replied. "You're not to blame… you saved their lives. Hopefully, I can save hers. There's far too much sedative in her blood for her size. Its going to get ugly before it gets better."

"Damn it!" Dominick paced back and forth. His clothes ripped, soaked in his own blood.

"I'll take care of her," Ms. Ellingbee replied in a calm voice. "It's going be a grueling night."

"Can I help?" Dominick asked.

"In the corner is the emergency care pack. Set up an I.V. drip. Are you familiar with setting up an EKG?"

"Yes, I've been trained as a field medic and for emergency care. Consider it done," Dominick replied. "I knew I should have stayed home instead of taking this case." Dominick, despite being worried about Elly's health, was overly annoyed that the incident even happened. "Those damns kids weren't supposed to be wandering around the mansion!" He slammed his hand against the children's dining table in anger, leaving behind a small handprint of blood.

"Look," Ms. Ellingbee shot a withering glare at Dominick, "what's done is done. Leave it in the past. Let's focus on getting this girl better." Patricia noticed the blood that dripped from Dominick's arm. She had been so worried about Elly that she hadn't even noticed how hurt Dominick was.

"You're bleeding," she said, "…a lot."

"It's nothing," he stated matter-of-factly. "I'm fine."

"Don't pull that superhero act on me," said Patricia sternly. "What good are you to me if you pass out while I'm tending to Elly? Get over here and let me patch you up before it gets any worse."

༄

Margot followed Hunter down the hallway. She didn't have to go far before she found him sitting against the wall sobbing uncontrollably with his head folded into his arms.

"Hunter…" Margot said, her voice soft, comforting. She took a seat next to him on the floor and put her arm around his shoulder. "Elly is in good hands. It was an accident. It wasn't your fault."

"She followed me…" Hunter cried. "I shouldn't have snuck out…"

"That's true," Margot frowned. "But what's important is that you're safe now, and Elly is with Patricia. She'll make her better, I promise. She's safe now."

Hunter didn't respond, instead he continued to sob quietly into his arms. He felt so far away from home, so lonely. None of this would have happened if his parents hadn't been on that stupid plane when it crashed…

"You know something, I'm going to break some rules here, but I want to show you something that might cheer you up." Margot stood up from the floor, offering her hand to Hunter. "C'mon, it's okay."

Hunter held Margot's hand as she pulled him up off the floor and led him back towards the elevator.

"I don't want to go back there," Hunter said hesitantly.

"Well, we're not going downstairs. I'm going to show you the Administration Quarters. That's where Ms. Ellingbee and I live. This second level is the Academic Level, where we house our guests and some of our students," she explained.

"Students? This place is a school?" Hunter sniffled, trying to catch his cool.

"Yes, school, training facility, as well as many other things. As you know, you and your sister now live here with us, and we'll be providing your education."

The elevator doors chimed open. Hunter hesitated, but he felt safe with Margot and entered the lift alongside her. She hit the button labeled "3 Administration Quarters." The elevator took its course upwards for a few seconds until the doors opened once again. They walked out into a large bright room filled with white tables and chairs.

"This is the mess hall," Margot explained. "Each of our quarters has its own dining room, but a few times a week the staff likes to get together and eat here. It's also where we celebrate holidays and birthdays."

The room was nothing like the bland cafeteria from his middle school, which was the gymnasium transformed into a large room filled with tables and chairs for eating. Instead, this room was adorned with a myriad of décor that was very different from what he had been exposed to in the other levels of the mansion. There were no gargoyles or mounted heads of strange creatures, nor any futuristic giant computers. The room was much more modern, with two sixty-inch, flat-screen televisions at either end of the room, showing a twenty-four-hour news channel.

Hunter noticed that on one side of the room there was a long counter, a huge metal sink that had a sprayer hose on it, a refrigerator, microwave, and a very state-of-the-art stove. The opposite wall held six windows that looked down onto one of the many greenhouses on the estate. Even in the cold wintery weather, Hunter saw a plethora of bright green plant life inside the large, glass-walled building. The flora inside the glass structure looked like the rainforests Hunter had learned about last year in his geography class.

"That's the eastern conservatory, the 'Demeter Station' as we call it. We're seeing fascinating breakthroughs in the field of botany. The Belmonte Estate studies many different aspects of life. Botany is only one of many." Margot couldn't help but smile as she spoke, peering out the window with Hunter. "We study, collect, and protect just about everything that the world has to offer. I like to think we're making a difference."

"Botany?" Hunter asked. It seemed that the mansion was no place for children with their fancy computer rooms and large glass buildings housing enormous plants. He had heard the word 'Botany' before in school, but he didn't really know much about it.

"Yes, botany is the scientific study of plant life," Margot answered. "We've recently had a few breakthroughs in medicine. We have plants growing that no one else in the world has seen or would even believe existed. That's what makes us special."

"What else is studied in the mansion?" Hunter asked, trying to keep his mind off of other pressing matters.

"Well, that list is a long one, and a confusing one at that." She laughed a little trying to explain. "Let's say there are many secrets around the estate. There are even things that I'm not at liberty to know, but I can tell you that we've been doing this for generations and have helped many people in many different ways."

"I see. It all seems scary to me," Hunter walked away from the window and took a seat at one of the tables. The excitement and tragedy of the night had left him exhausted. His eyelids grew heavy, he rubbed them fighting off a large yawn.

"Well, I assure you, the only reason you and Elly are stuck in your room is because of something outside the norm. In over a hundred years, we've never had an incident like this." She pulled out a chair taking a seat opposite Hunter. "That creature roaming around the mansion will be taken care of shortly. Anyway, all the mysteries and scientific stuff going on around you isn't scary. We're trying to help people, sick people who are suffering from things modern medicine can't help them with. We're not just helping people either, but all sorts of animals and wildlife too." She smiled and took Hunter's hands into her own. "Hunter, we want to help. Right now, you're too young to fully understand what is going on around you. That's why when we bring in young people like you we don't go into detail about what *exactly* the Belmonte Estate is all about because it would be far too confusing. We ease you into it, by the time you're your parents' age, you'll have the knowledge and understanding to fully appreciate and partake in what we do; making the world safer, better for all its creatures, big and small."

"Okay…" Hunter replied with a faint smile. He could feel her sincerity, the excitement when she spoke. Despite the positive notion, he still felt uncomfortable and alone. He had never asked to come to the Belmonte Estate. He would much rather be home with his parents, with his friends… with Elly, who wasn't hurt because of something he did. Making the world a better place seemed like a wonderful thing to do, but who was making *his* world any better? He knew he was being selfish, but he didn't care about the world or helping sick strangers get better. He would trade all of that to get his family back.

"Anyway, the cafeteria wasn't what I wanted to show you." Margot stood back up, grabbing Hunter's hand with excitement.

She led him out of the cafeteria and through what Hunter assumed was some sort of adult games room. His eyes momentarily lit up with enthusiasm at the sight. The first thing he noticed was the three tournament-size pool tables. Hunter loved playing pool with his parents. The sudden sight brought back wonderful memories of his parents swirling in his mind. They had a pool table in their basement at home, he remembered his father spending weekends with Hunter teaching him how to play. His father always told Hunter that he was a natural, that with practice he could become quite a good player. He beat his dad once, and he never let him live it down.

Hunter then turned his attention to the walls of the game room. They were fitted with huge flat-screen televisions broadcasting twenty-four-seven sports channels. The room offered more than pool and television. Hunter also noticed a few ping-pong tables, a large oak poker table, and a giant foosball table. Hunter didn't care where Margot was taking him; this room was more than enough to cheer him up. He was excited, once Elly got better, he wanted to bring her back to this room and teach her everything his dad had taught him about pool.

"I thought you'd like the lounge room," Margot said, noting his interest.

"It looks fun. My dad taught me pool."

"Your mother was a good pool player too," Margot added.

"Did you know them well?" Hunter had forgotten Margot knew his parents.

"I knew them well enough to know how much they loved you. That's what I wanted to show you." Margot led Hunter through the game room and into a wide hallway that resembled the hallway outside his room. They passed a dozen or so doors before Margot came to a stop.

"I think you'll like this room." Margot smiled, she typed in a six-digit number on the keypad next to the doorframe. The lock mechanism unhinged, the door opened. Hunter couldn't help but wonder what on earth she wanted to show him after everything else he had seen.

Margot lead Hunter into the room, he was confused. Why was Margot showing him this? He looked around in bewilderment. It was a plain, modern, cozy, little living room. Unlike Hunter and Elly's room, which was one giant bedroom, this was actually more like an apartment. Fully furnished, equipped with a small kitchen, two bathrooms, a main bedroom, exercise room, dining room, and living room that had a fireplace. The apartment was very clean, Hunter guessed it hadn't been lived in for a while.

"Take a closer look around," Margot followed Hunter around the quarters.

He continued on through the living room into the kitchen. On the fridge, he found a magnet holding up a letter he had written to his parents before they had left on one of their anthropology trips last summer. *What it was doing here?* Hunter looked at Margot with confusion. She gestured into the bedroom with a compassionate nod.

Hunter hesitated at first but made his way into the bedroom. The first thing that caught his eye was a series of picture frames hanging above the headboard of the bed. He instantly recognized them. He felt his stomach tighten, his hands shake. They were pictures of his parents. Some older, some more recent, in the middle of the collection of pictures was one large family portrait. He stared at that one the longest. He remembered the day the photo was taken. It was three days after his parents had brought Elly home from the hospital after she was born. It was also the first time Hunter had ever gotten to hold his little sister. He sat between his parents on their large green couch holding her in his lap with a big grin on his face. He remembered his parents saying that he was too young to hold her on his own, so she lay mostly on his lap with his parents holding her up for the picture. He remembered that Uncle Joe had taken the photo. Hunter was only three, but his parents told the story of the photo a lot. He had the same one hanging in his bedroom at home.

"I don't understand. Why are my parents' things here? Did my parents live here too?" Hunter asked Margot, who nodded her head.

"You know how your parents took a lot of very long trips for their professions as anthropologists?"

Hunter nodded. It was a regular occurrence for his parents to leave for business trips, sometimes for as long as a month at a time. He had grown accustomed to their nomadic lifestyle.

"Well, a lot of that time was also spent here doing research, collecting the data they'd get out in the field. Actually, before you were born, they lived here all the time. It wasn't until after you came into their lives that they decided relocate." Margot took a photo from the wall, she took a seet on the bed. She tapped her hand gently on the mattress next to her, signaling for Hunter to sit down. "I knew your parents from living here with them. My room is three doors down. They were so nice to me when I moved in. Like most of the others, they stayed here off and on when they needed to. They never stayed a day longer than what was required of them, always eager to get back home to you kids. They told me the story of this photo. They were so excited for you both to reach the age when they could share the mansion with you."

"They were?"

"Very much so." Margot flipped the frame over, carefully unhinging the back. "I wasn't supposed to show you this room, or even discuss my relationship with your parents until things settled down. I think the professor doesn't want the two of you getting confused over everything that's been happening. He's also very busy

71

right now and wants to be able to explain everything in person once the timing is right. Hopefully you can meet him soon."

"Margot?" a muffled voice spoke from the radio in her purse.

She took out her radio. "Yes, this is Margot, over."

"We have stabilized Elly. She is resting now and everything looks good. We're waiting for the sedative to work its way out of her system. We need to keep a close eye on her. Do you have Hunter with you?"

"That's great news, and yes, I do." Margot answered with a bright smile.

"Do you mind staying with Hunter in your quarters until Elly makes a full recovery? I'll be staying here in Hunter's bed to keep watch."

"Of course, I'd love to have a sleepover with Hunter."

"That Cusith was a great idea," Ms. Ellingbee added. "The pup hasn't moved from Elly's side. He's going to make a wonderful pet."

"I thought he'd be good for them," Margot answered.

"Tell Hunter not to worry, we'll save the discussion of his disobedience until after Elly is better."

"Will do," Margot replied.

"Thank you. We'll see you both in the morning, here in the kids' room, after breakfast," Patricia finished.

"What do you say we sleep here? You can have the bed, I'll sleep out on the couch."

Hunter smiled. A sleepover seemed like a fun idea. Even though he wouldn't admit to it, after everything that had happened in the last few hours, he was too worked up to sleep alone in a strange place.

"You can have that photo, but keep it safe." Margot took the photo out of the frame, handing it to Hunter as a keepsake. "Keep it close to your heart, always."

She gave Hunter a big hug before turning off the bedroom lights and making her way to the couch. To Hunter's surprise, sleep came fast.

Chapter 6
Uncle Joey

Hunter woke in his parents' old bed with the picture Margot had given him clutched tightly in his hand. He rubbed his eyes, folded the picture up and placed it safely in his wallet. The delicious aroma of bacon filled the room, for a second, he pictured his mother at home in the kitchen cooking breakfast with bacon, eggs, pancakes, and all the trimmings to go with it. His mother would always make huge Sunday morning breakfasts. He thought for a second that he would walk out into the kitchen and find her there over the stove flipping the bacon strips, dishing up pancakes onto his father's plate while he skimmed through the Sunday newspaper at the table. Memories like these sneaking into his head made him smile and want to cry at the same time.

"You're awake. Good morning." Margot poured Hunter a glass of orange juice. "I hope you like bacon."

Hunter smiled; he took a seat swallowing down a big gulp of orange juice. Margot filled his plate with scrambled eggs, his stomach growled at the delightful smell.

"When you're done, we need to go check on your sister. It was a late night for you, you slept past noon."

Hunter didn't talk much; he was too busy enjoying the breakfast. All the excitement of the night before had left his stomach aching for food. Once his meal settled, his mind rested on thoughts of his little sister, he wondered how she was doing.

"Ready?" Margot asked.

Margot led the way back to Hunter's room. They rounded the

corner to the sound of a familiar voice. Hunter smiled, could it really be?

There he was…

"Uncle Joe!" Hunter yelled in excitement. He ran to his uncle with his arms out wide for a hug.

"Hunter! Buddy!" Joe knelt down, giving his nephew a big bear hug of an embrace. Hunter felt safe in his uncle's arms. Something he hadn't felt since coming to the mansion. He had missed his uncle and could tell his uncle wasn't his normal jovial self. He looked worn down, tired with thick dark bags forming under his eyes. Joe was of average height and a slight bit overweight. He would always tell Hunter a college student's diet of dehydrated microwaveable noodles and day-old pizza made it impossible to be thin. He had unmistakable dark black hair and even darker brown eyes to match, a Jakobs' family trait. When he took Hunter out to the mall or local grocery store, people always mistook Hunter for his son, they looked so much alike. Joe's skin was paler than usual too, his normally well-trimmed facial hair had turned into a heavy beard with a slight hint of grey beginning to set in. Hunter thought it looked like his uncle hadn't slept in weeks.

"I'm so sorry about Elly," said Hunter, looking over at his sleeping sister. "Is she doing better?" He felt the guilt rise in his stomach again, forcibly trying to hold back the tears. Hunter was never one to cry, especially in front of his uncle.

"She's stable," Ms. Ellingbee replied. "Thanks for your help, Dominick."

"Yes, thank you. I'm so glad you were here when I couldn't be." Uncle Joe shook Dominick's hand. "You have no idea how much we owe you."

"It's no problem," Dominick stated. "I got some stitches, a few permanent scars, all in a day's work though, right?" His voice turned stern as he looked at Hunter. "But, none of it would have happened if these kids had listened." He gave Hunter a disgusted look. "They never should have been wandering around the mansion."

"No worries, Dominick," Patricia interrupted. "The proper

discipline will be administered."

"Well then, if you'll excuse me. I have a score to settle." Dominick gathered his hunting supplies, his laser scope rifle, backpack, and medical provisions. "Stay out of trouble, kid." He nodded towards Hunter and stomped out of the room.

"He's pretty upset with you guys," Uncle Joe said.

"Don't worry about him. When it came down to it, he was here for Elly when she needed it," Patricia replied. She dampened a small cloth with ice-cold water, rang the excess water out of it, gently applied it to Elly's forehead. "She's running a little fever, nothing serious though. As long as we continue to manage it, she should be fine."

"Uncle Joey, you don't look too good," Hunter intervened.

"Well, it's been a rough few weeks for me. Patricia called me late last night with the news about Elly, and on top of not getting enough sleep... I thought I told you guys on the phone to listen to Patricia? What were you thinking sneaking out like that?" He felt exhausted, he plopped down on the bed next to Elly, who seemed to be sleeping peacefully through her fever. Uncle Joe ran his fingers through his thick beard, letting out a sigh.

"They were *not* thinking," Margot added.

Joe hadn't seen her walk in, he was a bit startled by the sound of her voice.

"Err... I'm sorry?" Joe replied with a faint smile.

"They've been stuck in this room for the better part of the week. They were going stir crazy. Hunter, you're sorry for disobeying, aren't you?" She smiled at Hunter.

"I am, really," Hunter replied.

"Okay, Hunter, we can talk about it later. I'm glad you're safe and Elly is doing well." Uncle Joe stood up from Elly's bed, ruffling Hunter's hair playfully. "I'm sorry, but I don't think we've met." He turned to Margot and extended his hand.

"Umm, my name is... err... Margot." Her face flushed.

"I don't recall meeting you before," Joe fixed his collared shirt, a bit embarrassed by his scruffy appearance.

"No, I've only been here at Belmonte Estate for a few years. I've heard about you though," she answered.

"Well, Margot..." Joe smiled at her. "I hope it was good things." He laughed nervously.

"Of course," she answered. "Nothing too embarrassing, I promise."

"Good, because there are a few doozies floating around these old walls." Joe took back his seat, next to Elly, checking her temperature with his hand. She was still pretty warm to the touch. He let out another frustrated sigh. Between the loss of his sister, and the loss of a good friend in her husband, coinciding with his niece and nephew moving to the Belmonte Estate, he couldn't help but feel much like his young nephew, lonely. It had been an emotional rollercoaster of a month for the remaining members of the Jakobs family. He hadn't told anyone, nor would he ever admit to it, but he was upset that his sister had picked Professor Claudio Calenstine to be the children's guardian. Joe had loved them like his own children, he could really use them in his life right now. He also wasn't very happy about them being raised in the mansion.

"Well, can someone fill me in on what is actually going on here? Things have definitely changed since I left." Joe looked to Patricia.

"Yes, of course. Follow me, we can talk in private." She motioned towards the bedroom door with a wave of her hand. "It's been quite some time since you've set foot here at Belmonte. It will take some catching up, not just on the current situation either, quite a bit has changed."

"Hunter, are you okay to stay here with your sister?" Joe asked.

"Don't worry; I'll stay with them while you catch up with Patricia," offered Margot.

"Oh... well, thank you." Joe smiled as he and Patricia left the bedroom and made their way down the hall to speak in private.

"Margot," Hunter scratched Trayer behind his ears as he spoke, "when we snuck out last night, we saw something in the library." He had been itching to ask about the giant robot they had seen, he wasn't sure if it was a good idea.

"Yes, the Beast of Bladenboro. I'm sure it was scary."

"Well… uh… yes, that was scary," Hunter answered. "But, we saw… well, we saw something else down there. Another monster… A *big* monster."

"What? You couldn't have. We'd know if there was something else out." Margot was worried by Hunter's claim. There had never been a breakout in the mansion before the Beast of Bladenboro had gotten out. One breakout was a big enough deal. If another creature had escaped, it would surely be a sign of worse things to come.

"No, seriously… there really was," Hunter explained. "It was huge, um… like a machine or something. It had glowing blue eyes."

"Oh!" Margot let out a sigh of relief. "That's Plato," she answered.

"Plato?" Hunter frowned, he was obviously missing something.

"Oh, well… umm… he's an Automaton," she answered as if Hunter knew what an Automaton was. "Actually, he's our librarian." She chuckled a little. "He also takes care of the sublevel cells…err… by that I mean he takes care of the lower levels of the mansion."

"An auto… what?" Hunter asked.

"An Automaton. I suppose you could call him an android if you're more familiar with that term," she explained.

"He's a *robot* then?" Hunter's mouth fell open in awe.

"Yes, we were going to introduce you soon, during the Orientation. Meeting a walking, talking robot can be a bit… well, hard for some people to handle." Margot's mouth pursed tightly. "Why did you think he was a monster? He's such a nice robot."

"Well… it was chasing us, so we ran away thinking it wanted to hurt us. That's when we ran into Dominick and the ugly monster with wings."

"Great," Margot chuckled. "He wasn't attacking you. He was probably trying to take you back to your room. He knows you're not to be wandering around the mansion. He's a gentle giant. To be honest, you probably hurt his feelings running away from him."

Hunter questioned the concept of a robot having hurt feelings; he always thought robots were void of emotions. That's what he had learned from all the sci-fi marathons he had watched with his father.

Then again, he never thought they were real either. "Robots can't have feelings; they're not human, right?"

"Well… Plato is sort of state-of-the-art." Margot paused for a second, trying to think of an easy explanation of how the robot operated. "You see… we didn't build Plato, we found him buried under tons of stone rubble in an archaic crypt deep in the sea. Actually, he's quite ancient, so I suppose saying he's state-of-the-art is a bit misleading. That's also why he looks a bit scary if you don't know any better. He comes from a different time and place."

"So how does an out-of-date robot have feelings?" Hunter was still quite confused.

"Er… well, I guess they're not real feelings. Plato has been learning the complexity of human emotion through syncing up with the Internet, he usually gets it right. So, you're correct, they're not real emotions per se, but in order to understand us, he attempts to artificially display feelings and affections."

"So, how can he be state-of-the-art and ancient?" Hunter felt quite excited about Plato's existence. *An ancient robot that walked and talked like a person?* His father would have been so excited.

"Um, well… it's a bit confusing until you learn a bit more about what we do here in the mansion. Put it this way," Margot explained, thinking carefully on how to clarify the elaborate concepts to a young child. "You see, we didn't create Plato. If we did, it would have been state-of-the-art to our current limitations. This is where it gets tricky; *our* state-of-the-art is nothing near as advanced as Plato's state-of-the-art when he was made. We don't have that sort of technology at our disposal yet," she explained. "Someone else created Plato. Someone that was far more advanced in the science of robotics than we are today. You see… well… Plato was made a long time ago by an advanced ancient civilization that has now been lost to time."

"That's impossible." Hunter was confused.

"What is?"

"An old civilization couldn't make that thing."

"Well, see, that's just it. If I told you about an ancient civilization that was far more advanced than us, would you believe me?" She

78

quizzed.

"Um… well, I guess not, no…" Hunter thought for a second. "If there was such a thing wouldn't we have been taught that in school?"

"No, because modern people think in general terms, such as myths and folklore, unwilling to accept that there may be truth within these stories. They laugh at the idea of an ancient civilization superior to our own. It's a bit frustrating for people like us who seek out the truth." Margot continued, "Plato *is* proof, but if we were to go public about his presence, he'd be taken away. And who knows what the government would do to him. Dissect him probably, and Plato is far too nice for that."

"We thought he wanted to kill us." Hunter was embarrassed. He felt like a jerk hurting a giant robot's feelings.

"You should have introduced yourselves. He loves children." Margot smiled.

Margot and Hunter sat next to Elly watching over her while she slept. Together they played with Trayer and patiently waited for Patricia and Joe to come back from their conversation. Hunter was thrilled now that his uncle had come to stay with them at the mansion, and it showed with his newfound smile. Yet the downtime endured while waiting for his uncle to return found Hunter wondering about the long list of questions that haunted him about the mansion.

He thought of the weird symbol he had seen on the computer screen. He wondered what it stood for, what it meant… He wondered about his family and what sort of connection they had with the mysterious estate. He thought of Margot and how happy she made him when she had shown him his parents' quarters. How the photo she had given him made him feel closer than ever before to his beloved parents despite their loss, but even that slight ray of hope was engulfed with shadows. He couldn't help but wonder why they had a second home in the mansion in the first place. What did they do when they were here anyway? Why was his mom referred to as a "Seeker" in that email, and what the heck did that mean anyway? So many questions weighed on his young mind, and yet they didn't end there.

He had been attacked by a winged beast, some sort of treacherous monster that had the body of a giant purple cat and the wings of a bat. It was nothing like any animal he had ever seen or read about.

His mind turned to Professor Claudio Calenstine, his new guardian, who he hadn't even met yet. He wondered what his new guardian was like and why anyone would want to live in such a strange place. Despite all these illusive questions, he didn't dare ask Margot for answers. He was already in trouble for getting his little sister hurt. Nobody knew he had read the documents on the computer, and he preferred it stayed that way.

"Hunter," Elly whispered from her bed, her voice cracking as she spoke.

Hunter jumped from the sound, a bit startled. "Elly?"

"Are you okay, dear? How do you feel?" Margot rushed over and took hold of her hand. It was warm and clammy.

"Wh… err… what… happened?" Elly's words were soft. She could only manage a light raspy whisper. She spoke, but she didn't have the strength to open her eyes.

"You were in an accident, Elly. How are you feeling?" Margot added, but Elly didn't respond.

"What's wrong, is she okay?" Hunter grew agitated. "Why isn't she answering?" He began to pace around her bed, his face struck with worry.

"Shhh," Margot whispered. "She's fallen back to sleep, Hunter. It's okay, it's good that she came, even for a second. That means the sedative is wearing off and she's getting her strength back. Patricia will be delighted to hear the news."

"Here," Hunter took the wet towel Margot had dampened. "I'll hold it on her forehead."

"Thank you. You're a good big brother," Margot smiled. "So, your uncle… you seem very close to him."

"Uncle Joe is great. I wish we could have lived with him instead of in this mansion, but he said we couldn't."

"Well I'm sure he wanted to." Margot chose her words carefully. "I know your parents were very excited for you and your sister to live here at the estate."

"I guess," Hunter replied.

"It's true! They couldn't wait for the day they could share the magic of the estate with you."

"Really?" Hunter found that hard to believe.

"And I'm sure Joe had his reasons for not being able to stay with you and Elly."

"Well, he always says he's a poor college student. He's not even a student anymore. We went to his graduation party last year so he can't use that as an excuse." Hunter explained.

"Oh?" Margot cracked a smile. "Is that so?"

"Yeah, and he usually doesn't have that giant beard. He looks kind of scary with it."

"I sort of liked it." Margot smiled.

Another hour passed before Uncle Joe and Patricia made their way back to the bedroom. Patricia was elated to hear that Elly had momentarily regained consciousness. Yet despite the good news, the stress on Joe's face was quite evident, even to Hunter's young eyes.

"You look tired," Margot noted.

"Is it that noticeable?" Joe responded with a heartfelt smile. "With everything that's been going on, and the helicopter ride over here, I'm beat."

"Uncle Joe is afraid to fly." Hunter laughed.

"Yes, I'm also deathly afraid of bugs and heights." Joe laughed back.

"No wonder you decided to leave the mansion." Patricia checked on Elly's status.

"Well, I suppose you could say that."

"How long were you here for?" Hunter asked.

"Long enough." Joe cracked a small smile as he thought back to his childhood. "I grew up here, like you and your sister will."

"Really, you did?" Hunter was shocked at the news.

"I did. Your grandparents raised your mother and me here for much of our childhood."

"Would you and Hunter like to continue this discussion over

lunch?" Margot offered. "I wouldn't mind preparing you something upstairs."

"I'd love something to eat," Joe said, nodding.

The group left the room following Margot up towards the dining area. Joe hadn't realized how hungry he was. If there was anything he missed about the mansion, it was the delicious food. College had ruined his diet; he hadn't eaten a three-course meal in years. The mansion had changed so much in the past ten years, very little was as he remembered it. When they entered the dining room, he peered out his favorite window from his youth. He was shocked to see the flora-filled greenhouse sitting where he used to play games of kickball outside with his friends. He couldn't believe how much new technology had been incorporated into the dusty old mansion he remembered. He settled down at one of the white dining tables alongside Hunter as Margot began preparing lunch for the three of them.

"I see they added a new greenhouse where I used to run amuck," Joe said.

"Yes, it's quite new. We needed a controlled ecosystem for some of our new research," Margot explained readying a pot with boiling water.

"There are actually televisions now too," he joked.

"Not in our room," Hunter mumbled.

"Parts of the mansion have been upgraded with internet, and yes, cable as well." She laughed a little. "Many more people live here all year round, and the professor thought it would help them feel more at home if we modernized the place."

"I see," Joe responded. "Pretty nice lady that Margot, don't you think?" he whispered to Hunter.

Hunter smiled back. He thought she was nice too, but he felt like his uncle had an entirely different meaning.

"Kinda cute too, right?" Joe playfully punched Hunter's shoulder.

"Err… I dunno… I guess," Hunter shrugged off the question.

"Knew I should have taken the extra ten minutes and shaved this gnarly beard off." Joe ran his fingers through his facial hair. "What do you think? Is it me?"

"Margot said she liked it," answered Hunter, feeling a little uncomfortable.

"Really?" Joe looked over to Margot preparing a hearty lunch of grilled cheese sandwiches and what smelled to him like a pot of tomato soup. "Anyway, despite all the craziness you and your sister got into last night, how has your stay in the mansion been so far?"

"Terrible," Hunter answered bluntly.

"That surprises me." His uncle frowned. "This place is full of trouble for kids your age to get into. As much as you and your sister should be grounded for sneaking out last night, I understand why you did it. When your mother and I were here as kids, we always got into trouble."

"Were you my age when you lived here?" Hunter asked.

"Yep, we sure were. Your grandparents were always disciplining us."

"How come you guys never told us about this place?"

"Well... because it's not allowed." Uncle Joe scratched his chin trying to put into words what he was allowed to say, which was a bit difficult under the circumstances.

"What do you mean?" Hunter pushed on.

"It's hard to explain, in fact it's one of the reasons I left. Hard to trust a place always full of secrets, ya know?" Joe spoke in a hushed voice. "But, to honor your parents' wishes, I will play the game and watch what I say."

"That's what everyone says." Hunter grew annoyed. "'We'll tell you later, you'll meet him soon, you'll get answers when the time is right,'" Hunter whined.

"I understand... I really do," Uncle Joe replied. "It was the same way when your mom and I were younger." Joe cracked his knuckles uncomfortably, a bad habit he picked up when he felt uneasy. "I can tell you that this place keeps its secrets for a good reason. There are a lot of um... well... highly classified and sometimes even dangerous things going on within these walls. In order to keep the mansion private and concealed from the world, they live by a very secretive code. I can tell you that you'll learn a lot about why you're here, very soon. In a few days, everyone will have arrived, and you'll slowly get some answers. Until then, I suggest we sit back and go with the flow."

"Why are there more people coming?" Hunter asked.

"Haven't they told you anything? In a couple of days, once everyone who has been invited shows up, there's an Orientation where you'll learn a brief history of the estate. You'll get a quick tour, and at the end, you'll have to make a big decision."

"What sort of decision?"

"The same one your mom and I made. The same one your grandparents made before us. It's written in you and your sister's fate. It's sort of a family tradition."

"Lunch is ready!" Margot interrupted. She carried over a platter of delicious-smelling grilled cheese sandwiches accompanied by a slow-roasted pot of rich and creamy tomato soup. Hunter and Joe were both eager to fill their bellies. The delicious aroma made their mouths water.

"Hope everyone is hungry. It's nothing fancy, but one of my favorites."

"Are you kidding?" Joe beamed. "I've spent eight years in college. Anything that's not made with dehydrated noodles and prepackaged seasoning is a feast." He took a sip of the steaming hot soup. "Oh man... heavenly," he smiled.

"Well, thank you." Margot blushed.

"Grilled cheese is my favorite too," Hunter added. He took a giant bite, spilling the delicious melted cheese onto his chin.

"So, you decided to leave the mansion for college?" asked Margot.

"Umm, well... Yeah, sort of. I finished my master's degree in creative writing," Joe replied, speaking between mouthfuls of food.

"Really, a writer? That must be why you have that beard." Margot laughed.

"Err... Well, not exactly," Joe said, chuckling. "I call this my stress beard. Too much has happened in the last month to worry about small things like lining up my facial hair evenly."

"Uncle Joe is a great writer," Hunter interrupted. "He always writes Elly and me into his stories. My favorite was when he made me a superhero with powers to fight off evil monsters."

"Really?" Margot teased. "Written anything I would have read?"

"Not unless Hunter was selling the copies online and taking all my royalties," Joe joked. "Actually," Joe's voice got a bit more serious, "before their parents..." he stumbled for a second, forgetting momentarily Hunter was with them, "...well you know, before all these terrible things happened around us, I was offered a job at my college to teach."

"How exciting!" she exclaimed.

"I didn't know that, Uncle Joe," said Hunter.

"Well, I had to turn it down."

"What, why?" Hunter asked, taking sips of the steaming soup. "You've been in school forever."

"Well, buddy, sometimes life throws you curve balls, and you have to read adjust your batting stance."

"Oh," Hunter replied, not really understanding the euphemism.

Margot didn't respond, instead she frowned ever so slightly as she finished her meal.

The three of them ate in silence until they finished. Hunter and Joe were both thankful of Margot's kindness, and now their bellies were filled to the brim with her delicious food. The afternoon had been nice for Hunter and Joe. Joe missed his niece and nephew dearly, and although he wouldn't show the kids, he was struggling miserably with the death of his sister. It was therapeutic to spend time with his nephew.

When Joe received the call that Elly had been hurt, he had experienced his first ever panic attack. He had been alone for almost two weeks locked away in his small downtown apartment. He found himself only willing to leave for the funeral service and a couple of food runs. Even then, most of his money went uncharacteristically to booze. He had found himself in a dark place he had never been in before. His only way to deal with his pain was by drinking away what he couldn't deal with. He was watching himself turn into someone he desperately didn't want to be. Yet, he didn't have the strength to make the change.

Joe had originally planned to depart for the mansion within a few days. He made a promise to himself; to clean up his act and to be emotionally strong enough to take care of his niece and nephew while he visited. He never thought he would wake up in the middle of the night to board a personal helicopter a few hours later. Flying was one of his biggest fears. Before he left, he took a shot of whiskey to ease his nerves. He was thankful Elly was doing better; thankful to be around his family, but he was ashamed to have shown up in his current condition. Even now, there with his nephew, he felt the urge. He realized he wasn't ready to return to the mansion yet, and raise his niece and nephew, especially under these circumstances.

"Hunter, be a pal and take care of the dishes. Margot was nice enough to make us food. You can take care of it."

"Okay." Hunter would normally argue over the daily chore of dishes, but he still felt terrible about sneaking out and getting Elly hurt; and he couldn't believe he hadn't been grounded yet. He gathered the dishes and ran the hot water in the sink, applying a liberal amount of dish soap.

"That was easier than expected. Any normal day and I'd have to ask him at least three times." Joe chuckled.

"That was sweet of you," Margot added, ignoring the joke.

"What? Putting Hunter to work on the dishes?"

"No… um… you know. How you gave up that job as a professor to be here with them. They need you here. Hunter is a different person when he's around you. I think it makes this transition a bit easier for him."

"To be honest," Joe looked over at Hunter who was washing out the soup bowls, "as much as I would like to think I made the choice to be here for them, I'm pretty sure I need them more than they probably need me. I was a mess before I got here." Joe took a second… "Honestly, I'm still a mess. Coming here and seeing their faces though, even Elly's, who's lying up in that bed sick, they make me want to get better."

"They seem like good kids." Margot reached out her hand and

placed it on Joe's sympathetically.

Joe found himself affectionately squeezing hers without realizing it. He found himself looking into her eyes; they were dark blue and slightly infused with a hint of speckled grey. He had never seen eyes that color before. He found them fascinating, hard to pull away from.

"I'm all finished," interrupted Hunter.

Joe jumped, Margot quickly pulled her hand away. She cleared her throat nervously and smiled at Hunter, who walked back over to the table. He took a seat next to his uncle, completely oblivious to the moment.

"Uncle Joe, they have an awesome game room. Want to play something? They have a pool table like at my house."

But before Joe could agree to a game of pool, Margot's radio interrupted them.

Hunter frowned at the distraction. He had been eager to play in the game room since seeing it the night before.

"Margot, are you still with Joseph?" Patricia chimed in over the static of the two-way radio. "I thought he would like to meet me downstairs to welcome Benjamin and his son, Alistair Jenson, as they arrive. They've been dropped off at the gates."

"Ben is here?" Joe beamed with excitement. He quickly stood up from his chair, ready to run downstairs.

"Copy that, Patricia. I'll look after Elly while Joe and Hunter meet up with you downstairs."

"Who's that?" Hunter asked. He recognized the two names from the computerized message he had read.

"Ben was my best friend when I lived here as a kid. Man, we were always getting into trouble. You know he has a boy your age, you might have a new friend."

A new friend, Hunter thought. He was a bit nervous about meeting someone new. He was never comfortable at forced social moments like these. However, the thought of befriending someone his age in this strange place put him a bit more at ease. Maybe things were finally starting to turn around for him.

Chapter 7
A Friendly Reunion

Hunter found himself, once again, staring at the large front doors where he and Elly had first entered the bizarre mansion. It had been almost a full week since that fateful rainy afternoon when they were dropped off at the mansion's front entrance. But to Hunter, it felt like it was just yesterday.

The sight of the magnificent oak doors brought back a flood of painful memories. Hunter remembered how awkward the taxi driver was during the long, tiring drive through the immense forest, and how bitter and desolate he felt from being taken away from the only home he had ever known. At least now, Hunter was standing in front of those colossal doors alongside his beloved uncle. They stood there, the two of them awaiting his uncle's friend's arrival. He felt a sense of comfort being with Joe, like he had finally gotten his family back.

Hunter and Joe peered through the large bay window near the front doors. It wasn't too long before he saw the bulky iron gates open. He watched as the friendly caretaker, Ms. Ellingbee, who was smiling as always, quickly welcomed two shadowy figures into the estate grounds. Hunter couldn't see the two clearly, but his uncle must have had better vision because the moment they came into view, Joe's eyes lit up with excitement.

"That's them!" Joe's voice boomed. "I haven't seen Ben in years." He quickly unhinged the smaller hidden door within the larger double-framed entrance as Ms. Ellingbee had the day Hunter and Elly entered the mansion. "C'mon, let's go meet them."

"Oh," said Hunter a bit too nervous to allow any excitement to get the best of him.

He decided to stay behind. He waited eagerly, watching as his uncle walked out into the wintery mid-afternoon to meet his friends. Hunter hadn't worn his jacket and didn't feel like venturing into the bitter cold to meet a couple of strangers. In fact, Hunter wasn't all that thrilled to meet anyone new at this point. He would rather stay up in his room and watch over his little sister.

Uncle Joe quickly jogged through the snowy courtyard to meet up with Patricia and their new housemates. The snow had started falling in earnest as it grew ever closer to winter. Hunter watched contentedly from the warmth of the mansion as the large snowflakes fell from the grey sky, leaving behind a wintery white blanket across the sprawling courtyard.

"Joe? You sly devil! How long has it been?" Benjamin ran up to Joe and the two men embraced each other with a hearty back-slapping hug. Benjamin was about a foot taller than Joe with a much slenderer frame.

"About a decade, right? Either way, it's been too long, my friend, and this must be your better half?" Joe threw out his hand for a 'down-low' high-five towards the young boy standing next to his father. The blonde-haired child responded with a faint smile and a quick slap.

"Alistair, right?" Joe asked.

The boy nodded. He stood a little taller than Hunter, a skinny kid with blonde curly hair. Much like Hunter, he had a thick pair of glasses that sat atop his cold red nose. He sniffled a bit from the cold and did his best to keep up with the adults as the group made their way up through the courtyard, back towards the mansion.

"Yes, this here is my boy genius," Ben said proudly. "He knows more about computers than his old man. Plato may have found his replacement."

"Awesome!" Joe smiled. He could feel how proud Ben was as he spoke of his son. "I can't wait for you to meet my niece and nephew." Joe pointed towards the mansion, where Hunter stood staring back at them.

"Now, you boys better behave," Ms. Ellingbee added with a playful smile. "And I'm not talking about you, Alistair. Don't let these two 'adults' fool you. Your father and Joe always seem to find trouble." She winked at Alistair, who chuckled in return.

"Come on now, Patty. We weren't that bad, were we?" Ben playfully punched Ms. Ellingbee on the shoulder, and she gave him a stern look, clearly not amused.

"Don't think I forgot about the night you two snuck out and dyed all the young girls under garments bright pink," she added.

"Gross, you did that, Dad?" Alistair's lip curled.

"Well…" Ben smiled slyly. "…It was Joe's idea."

"That was like… err… fifteen years ago. We've matured since then," Joe added.

"Yeah, we're a couple of model citizens," Ben boasted. He grabbed Alistair and swung him up onto his back, giving him a piggyback ride up to the mansion entrance.

"Wow, this place is huge." Alistair's jaw dropped at the surroundings. He stared up at the towering double doors, like Hunter, feeling a bit in awe at their sheer size.

"Well, here we are; let's get inside and warm up." Ms. Ellingbee gestured towards the door kicking the snow off their feet. She closed the mighty doors and locked them behind her.

"It's good to be back." Ben let out a sigh of relief.

"Wow… is this really the place?" asked Alistair.

"Yep, this is it, my boy, your father's secret getaway."

"It's creepy." He thought the mansion looked big from the outside, but this room alone, made him feel small. Alistair looked all over, amazed at its eerie contents. The strange gothic designs imprinted on the big double doors and the weird, mounted animal heads on the far wall. He hadn't even realized Hunter was standing next to him until he took a step back to get a better view of the large stained-glass window on the eastern wall and almost tripped over Hunter's foot.

"Alistair, this is my nephew, Hunter." Joe smiled.

"Hello," the boys said in unison.

"So, I can imagine the mansion has changed quite a bit since you last stepped foot in it, aye?" Ben took off his scarf and gloves, shaking off the snow.

"You could say that," replied Joe.

"Well, if you boys don't mind catching up in your rooms, we're under direct orders to remain in our quarters until further notice," Patricia interrupted.

"Oh yeah, I forgot about the email Plato sent me," Ben stated. "Any idea how the security breach happened?"

"Still looking into it. Plato hasn't found anything yet, but you can ask Hunter about the seriousness of the situation."

"What's that now?" Ben's head cocked slyly to the left with an intrigued smile.

"Umm... let's follow Patricia up to your room while Hunter explains." Joe nodded to Patricia, who eagerly waited to press on.

"Time is of the essence," she added.

"Do I have to?" Hunter didn't like the thought of revealing how his sister got hurt, and he felt a bit shy about sharing his troubles with strangers.

"I think Ben might enjoy what you have to say," said Joe, hiding a smirk from Patricia.

The group moved on from the main foyer and up towards the balcony level, where the elevator sat waiting.

"Well," Hunter started, "I snuck out last night to explore the mansion. Of course, my little sister followed me even though I told her not to." Hunter went on explaining the situation, pinpointing all the reasons why he shouldn't be blamed for his sister's injuries.

"You're kidding me!" Ben was amazed at the story. A beaming smile grew across his face as Hunter explained his little adventure. "You haven't been here for a week, and you already snuck out? That's fantastic!" he exclaimed loudly, giving Hunter a high-five. Hunter was completely caught off guard by his enthusiasm but was happy to oblige the friendly gesture. Alistair and his father both seemed to be very friendly. Hunter felt bad for being worried about meeting the two. He should have known Uncle Joe would have awesome friends.

"Benjamin!" Patricia frowned at Ben's response, shaking her head in disbelief. She continued in a very motherly tone, "You're a role model now. I don't think you should be giving high-fives to children for sneaking out and getting into trouble, especially with you-know-what on the loose. His sister could have died, you know? She is in bed now injured from their misjudgment, lucky to be alive."

"Oh… um, yea, of course. Sorry…" Ben stumbled over his words, a little embarrassed over his immature display in front of Patricia, who was definitely a mother figure to both Benjamin and Joe. He leaned towards Hunter and whispered, "Still a pretty admirable feat. Like uncle, like nephew, I suppose," he added softly, away from Patricia's ears. "So, good old Dominick was called in to take care of the cryptid?" he readied his voice for everyone to hear.

That word set off a strange feeling in the pit of Hunter's stomach. Cryptid, what on earth was a cryptid? That one single word had haunted Hunter's mind ever since he had read about it in the mysterious email.

"Well, everyone capable of eliminating the threat was out preparing for the festivities or on other business needs, this time of year the Estate gets pretty empty. Professor Calenstine wasn't happy about calling Dominick's group in, but he'd hoped to get everything sorted out before everyone showed up, I think he is hoping to patch things up with him as well... We see how that turns out," Patricia explained as the elevator door opened. The group squeezed in, continuing their conversation.

"Well, it'll be fun once Abram gets here," Ben said jokingly.

"Those two still hate each other?" Joe asked.

"Are you kidding me? My cousin holds grudges like none other. Not to mention, Dominick isn't exactly the nicest guy in the world. I'm glad he's from Abram's side of the bloodline and not mine. We keep it pure, right, Alistair?"

Alistair nodded, not quite understanding what was going on.

"Who are they talking about?" Hunter whispered as the grown-ups continued their conversation. He had heard the word 'bloodline' tossed around a few times in the mansion, but he didn't quite understand what was meant by it.

"I dunno," Alistair answered, a bit perplexed as well by the meaning of 'keeping it pure.' "Abram is my uncle. He works here with my dad. I don't know who Dominick is though," he whispered back.

Hunter found it interesting that Alistair's dad and uncle both worked in the mansion where his parents also had a second home. Hunter wondered if, perhaps, his parents worked here in some capacity as well and it wasn't a room for rent when they left for their expeditions. He was excited to get a chance to speak with Alistair alone and find out if he knew anything more about the strange mansion.

"How about we go to Hunter and Elly's room so you can meet my niece? I want to check up on her anyway," Joe suggested.

"We'd love to," Ben answered. "Kim and Geoff always spoke so highly of them." He paused for a second; he hadn't given it too much thought that Hunter had lost his parents, and Joe had lost a dear friend and his sister. He had gotten lost in the moment of reuniting with an old friend, having forgotten about all the heartache their family was dealing with. It wasn't until then, that the dark truth of the current situation settled in around them. Hunter immediately felt the mood change.

"That's a great idea," Patricia said, lifting the natural tone of her voice a pitch higher to try and lift the mood a bit. "I'll go whip up some of my famous marshmallow mint hot chocolate."

"That sounds amazing!" Hunter smiled.

"Yeah! Can I have extra marshmallows?" Alistair beamed with excitement as well. Hot cocoa was just the thing he needed to warm up from the bitter cold.

The group settled in the kids' room where Trayer excitedly jumped onto Hunter's shoulders and knocked him to the floor. Trayer's excitement got the best of him, his tongue followed suit with a slobbering assault of licking, playfully nibbling on Hunter's face. Trayer had been by Elly's side since they brought her back from the library unwilling to leave her, not even to eat his dog food.

"Err… is that dog safe?" Alistair hesitated taking refuge behind his father's back.

"That's a Cusith," Ben answered his son, bending down to allow Trayer to sniff his hand. "Don't let his size scare you." He scratched Trayer's belly and the dog rolled over, delighted. "Old Bernadine had her pups. I'm guessing she didn't make it... I'll miss that old dog." Ben's voice was sad at the thought. Bernadine was Trayer's mother.

"They said he was the only puppy to make it," Hunter added, noting the sadness in Ben's eyes, something he was getting used to seeing.

"Well then, you have a very important pet to take care of. He may be the last of his breed in the entire world." Ben stood up, pushing the grief from his voice.

"That's sad." Alistair had warmed up to the pup and was scratching Trayer's ears.

Joe sat next to Elly on her bed, hoping to see improvement. She appeared to be sleeping peacefully, tucked snuggly into her bed sheets. He placed his hand on her forehead. Her fever had broken which was a good sign.

When Joe had first seen Elly that morning, his niece's face had been pale and clammy. Thankfully, it had returned to its natural pinkish hue. He had been worried for a while. He wasn't sure how he or Hunter would have dealt with the sudden loss of Elly. The three of them were going to be relying on one another for quite some time to come.

"Here we go." Patricia entered the room with a platter of steaming-hot mint cocoa, topped off with melting marshmallows. The delicious sweet fragrance warmed Benjamin and Alastair's still freezing bodies.

The drink brought back fond memories of Hunter's parents. They would always share a cup of hot chocolate with the kids every Christmas morning before they were allowed to open any presents. It was a bittersweet memory. He was happy he had so many fond memories, but they always left him hurting more than helping. In fact, Hunter had decided he hated how everything he seemed to do brought up some lost memory of his parents. He really wished he could forget about them forever and not have to deal with the dulling pain that continuously crept up on him. Suddenly, his hot cocoa lost its flavor.

"Why don't we let the children be for a while? Elly is doing well, and I can show you Joe's new living quarters," Patricia suggested.

"Please tell me you moved him next door to me." Ben smiled.

"Hunter, please take care of Elly for us until we get back, and have fun with Alistair." Joe waved shutting the bedroom door, leaving the children alone for the first time since the accident.

"What happened to your sister?" Alistair asked, sipping on the hot chocolate.

"Well, I snuck out of here last night to explore the mansion. Nobody would tell me and Elly anything about this place. They locked us in here like prisoners. She followed me despite me telling her to stay back, then we got attacked by that monster that's running around here, and she got hit by some kind of dart," Hunter explained.

"Wow! That sounds…" Alistair hesitated for a second, "…scary. She's okay now though, right?"

"She woke up for a bit earlier, so I think so," Hunter blew on his cocoa to cool it down.

The two kids sat at the table near the large window overlooking the mansion's courtyard. Hunter watched a couple of different families make their way into the mansion. Each family was greeted by a different person. All of the families seemed to have a child around Hunter's age. He and his sister had been here for almost a week and had seen no one coming or going from the mansion, so he found the recent events a bit perplexing.

"Looks like you're not the only ones showing up today," Hunter said, curious over the sudden flood of people arriving.

"There should be a few different families showing up. That's how it works," Alistair answered.

"How what works?"

"You know, the mansion," Alistair explained. "My dad told me every generation has a chance to come to the mansion. He said it's our generation's time."

"Really?" Hunter was baffled. He had never been told such a

thing. He wasn't even sure what Alistair meant by 'their generation's time'. *Time for what?* He wondered.

"Didn't your parents tell you about tomorrow?"

"No, they died a few weeks ago." Hunter stared into the bottom of his now empty mug. He wondered if his parents had meant to tell him about the mansion and the whole generation thing. Maybe they didn't have the chance.

"Oh, I'm sorry…" Alistair frowned. Hunter knew it wasn't a fun conversation for anyone to take part in.

"What else do you know about this place?" Hunter asked, breaking the awkward silence.

"Not much, my dad works here. He's an archeologist or something like that. He goes around the world and digs up old cities and animals and stuff."

"Really? My parents were anthropologists," Hunter explained.

"What's an anthropologist?"

"My mom told me she studied different cultures and how they live."

"They sound similar, huh?" Alistair noted. "Maybe we get to become anthropologists or archeologists tomorrow."

"Maybe…" Hunter answered, though he doubted it.

"So, what do you do for fun here?" Alistair asked.

"Well, Elly reads all those boring books on the shelves. I sit around and play with Trayer; that's all there is to do, really."

"There's not even a computer or a television in here?"

"When I snuck out, I found a room full of computers. It was huge," Hunter added, raising his hands as high into the air as he could to signal how large the screens were.

"Really?" Alistair's eyes lit up. He was, indeed, brilliant with computers. Since the moment he could read, he had been on a computer learning how to operate them. For Alistair's tenth birthday, his parents had given him his first PC, and after a year of learning it inside and out, his parents had upgraded him to a laptop. That's when he learned how to take apart and put together his old desktop computer. Computers and technology fascinated him, he wanted nothing more than to get his hands on this, supposedly, giant collection of computers.

Hunter explained to him in detail how he used the wadded-up paper to escape from his quarters, the hidden room they found in the library, the giant robot that Margot had said was the librarian, and of course, the computer room where he had found the weird logo and the letter Alistair's dad had written to Plato. Alistair was ecstatic by the end of the story; a real walking and talking robot was more than he could have ever dreamed of.

"Did your dad tell you about the Orientation?" Hunter went on. "My uncle mentioned it but didn't say too much else about it."

"An Orientation?" Alistair questioned. "Err… no. But he said there was going to be a party for everyone with lots of food, and that all his friends would be there."

Hunter liked the idea of an Orientation party filled with food and friends. When Elly and Hunter first arrived, Hunter assumed they would be the only children in the mansion, at least he didn't think such a cryptic and gothic-looking place would be very kid oriented. After meeting Alistair, he thought differently. Things wouldn't be so bad if his uncle stayed to live with him at the Belmonte Estate, and he had Alistair to keep him company. Not to mention that with all the new people arriving, there could be even more children his age coming to stay.

"Hunter?" Elly's whispered.

"Elly? You're awake again!" Hunter ran over to his sister's bedside, almost getting knocked over by Trayer, who jumped up from his sleep at the sound of Elly's frail voice.

"I had nightmares… about mom and dad…" she answered. She was much more awake than she had been previously.

"It's okay. Trayer was here watching you the whole time. He never left your side."

Trayer jumped up on Elly's bed burying his head beside her, snuggling his warm snout under her armpit. Elly giggled weakly.

"How do you feel?" Hunter asked. "Can I get you something? Oh, and Uncle Joe is here! He should be back soon." Hunter didn't know where to begin he was so excited to see his sister awake and talking.

"Uncle Joey is here?" Elly asked, excited by the news. She hadn't seen her uncle since the funeral service.

"Yes, and this is my new friend Alistair," Hunter added, pointing at Alistair.

Elly hadn't noticed the young boy with curly blonde hair sitting at the table next to the bed.

"Hello. Um… I'm sorry you got hurt," Alistair said, a bit lost for words. "Hunter told me what you guys did. That was pretty brave of you."

"I don't remember much," Elly's mind was still a bit foggy from her injuries. "I remember running from the robot…"

Before Elly could say anything else her Uncle Joe, Benjamin, and Patricia returned to the room with dinner for everyone. Elly's stomach rumbled at the sweet smell of garlic-roasted pork chops with cheddar and chive potato crispers delightfully played with her senses.

"Heavens, you're awake again!" Patricia smiled, swiftly setting down the meal on the table and rushing over to her. "Tell me, dear, how do you feel?"

"Hungry," she answered, "And a little confused."

"Elly, I rushed over here as soon as I got the call that you'd been hurt," Uncle Joe explained, holding his niece's hand.

"Uncle Joe, are you staying here with us now?"

"Err… well…" Joe thought for a second, he hadn't really planned that far ahead. Everything had been happening so fast. He knew it was supposed to be a parent that went through the Orientation and the potential forthcoming 'Enlightenment' with the next bloodline. He wasn't even sure if they would allow an uncle to take the place of the parent in the process. "We'll have to wait and see… it sort of depends…"

"Depends on what?" Elly's voice was now gaining strength.

"Well… Professor Calenstine is technically your guardian, and the mansion works with specific rules, so it all depends on what happens tomorrow."

"I don't understand, what's tomorrow?" Elly asked as Patricia brought her over a large plate of pork chops and potatoes.

"Do you think you can eat?" Patricia interrupted.

Elly nodded, her eyes wide with excitement at the sight of the meal, eager to taste the delicious smelling foods.

"Good, it's important to get your strength up," Patricia said in a serious tone. "I know that we've kept a lot from you kids about the estate and why you're here. We all understand the hardships you two have endured in your strange new home and dealing with the pain from your loss. Regardless of where your parents are now, and I assure you they are watching over you, this is where they wanted you to be. Tomorrow is the big Orientation where everything will be explained, and you'll have an official tour of the estate to answer even more of your questions."

The night grew late, and Patricia stayed with the children to make sure they were both comfortable and that Elly stayed in good spirits. Benjamin showed Alistair to his room three doors down from the kids, and then quickly retreated into the upper levels of the mansion with Joe to catch up and reminisce over the past ten years.

Hunter had grown eager for the following day's festivities. He had seen a lot of people showing up at the mansion, and if they were all as nice as Alistair, then he was excited to meet some more potential friends. It had been a long week for both him and his sister, but for all the dark things that had been thrown their way, things finally seemed to be turning around. Hunter and Elly both hoped their uncle could stay with them at the mansion so they could be a family once again. A family, Hunter thought, he wasn't sure he would ever feel that way again.

Elly had fallen asleep easily, and Trayer snored as loud as ever at the foot of her bed. Hunter on the other hand tossed and turned in his bed. Tomorrow was the Orientation, maybe he would finally get to meet their new guardian, Professor Calenstine. He was excited to finally get some answers, but even more, he was excited to put this terrible week behind him and move on.

Chapter 8
The Brunch

A loud rustling noise woke Elly from a deep sleep, a welcomed distraction that stirred her awake as she struggled with another of her recurring nightmares. Elly dreamed once again of her dead parents. She sat with them at the dinner table, their eyes void of all life, mindless shells of her parents. She would talk to them, but they would ignore her, staring lifelessly at the walls. She awoke in a pool of sweat, the dream always left her with a crippling sense of overwhelming despair and depression.

There was a brief moment of peace, a second when she had woken up where the dream world and reality fused together into some sort of hyper reality. In that split second, her parents' death was the nightmare, reality would have her waking up at home, cozy and comfortable in her bed. Her brain told her that the loud noise must have been her parents coming home from one of their many trips overseas. Their death, the scary mansion, the beast that attacked them, all these terrible things were the dream. She convinced herself that when she opened her eyes, everything would be back to normal. A moment of relief…

"Elly, rise and shine!" The voice of Patricia Ellingbee brought Elly out of her daze. "You're running late; Hunter and Alistair are already downstairs." Patricia laid a beautiful yellow dress across the foot of her bed. "I found this darling dress in your closet, it's perfect for the brunch."

It was no dream. This was her reality.

Elly recognized the yellow dress. It was the one she wore on Christmas Eve last year for the late-night church service. Afterwards, her father drove them all over the city looking at Christmas lights. She remembered they drove downtown to a giant building called the 'Water Works.' It was the epitome of beautiful. Every year, the city constructed a huge Christmas tree and brilliant display of Christmas decorations. Elly's father had told her it was on Christmas Eve fifteen years ago when he proposed to her mother right before the giant Christmas tree. It was a bitter winter, he swore the only reason his knees had shaken that night was due to the cold. Elly thought the place was magical. That was the last Christmas they would ever spend together as a family. She hadn't worn the dress since, her mother packed it away for safekeeping.

"Are you excited?" Patricia asked.

"About what?"

"The brunch, It's the first time you'll get to mingle with the rest of the mansion, including all the new children. It's part of Orientation day," she explained.

Elly didn't quite understand why groups of children were coming to the creepy old mansion. On the bright side, at least she was allowed to leave the room.

"Do you feel well enough to join in the festivities?" Patricia realized that Elly had spent the last two days in bed recovering from her injuries. She didn't want to push her too hard, despite how important the day's festivities were.

"Yes!" Elly shouted, quickly jumping out of bed. There was no way she was going to spend the entire day stuck in the musty old room while her brother and his new friend got to have all the fun. She slipped into the pretty yellow dress.

"Oh, let's do your hair up. First impressions are always important." Patricia smiled; she seemed to have more energy than normal.

"You seem excited," Elly noted while Ms. Ellingbee curled her hair.

"Oh dear, is it obvious? This is how I act when I'm nervous."

"Nervous? About what?"

"Well, because the big Orientation dinner is later tonight. It's my duty to run it, making sure all goes according to plan. I'm the master of ceremonies for the event and with all these things going wrong…"

"I'm sure everything will go great. It sounds like fun."

"Professor Calenstine doesn't trust anyone else with it. It's a big honor for me." Patricia sprayed hairspray on Elly's curly red bangs. "Look, you're a doll." She smiled, holding up a hand mirror.

"So, what is a 'brunch' anyway?" Elly bounced her bangs with her hands.

"Well, follow me and I'll show you. Like I said, you overslept, and we're late."

Elly couldn't believe what she saw once the main elevator doors opened onto the main foyer. She remembered the room perfectly with the two beautiful unicorns, the wall mounted with the heads of strange creatures, and the two staircases leading up to the balcony where she and Ms. Ellingbee now exited the elevator. That was all the same, but the rest of the room was elegantly decorated to the finest degree. It reminded Elly of the magical ball her mother would read about in her favorite fairy tale. Silver and gold balloons with matching streamers decorated the foyer brilliantly.

The giant buffet tables downstairs were stocked with more food than Elly had even seen in her life. There were roasting pots of six different soups, a giant salad bar with all the fixings. She counted ten different kinds of breads, herb-roasted chicken, pickled bologna, bacon-wrapped scallops, and so much more! There were even exotic dishes she had never seen before. The wonderful scent hit her nose the very moment the elevator doors opened.

Elly knew that where there was food, there would be her older brother, stuffing his face with the delicacies. It didn't take long for her to spot Hunter standing next to one of the buffet tables with Alistair and a girl who looked about his age. They were eating heaping plates of food and laughing, except for Hunter, who was a bit red in the face, fidgeting with his hands behind his back.

Elly hadn't wanted to wear her yellow Christmas dress until now.

Everyone she saw was dressed up for the occasion. Hunter was even wearing his suit, which he seemed to have already grown out of. His sleeves lay a bit too high on his arms, his pants showed a bit too much ankle. She figured Patricia must have forced Hunter to dress up. Elly knew he hated wearing a tie. The adults were all dressed up as well. The women wore elegant gowns, varying in colors, and long velvet gloves.

Elly found Uncle Joe standing next to Margot and Alistair's father, Ben. She knew Uncle Joe hated dressing up as well. He was the only adult in the group wearing blue jeans. At least he was wearing a plain, solid black dress shirt and tie.

"Everyone looks so pretty," Elly made her way down the stairway and into the heart of the party.

"As do you, my dear. Now, go meet some new friends. Everyone from the mansion is here, so there are plenty of new people for you to meet."

Elly made her way through the swarm of strangers, all of whom appeared to know who she was, which was a bit unsettling, as she had never seen any of these people. How on Earth did they know her? They stared and whispered secretively. They weren't obvious about it, but Elly could tell. She felt the hidden fingers pointing at her, the eyes watching her, she knew what they were talking about. Her parents, the plane crash, how they were now orphans living here at the mansion. She did her best to ignore them and pressed on.

"Uncle Joey!" She found her uncle first, who she hadn't really gotten to see since his arrival. Uncle Joe smiled brightly at the sight of his niece finally up and walking for the first time since he got there. He picked her up and swung her in his arms like a princess.

"Glad to see you finally decided to wake up, lazy butt," he teased.

"Elly, you look adorable," Margot said, smiling. "I love yellow, it reminds me of summer."

"Thank you." Elly blushed. "I like your dress too. It's beautiful."

Margot wore a long black gown with a thin veil that partially covered her face and black open-toed shoes to match. Elly thought that she was the prettiest grown-up of the bunch.

"Not too shabby of a food spread, aye?" Benjamin offered Elly one of the many cookies and brownies towering on his plate. Elly obliged and picked a caramel-covered walnut brownie, taking a huge bite.

"Now, make sure you get some real food too. There are a lot of healthy choices in that buffet," Joe added. "You're not allowed to eat cookies and cakes for lunch, like your Uncle Ben does."

"He's my uncle?" Elly asked through her mouthful of brownie.

"Well, he's the closest I have to a brother, so yeah."

"Great culinary role model," Margot joked.

"Hey, all I'm saying is… Give me the choice between cake and carrots, and well… cake will always win." Ben crammed an entire piece of cherry-glazed double chocolate cake in his mouth. He gave a goofy smile, barely holding all the cake in his mouth, making Elly laugh.

"He told me last night that his wife doesn't let him have sugar in the house. So he makes up for it here," Joe explained. He then pointed out Hunter at the other end of the buffet table. "Go say hi to your brother and your new friend Alistair."

"Okay." Elly danced her way playfully through the maze of people toward them.

"She seems to have gotten her energy back." Ben wiped away the excess of chocolate frosting coating his chin.

"We were pretty worried about her that first night. It was touch and go," Margot explained, sipping on her white wine. "You couldn't tell from today that she almost died two nights ago. That little girl is resilient."

"It's in her blood." Joe smiled.

∽

Elly was amazed at how many people were at the luncheon. The children had been at the mansion now for over a week, and they hadn't met more than a handful of people. Elly guessed there were easily a hundred guests wandering around the main floor enjoying the festivities. She wasn't sure where they had all been hiding, or if

104

they had all arrived the day earlier, but the mansion was now full of bust bodied people of all ages.

"Elly," Hunter yelled her name.

"Hello," Elly walked over to Hunter, Alistair, and the girl she saw earlier.

"This is my cousin, Olivia Lee-Kay," Alistair introduced the two.

"Just call me Liv," she corrected with a pleasant smile. Liv was twelve, and the daughter of one of the most respected figures on the estate, Abram Williams Winters. She was tall and slender; her father always telling her she had blossomed into a beautiful young woman a bit too early for his taste. Liv often was mistaken for being older than she really was, though she hated it when people made reference to it. Liv shared Alistair's blonde hair and soft blue eyes. Elly thought they could easily pass as brother and sister.

"It's very nice to meet you," she shook Elly's hand. "Your brother told me you'd been hurt. Are you okay?"

"Oh yes, I'm feeling much better. I don't remember too much of it, anyway."

"Um, Liv," Hunter interrupted, "...can I get you some more punch?"

Elly shot her brother an annoyed look for butting in, he returned it with a sympathetic shrug.

"Sure, thank you." Liv smiled back, handing Hunter her cup.

"C'mon, Alistair, follow me." Hunter pulled his new friend away from the girls.

"How come you didn't tell me?" Hunter whispered, nervously pouring two plastic cups full of fruit punch.

"Umm... tell you what?" Alistair asked a bit puzzled over the accusation. "Are you going to pour me one too?"

"That your cousin was a girl!" Hunter poured a third glass handing it to him a bit forcefully, spilling a tad on the floor.

"What do you mean? So, what? She's a girl," Alistair stated. He could tell that Hunter was a bit edgy.

"I mean... c'mon... I would have liked to have known. You know, umm... been prepared."

"You're being weird," Alistair chuckled. "Prepared for what? Is that why you've barely said anything since my dad introduced you to her?"

"Well, no, that's not why…" Hunter turned red. Liv was undoubtedly pretty, beautiful even. He had had crushes before, but he'd never spoken a word to any of them. Now he had been cornered in an awkward situation where he was forced to try and make small talk with a pretty girl. Instead, he stood there laughing over every small joke, fiddling with his sweaty hands behind his back.

Hunter knew that Alistair didn't understand, he just wished he had a heads up so he could have had stayed up all night practicing what to say…

"Your brother is pretty quiet." Liv pulled out two open seats for her and Elly to sit.

"Uh… he is?" Her brother was known for having the gift of gab. He would never shut up around the house.

"He seems nice though. Is he shy?"

"Ha, no," Elly joked. "My brother is a loud mouth."

"My dad told me what happened. I'm really sorry about your parents."

"Oh…" Elly didn't like talking about her parents, she ignored the sentiment, changing the subject. "Who's your dad?"

"He's right over there, it looks like he's arguing with my uncle again." Liv pointed across the room to a tall, well-tanned, muscular man. He had thin, balding hair that was pulled tightly back into a ponytail. His name was Abram, currently he was engaged in a heated conversation with Dominick. He was in his mid-forties, a bit older than Elly's parents. His face curled up in disgust as he pointed his finger in Dominick's face.

"You're an insult to the families!" Abram's voice cut through the murmurs of the crowd, causing the party to come to a sudden halt. Everyone turned their attention to the fight.

"Right!" Dominick mocked. "I'm the insult? Because you were lucky enough to be born eight years before me and blessed by the bloodline," he yelled back.

"You're an insult for betraying the Seekers. You're nothing but a damn sell out!" Abram got into his younger cousin's face. The two stood nose to nose, both men's eyes wild with anger.

"I was never a Seeker! Remember?" Dominick shot back. He stared into Abram's eyes with a jealous rage. "Seekers are only for the chosen, remember? So, your precious little secret society can go to hell!"

"How dare you insult our family?" Abram clenched his fist, the vein in his temple was throbbing.

Ben had shot through the growing crowd, he grabbed his older cousin by his arm preventing him from throwing a punch. He nearly didn't make it, Abram had already pulled back ready to let his fists finish the conversation. Patricia had also made her way into the midst of the dispute, wedging herself between the two men.

"Both of you stop it! Act like adults!" Patricia barked, her face flushed with embarrassment. "Dominick, don't you have a job to do?" she asked.

"This isn't over, Abram, not by a long shot. I'm not your little lackey anymore." Dominick turned his back and stormed out, pushing aside anyone in his way.

"Calm down, cuz, it's not worth it. Let him go," Ben attempted to cool Abram down.

"I'm… I'm sorry." It took Abram a second to realize the scene he had caused. "Sometimes my anger… it gets the better of me."

"Please, everyone, enjoy the party. I assure you, everything is fine," Patricia attempted to regain control. "We will speak later, Abram," she whispered.

"What was all that, about?" Hunter handed Liv her drink.

"Oh my God… I'm so embarrassed." Liv hid her face in her hands.

"It's okay," Elly said, smiling. "It wasn't that big of a fight. I doubt most people even noticed." Elly knew that was a lie. The entire party had stopped and turned its attention to the quarrel, now that it had ceased, the gossip began. At least they weren't talking about Elly anymore.

"That's not true, everyone grouped around them. It was so childish!" Liv sighed.

"Children," Margot and Patricia made their way over with Uncle Joe and Benjamin following closely behind. "Are you guys okay?"

"Just embarrassed," Liv answered.

"I'm sure your father is sorry, Liv," her Uncle Ben replied. "I'm sure you know the history between your father and Dominick. There's a lot of bad blood there. I'm surprised Professor Calenstine even hired him."

"He didn't have to act that way in front of everyone in the mansion." Liv's eyes filled with tears.

"Come now, dear, come with me. You're going to smear your makeup," said Patricia. "It's going to be all right. I'll make sure to yell at your father for you," Patricia chuckled.

Patricia left with Liv, leaving the group behind to finish eating their brunch. Hunter felt a sense of relief now that Liv had left, although he felt terrible for how upset she had been. At least now he didn't have to worry about everything he said, before he said it.

"What was that fight about anyway?" Elly asked. "Dominick saved us from that monster. He can't be a bad person."

"Well, there's a bit more to it than that, it's…uh…complicated to say the least. Maybe we can fill you kids in later," answered Ben.

"Interesting day, so far." Uncle Joe took a seat next to Margot. "Wonder what's going to happen next?"

"Oh my!" Margot's face lit up, a bright smile stretched from ear to ear, her attention was drawn across the room.

Joe frowned, unable to figure out the sudden change.

"He came?" She got up quickly from the table, her hands trembling with excitement. "he actually came!"

"Who came?" asked Joe.

"He did," Ben pointed over Joe's shoulder.

A striking young man entered the room, immediately all eyes fell upon on him. He was dashingly handsome, wearing a stylish white tuxedo with a dark, red velvet vest. He smiled, nodding to the usher who took his jacket and scarf. He entered into the sea of people, his eyes peering through the party, looking for someone... Joe sat by, watching as the beautiful Margot flew into the man's arm. He swung her around, kissing her deeply, in front of everyone.

"That's Sebastian," answered Ben. "Sorry, I thought she would have told you"

"Sebastian? A boyfriend?" asked Joe.

"Well, a fiancé actually," Ben replied.

"A fiancé, really? That's so neat!" Elly was excited.

"What's wrong, Uncle Joey, you look upset?" Hunter asked.

"No... of course not," Joe replied, a little taken aback at the sight. "Nothing to be upset about, right?" He turned away from the sight forcing a smile.

"C'mon, bud, let's go grab a drink," Ben patted his friend on the back. Uncle Joe obliged without saying a word to the kids.

"I need a stiff one," Joe whispered.

"We'll see about that," Ben looked over to the kids. "We'll be back soon," he noted.

"Okay," said Alistair.

"Uncle Joe seemed sad," Hunter finished off the last sip of his punch.

"I think he has a crush on Margot," Alistair answered. "Did you see his face when she jumped into that man's arms and kissed him."

"He shouldn't be sad, weddings are fun," Elly added.

"I guess..." said Hunter, "...unless the person you like is marrying a stranger."

"Sssh, she's coming," Alistair whispered.

Margot and Sebastian held hands as they made their way over to the children's table.

"Children, where did Joe and Ben go? I wanted to introduce everyone to Sebastian Bell," said Margot.

"Umm... well, they left," Hunter said, feeling a bit uncomfortable.

"Oh..." Margot looked disappointed. "Well, Sebastian, this is Hunter, Elly, and Alistair. Kids, this is Sebastian. He surprised me today by showing up."

"Hi, kids, I've heard a lot about you." Sebastian's voice was deep and strangely alluring.

"Hi!" Elly caught herself staring into his mysterious grey eyes.

"Well, aren't you the prettiest girl in the room." Sebastian smiled. "If Margot isn't too jealous, would you honor me with a dance?"

"Oh, well of course not," replied Margot.

"After you, my dear." Sebastian held out his hand.

"I don't know how to dance…" Elly frowned.

"Well, Sebastian's a great teacher."

"Okay then." Elly stood up and was whisked away by Sebastian onto the dance floor.

"Margot, we didn't know you had a boyfriend," Hunter said.

"Oh, I'm sorry. I guess with everything going on, I didn't think of it." Margot didn't quite know what to say. "He's been on a trip overseas for months now. He completely surprised me. I didn't expect him home for another month."

"Oh, okay," Hunter replied.

The rest of the brunch was a bit uneventful, which was okay with Hunter and Alistair, who both spent the rest of the quiet afternoon alone, wondering about the big mysterious 'Orientation' dinner later that evening. Hunter was ready for some answers, he was excited to finally meet his elusive new guardian, Professor Calenstine. Once the dust settled and the brunch withered away to a few lingering guests picking at the crumbs and leftovers from the buffet table, the children decided to make their way back to their room.

Chapter 9
Dog Messes

Trayer was delighted when the children made their way back to their quarters. He had grown restless being alone in the room for so long. The pup couldn't contain his excitement, his large thick tail wagged uncontrollably, knocking everything over in its path.

Unfortunately, the children were not quite as happy to see the behemoth puppy who eagerly awaited them. The children were shocked at what they saw, their mouths fell open at the mess that sat before them. Their room was a whirlwind of disaster. The floor was covered in pieces of what had once been their bed sheets, their pillows were tattered and tossed everywhere, completely ripped to shreds. To Elly's greater misfortune, even her mattress had been chewed on and wrecked by Trayer's puppyish assault.

"Trayer!" Hunter yelled, the young pup jumped onto him. Using Hunter's shoulders for leverage, the dog stood on his hind legs licking his face. "Get off me, you stupid dog!" Hunter pushed the pup off of him in a fit of anger. Trayer whimpered sadly, head down with guilt.

"Oh man… Why would he do this?" Elly moaned, standing over what was left of her once comfortable bed. It was chewed all the way through to the spring coils.

"I think he got lonely," said Alistair, chuckling softly. However, Hunter and Elly didn't see the humor in the situation. "Well, he is a puppy, he was left alone for hours up here. Poor dog," he continued. "At least he didn't…oh, never mind, he did." Alistair had a disgusted look on his face, plugging his nose with his thumb and index finger.

"Grrrooosss!" Elly frowned at the sight of a giant pile of dog waste in the corner of the room. The smell hit her nose, she felt like she was going to throw up.

"Don't worry, I'll pick it up," said Alistair. "I have a dog at home named Cerberus, I had to pick up his mess until he was housebroken. It took months."

Elly thanked him and helped, despite the foul smell. It's not a fun task cleaning up a pile of dog mess, especially one from a giant dog.

"Yuck… I guess we throw the rest of this stuff away." Hunter pointed to the clutter.

Hunter hadn't been able to get Liv out of his head since she left the brunch after the incident involving her father. His anger over the destroyed room quickly faded at the thought of Liv's pretty smile. He was worried about her. She'd been so upset when she left the group earlier that day. Although Hunter would never admit it, he silently hoped she would show up at their room looking for Alistair. Then again, he wouldn't know what to say or how to act, he worried he would come off looking like an idiot.

"Sebastian is so nice; Margot is lucky. He's like Prince Charming," Elly sighed, breaking Hunter's deep thought. She had thoroughly enjoyed dancing with Sebastian, listening to him talk about how much he adored Margot.

"He's okay, I guess," said Hunter, unimpressed with what he had seen of Sebastian.

"Yeah, he seemed to be laying it on pretty thick in front of Margot," Alistair added.

"You're just jealous," argued Elly, tossing the remnants of her pillow into a trash bag.

"Of what?" Alistair frowned. The simple idea of being jealous of Sebastian was a ridiculous thought.

"Because he's so perfect," said Elly, who danced around the room as if Sebastian was there leading her. "He's smart too. He travels around the world for the mansion researching things. He's been everywhere!"

"Awesome!" said Hunter sarcastically. "I say he's hiding something. No one is that perfect."

"Yeah, I agree," said Alistair. "Anyway, let's focus on cleaning your room so we don't miss the Orientation tonight."

"I don't see why you guys hate him," Elly argued, but the boys didn't respond. They ignored the comment and went on cleaning.

It had already been a long day for the children, now they found themselves working hard on trying to fix up their room before one of the adults came to check on them. Trayer stayed hidden in the corner with his head hung low. He wasn't a dumb dog; he knew the children were angry with him. He let out an occasional whimper, waiting for one of the children to call him over to play. They didn't.

"Children," Ms. Ellingbee's voiced chimed in over the rooms P.A. system. "Your party will pick you up for the Orientation dinner in two hours. If you need anything, please chime us and let us know."

"Okay, we will," Hunter replied.

"Well then, I will see you tonight. I hope you are all excited!" Ms. Ellingbee clicked off the loudspeaker system.

"Yikes! Only two hours to pick this place up," said Elly, worried.

"C'mon, it won't take too long. We have to work together," Alistair held open a large trash bag as Hunter shoveled shreds of bed sheets into it.

"So, I've been meaning to tell you guys," said Hunter quietly. "When we snuck into the hidden room under the library… well, I read a message on one of the computer terminals. It said that someone in the mansion must have broken through the security system."

"Really?" Elly asked.

"Yeah, Alistair, your dad was sending that robot, Plato, a message, and he said he thought it must have been an inside job."

"But, who would do that? Everyone seems so happy here," Elly stated.

"Dominick seemed pretty angry," said Hunter. "He's your uncle, right, Alistair?"

"Not really," Alistair answered. "Liv is my cousin, her dad is obviously my Uncle Abram, but their relationship to Dominick is from my aunt's side, and not from my family."

"So… like a second cousin or something?" asked Hunter.

"Yeah, I supposed that's what it would be called. I only met him a few times. He never seemed angry or mean though."

"Well, he seemed pretty angry with your uncle and the mansion," Hunter replied.

"But he wouldn't have had access. I'm pretty sure my dad told me they called him in after that monster had already escaped to try and get it captured before today's festivities."

"Hmmm…" Hunter wondered. Alistair was right, the only reason Dominick and Agent Roberts were even at the mansion was to try and capture the beast before the party.

"Who else is there that could have done it?" Elly asked.

"Well, the mansion seems really big. There were so many people at the brunch, it could have been anybody," Alistair explained.

A loud knock caught the children by surprise, Uncle Joe and Ben entered their room. Joe's mouth dropped as the kids frantically tried to hide the enormous mess.

"What on *earth* did you kids do?" Joe gasped.

"Guys, seriously, it smells terrible in here," said Ben.

"Trayer made a mess," answered Elly. "We tried to clean up as best we could…"

Trayer poked his head up at the sound of his name, only to let out another whine after seeing the obviously angry faces of Ben and Joe. Trayer could easily pick up on the tension in the room and wanted nothing to do with it.

"Well, we were checking up on you kids to make sure you're going to be ready for the Orientation," said Joe.

"We will be, promise," Hunter quickly answered.

"Yeah, we're almost done picking up anyway," added Elly.

"Well… I suppose we can help…" said Ben, feeling defeated, "You kids will never finish cleaning up this mess in time."

"Are you happy now, Trayer?" Joe shot a disgruntled look at the pup, who wagged his tail in response. He quickly ran over to Joe, forcing his long-wet snout into his palm, begging for his attention.

"Don't pet him, Uncle Joe. He's a bad dog," said Hunter.

"Well, he was all alone up here while we were all downstairs at the brunch," replied Joe. "Can't blame the pup for getting bored. He'll learn, won't you, big boy?" Joe scratched the mighty dog's ear.

"You seem happier, Uncle Joey," said Elly.

"What do you mean, of course I'm happy."

"Well, you seemed sad when Margot ran over to Sebastian," Elly clarified.

"Well…" Joe was at a loss for words and didn't care to elaborate on the situation to his niece.

"A little misunderstanding is all. Grown-up stuff but everything is fine now," Ben swept up the kids' room.

"Yeah, it's fine," Joe added. "Let's focus on getting this room of yours picked up."

"Dad," Alistair asked, "…what was wrong with Uncle Abram and Dominick? We were wondering why they got so upset."

"Oh boy," Ben took a seat on Hunter's bed and let out a sigh. "I'm not even sure where to start." "They got pretty angry with each other," added Hunter.

"Well, Dominick always wanted to be a part of the mansion. He grew up knowing his uncle, Abram's father, and your late grandfather, was a fearless adventurer who went on countless expeditions. So… he waited and waited for the chance to follow in his uncle's footsteps. Until finally both he and your Uncle Abram were asked to visit the Belmonte Estate, just like you kids. He figured that this was his opportunity" Ben went on to explain, "Unfortunately, the mansion only allows certain individuals that meet specific requirements to become what Dominick dreamed of. All he was allowed to do was join his older cousin's team and follow under his orders, that didn't last long. Things got pretty messy on Dominick's last trip… things have never been the same since. He left an angered and bitter man to start his own company. He found a financial backer through some mysterious deep-pocketed corporation, funding his group, the MFPA group."

"What's that stand for anyway?" asked Elly.

"Er…"Ben hesitated to answer the seemingly innocent question.

"You might as well tell them. Hunter and Elly already know about the Beast of Bladenboro, so it's not like these animals are secrets to them," said Joe.

"I suppose," replied Ben. "It stands for: 'Monsters and Fiends Protection Agency.' They basically follow leads on creatures like the Beast of Bladenboro, capture the creature and sell it for money to the corporation."

"What corporation? Why would they want a monster like that?" asked Hunter.

"Aten Corporation, and we don't know much about them other than when Professor Calenstine heard about the partnership, he was very upset. He even offered Dominick a place within the estate, but Dominick was too hardheaded and unwilling to look past his hatred for Abram. Not sure why he decided to contact him how, so many years later for this job..."

"So, there you have it," said Joe. "The mansion is not without its drama."

"And needless to say, Uncle Abram and Dominick don't care for one another."

Uncle Joe checked his watch, and the time was drawing near for the Orientation. Soon the entire mansion would gather to finish up with the last of the day's festivities. They would leave the children's room, take the elevator up to the fourth floor and enter the large ceremonial lobby.

Joe thought about the day of Orientation when he was Hunter's age. His parents had brought him and his sister to the mysterious mansion under the notion that they were going to visit their parents at work. He remembered feeling confused and lost during the strange Orientation. He hadn't a clue what his parents had dedicated their lives to. Joe couldn't help but be excited and a bit nervous for his niece and nephew. Though he hadn't a clue how they would react when the truth about their parents was revealed to them. Most kids are excited and curious when they found out about the mansion and all its secrets, but then again, most kids weren't told two weeks after their parents' untimely death...

Joe also knew they had been eager to unravel the secrets of the mansion and knew quite a bit more than they should have heading into the Orientation. Whatever the outcome, he knew it was out of his hands. He decided it was best not to over-think it and instead found his mind wandering to the image of Margot kissing her fiancé. Suddenly, he had the urge for a drink.

"Everybody ready?" asked Patricia Ellingbee. She and Liv burst through the kids' door with excitement. Hunter's heart sank deep into his chest as he saw the stunning Liv.

"Sorry about earlier, guys," said Liv, a bit embarrassed by her actions. She looked down at the floor, avoiding eye contact with the other kids.

"It's okay," Alistair noted. "Hunter was worried about you, though."

"Really?" Liv smiled.

"Err..." Hunter froze.

"Of course, he was, we all were." His uncle saved him.

Hunter wasn't sure if his uncle had done it on purpose or not. He hoped his shyness wasn't that noticeable, but he was thankful for the save.

With that painful moment of adolescence gone, the group hurried their way to the ceremonial hall.

Chapter 10
Orientation

Hunter hadn't been to the fourth floor of the mansion yet and was completely awestruck by what he saw. Dedicated entirely as one grandiose auditorium, the fourth floor was where they held the most important of festivities. The entire floor was one giant room. It was elegant in nature, its beauty indescribable. The children were awed by its splendor as they entered with the adults by their side. The room's walls rose high, seemingly into the heavens, where its ceiling domed at the top. There a brilliant crystal chandelier hung down from the heart of the ceiling, shining like a bright, beaming star. The ceiling itself was painstakingly painted to portray the universe surrounding its starred chandelier. Small planets and a myriad of twinkling stars glistened above. If Hunter hadn't known any better, he could have sworn he was staring out into the night sky.

The group took their seats and mingled quietly as they waited for the festivities to begin. There were about a dozen large rectangle tables that sat roughly thirty people each. The tables were decorated with the finest tablecloths and dinnerware one could expect from an ancient mansion. The food once again was astounding, somehow topping their previous brunch when it came to the selection of exotic and wonderful-smelling dishes. Hunter knew he would dine like a king. He was still full from earlier, but he couldn't stop himself from dishing up a large plate of broiled redskin potatoes garnished heavily with butter and chives, blackened chicken breast over rice pilaf, and of course a large slice of triple-thick chocolate cake.

The room seemed more than a typical room to Hunter, as if there was a hint of magic in the air. In front of the large tables stood an even bigger stage where Patricia Ellingbee stood in front of a podium. She tapped the microphone causing a deep thud to echo throughout the hall. Behind her, a giant carpet hung as the backdrop for the stage. It was a dark royal red, designed with a familiar logo that Hunter had already seen in the mansion.

"Elly," Hunter whispered as he choked down a big bite of potatoes.

"Gross," she frowned. "Chew with your mouth closed"

"That's the strange logo I saw below the library," he whispered.

"I know that logo," Alistair added. "My dad has it tattooed on his chest."

"Do you know what it is?" Hunter asked.

"No, only that he said that it meant a lot to him."

"Attention!" Patricia began, hushing the room into silence. She cleared her throat nervously as she stood in front of the room full of guests. You couldn't tell, judging from her stone face, but her hands shook uncontrollably behind the podium.

"Um… excuse me, attention please. Yes…" she hesitant at first, but quickly gained confidence. "Well, hello all. I'd like to start by giving a warm welcome to those of you who are new to our wonderful little estate. I assure you, everyone at Belmonte is quite excited and happy to see all our family, both old and new. I know that for some of you this is the first time you have ever seen the estate, and I am sure there are a million questions running through your heads, which I assure you we will address in due time. For others, those of you who call our wonderful little mansion home, who help us out with our day-to-day operations, we cannot thank you enough for all of your hard work and endurance through the years. We have established something wonderful here at the estate, and I am proud to call some of the brightest minds in the world today, not only my colleagues, but my family as well."

Patricia paused for a second to gather her composure. When listening to Patricia speak, one couldn't guess how utterly terrified she was. She had delivered the introduction of the speech with such perfection, and charm, that the crowd let out a loud round of applause and whistling as she shuffled her notes.

"—Tonight, is such a special night. A night that only happens once in a generation, filled with magic and wonderment. A time where we invite and open our doors to the next in line worthy of our secrets," Patricia went on, now piquing Hunter and Elly's interest. "I am very pleased to introduce to you the man who brought us all together, the Professor, Claudio Calenstine!"

Suddenly, a large fiery explosion shot fifty-foot flames from the middle of the stage straight into the air. The audience gasped in awe at the sight. The bright light from the chandelier gave way to the eerie blaze that faded from a dark orange to a brilliantly bright blue. A loud pop echoed through the hall that was almost unbearable to the younger ears. This caused many of the children to jump in their seats. The adults merely smiled as if they had seen this act before. A big mushroom cloud exploded above the bright flames and quickly disappeared. A lone floodlight opened on a mysterious man who appeared to have been in the center of it all. The audience applauded loudly, followed by a standing ovation from the adults. Hunter shot Alistair a quizzical look. The man at the epicenter of the explosion was Professor Calenstine. He smiled brightly at the audience.

Professor Calenstine sat in a wheelchair. To say he was old would not do justice; Hunter thought he looked more ancient than merely old. The professor was about as skinny and frail as any living man could be. He was also completely bald with prominent white bushy eyebrows. His wrinkly, loose skin dangled from his bones. He sat with a green folded blanked over his lap, covering his legs completely. From his outer appearance, Hunter thought he looked like he was on his deathbed, but then the old fragile man spoke. His words filled with life and excitement, his voice young and alive. It shocked Hunter, whose eyebrows scrunched together as his brain tried to make sense of the contrasting elements.

"I always did love a little magical flare," Professor Calenstine said with a wide smile and a hint of a chuckle. "Tonight, is a magical night indeed. Those of you who have appreciated this event in the past know it is not very often when we are able to welcome with open arms the next bloodline into our secret little club. We are here to welcome our new friends into the light and teach them of our collected family's heritage."

"Finally, answers," Hunter whispered to Elly. His uncle nudged his shoulder signaling him to be quiet.

"To say much has happened since the last Orientation is an understatement. Indeed, even the last month has weighed heavily on our souls as we mourn the loss of two of our Seeker family members. We must honor their memory and move forward, continuing to accomplish our goals. I am proud to say we have seen many gains in our field this year. Taken a stride forward into the forefront of the paranormal world with new technologies and evidence to shake the foundations of what society *thinks* they know. We continue to make the world a better place with the advances at our botany stations, even finding the mythological plant, Mandragora, which may provide a cure for Alzheimer's disease," the crowd erupted once again. Professor Calenstine waited for the audience to settle before he went on. "The study is still in its infancy, and I cannot speak too much more about the plant itself, but this breakthrough solidifies the reason I have dedicated my life to our beloved society. When the world turns its head away from legends, myths, and the paranormal, we are there to find the real answers. This is why we must maintain our secrecy from the world in order to retain balance."

"Paranormal?" Alistair whispered to Hunter. "Like ghosts?"

"I guess so," he answered, equally as confused.

"Tonight, is not about our advancements in the field. Rather, tonight is about thickening our heritage. The backbone of our society relies on the duties of our fearless Seekers. The ones who travel around the world to bring specimens back for us to study, *and* to save said specimens from extinction. To prove that the world still has many mysteries left to discover. Now it's time to introduce our new, potential, members to our Secret Seekers Society. My fellow Seekers, could you please join me onstage with our new guests?"

"That's our cue, big guy." Joe winked at Hunter with a smile.

"What?" Hunter asked, confused.

"You too, Elly, you're also a part of this. Your parents would be so proud right now," Joe added, standing up and straightening his clothes.

The children followed suit, reluctantly standing up with their Uncle Joe. Hunter felt the nerves in his stomach tighten. Elly felt her cheeks flush. Ben stood up with Alistair as well, who seemed quite comfortable with the sudden attention.

The children peered across the darkened auditorium, seeing only a few dozen of people standing up. Hunter peered behind him, Liv and her father Abram sat a few rows back. Hunter's heart pounded in his chest waiting to see if she too, would stand. Her father Abram stood with a wide, proud smile taking his daughter's hand. She looked a bit uneasy, nervously pulling her bangs away from her eyes. Hunter's hands tingled.

"C'mon, guys, it's our time," Uncle Joe lightly pushed the children towards the stage.

Elly thought she could hear a pin drop as they made their way up the extended aisle towards the stage. She felt every eye in the audience burning a hole into her back. She looked at her brother, who shrugged his, he had no idea what was happening, either.

The group of families made their way on stage. Hunter noticed the children were all close to his age, give or take a few years. He recognized only Liv and Alistair. All of them looked as uncomfortable as he and his sister, with the exception of Alistair, who seemed to be enjoying the attention. The floodlights were hot, Hunter felt the sweat dampen the ring around his collared shirt.

"Welcome, my friends," Professor Calenstine smiled. "I know you do not know who I am, but I assure you I have heard all about *you*. You see, you are not ordinary children. You are all a part of something bigger, larger, than anything you could have ever imagined. You were born into a secret family. Your ancestry can be traced back over hundreds of years to great and daring men and women who helped shape the world as we know it. A lineage of monster hunters and paranormal frontiersmen, a family tree filled with... Seekers."

Hunter's heart raced. Elly fiddled with her fingers nervously. Seekers, monster hunters... this is what their parents hid from them? They hunted monsters?

"Your guardians have chosen to have you follow in their own footsteps, and you shall live here through your remaining scholastic years alongside them. You will finish up your academic duties with the finest scholars the world has to offer. For I assure you, there is no other school in the world that will give you a better education," Professor Calenstine said with a serious tone. "These young children, beside me, will also be enrolling in our 'Enlightenment' courses. Where they will be taught everything, they need to know about what being a Seeker is all about. While other children will be watching movies about sparkling vampires, you will be learning the truth behind the creatures that American lore has romanticized into popcorn art. Yes, children, vampires are real." He paused for a second and let the children work through his words.

"This may come as a startling surprise too many of you, perhaps even a bit scary for you to understand but, there *are* monsters that go bump in the night; living, breathing creatures kept hidden from the modern world. There *are* mysterious objects out there that have magical qualities. Your families are the ones who study these creatures and objects in the field, hunt them down, and sift through what is fact or fake. You here on stage, you are the next in line to take over the bloodline from your parents. Congratulations!" Professor Calenstine applauded, the crowd quickly joining in.

"Vampires are real?" Elly looked at her brother with wide eyes, a bit of terror hidden within them.

"I guess so..." He turned to Alistair a few feet away. He seemed excited, too excited for Hunter's taste.

"Don't worry," Uncle Joe whispered to the kids. "Don't let the whole vampire thing scare you. They never come after humans. Ugly little bastards, but their scared of us. Trust me when I tell you, they are *not* what you think."

"Uncle Joey..." Elly began but was cut off before she could finish.

Joe caught the slight fear in her young voice. He remembered when he was their age, standing on the very same stage looking out at a sea of strangers. He remembered feeling a mixture of confusion and fear. It was not normal for a young child to find out all these monsters they grew up fearing were actually real.

"—Yes, we are so proud of you all standing up here," Professor Calenstine continued. "Your lineage goes back generations. The unknown is in your blood; your destiny is to seek out the truth shrouded in darkness. But of course, you will never be *forced* to live this lifestyle. Once you've graduated from the Enlightenment, you will then be asked to take part in a series of trials to finalize your step into our society. In the end, if you pass, you get to choose whether you stay and learn all the mysteries of the world, or go back to society none the wiser."

Hunter's brain was moving a mile a minute. A secret society? Destiny? A family lineage of monster hunters? So many questions with little to no clear answers.

"So, please, parents and guardians, as always, let us transition our new family members slowly. School will start up in one month's time. Until then, share your life stories with them. Begin opening up about the part of your life you were sworn to keep hidden for so many years. You have all been in their shoes. You remember what it was like when you became aware of your special situation. Use that as a tool to help aid them into a better understanding of what we do," Professor Calenstine took a small sip of bottled water and cleared his throat. "Children, you will get more answers soon. Tomorrow morning, we will begin our day with a small tour of the mansion for all of our new students. Those of you onstage are also formally invited to a luncheon with yours truly. I do hope you bring many questions as well as a hearty appetite. Until then, I would ask for the children to please go back to their seats and enjoy the rest of the evening. We have amazing food and spirits. Tonight, we celebrate a new era and dine with new friends!" Professor Calenstine lifted a glass of wine high into the airs. "Cheers!"

"Cheers!" The audience applauded.

The applause was cut short. An ear-splitting growl echoed across the stage, and Professor Calenstine dropped his wineglass, shattering it across the stage, spilling its dark red wine across the floor. Elly jumped back at the loud, piercing growl. She recognized it, as did Hunter, who stood with his legs frozen in fear. The audience gasped, this wasn't a part of the ceremonies. Their heads shot back and forth, looking for where the sudden noise had come from.

"Get the professor out of here now!" Ms. Ellingbee ordered.

Joe grabbed his niece and nephew and held them close. His eyes darted across the darkened auditorium. *Damn theatrics*, he thought. They had dimmed the lights to allow Professor Calenstine's magic trick to display better. It was too dark to see above the stage where the stagehands worked the lighting, curtains, and other props. The beast had to be hiding up there. It was hard to tell by the growl because it echoed and bounced across the stage due to the acoustics.

"Watch the kids!" Abram ran towards Professor Calenstine. "I'll get the professor to safety!" He grabbed Professor Calenstine's wheelchair racing him off stage. Hunter caught a glimpse of the professor's face as Abram hurried him to safety. Hunter thought the old man would be scared stiff by the thought a monster hunting the lot of them. He was surprised to see the professor's steady eyes, searching the auditorium, not a hint of fear in them.

"I got them!" Joe yelled back. He grabbed Liv's hand and pushed her close to the group.

"Joe, have you spotted it?" Ben shouted. He opened an emergency side exit side door and began ushering people out. "Stay calm, people!"

"No, I don't see it anywhere."

"Take the kids to the south exit, away from the commotion. I'll stay here and get these people out."

"C'mon, kids!" Joe pushed them back.

The children found themselves running through a wave of scared people going in the opposite direction. They followed Abram's route across the stage to the opposite end.

"We have to keep moving, but stay together. Don't get lost in the commotion," Joe yelled over the surreal mix of panicked people trying to get out.

Joe got the kids halfway across the stage when the giant beast soared from out of nowhere. Its giant black wings stretched out, easily twelve feet wide. Its thick muscular body hit the stage with a loud thud. Hunter could feel his heart pounding in his chest. Elly's eyes teared up as she stared, once again, at the awful-looking beast. Frightened, the children began screaming uncontrollably as they fled its menacing presence. They could smell its vile breath, it reeked of rotten flesh, the remnants of its last meal.

The beast stood ready to attack. Its large bulky head hung low, its hind end raised slightly, ready to pounce on its victim. It was a vile beast, with those green, soulless eyes peering at them. Originally, Hunter and Elly only saw bits of the beast as Dominick's flashlight had only caught glimpses of the creature during the darkened struggle in the library halls. Now, it stalked them out in the open, underneath the bright stage lights, showcasing the beast's smooth dark purple hair, its muscles flexing with anticipation beneath its mane. Elly couldn't fathom how powerful and strong it was. The wicked creature's lips curled, it growled quietly. Saliva foamed around its mouth and dripped onto the floor, almost as if it was purposely trying to intimidate the children.

Even though he had no idea how to fight off such an immense creature with no weapons, Uncle Joe pushed the children behind him.

"That's what you guys saw under the library?" Alistair asked in awe.

"Yeah…" answered Elly.

"When I count to three, I want you kids to run the other way," Joe demanded.

"What?" Hunter asked, dumbfounded at the thought of leaving his uncle alone to fend off the beast.

"I mean it," Joe ordered.

"We can't leave you," Hunter pleaded.

"One…" Joe whispered, trying not to make any sudden movements.

"Uncle Joey?" Elly now chimed in, also uneasy with the probable outcome of her uncle's plan.

"Two…" he said sternly.

"Guys, we should listen to him," Liv whispered.

"Three!" Uncle Joe jumped towards the beast.

"Run!" He yelled as he ran blindly towards the snarling creature. He closed his eyes and felt the sudden weight of the beast crash into his body. He couldn't see a thing, only a sudden flash of red. His entire body burned, something heavy was on top of him, the immense weight crushing his chest. He thought he heard his niece's cries, but he couldn't tell, the loud snarls of the monster were too loud to make out anything else. His body was going numb. There was pain, intense pain. Then there was nothing, blackness crept up around him.

Chapter 11
Anarchy

The massive automaton Plato waited patiently for his cue, underneath the large stage in a secret passageway. He was the first glimpse of the 'unknown' the children were to see during the Orientation. It had been somewhat of a tradition since his arrival at the estate. Plato was the perfect baby step into the mysterious world the estate would inevitably open up for the kids. He was a giant, lovable android with a heart of gold, the perfect icebreaker.

At first, Plato declined Professor Calenstine's invitation to the Orientations. Even though he was a massive robot with a highly advanced artificial intelligence (A.I.) system, he was very shy when it came to meeting new people. Well, as shy as an automaton could emulate using his human emotion shadowing mainframe. However, after much coercing from Professor Calenstine, and a simple promise stating that with every Orientation that Plato participated in, his shyness would decrease, Plato finally agreed. It only took three Orientations for Plato's human emotion shadowing mainframe to kick in and conquer his fear of public speaking. Of course, that translated to three human generations.

Now, Plato loved the attention he received when he was cued for his big entrance. He knew that, for these children, robots like him were merely fictional characters in books and movies. He loved their faces when he popped out from behind Professor Calenstine. Some children screamed, others cheered, most gasped in awe at his mighty size, but it always ended the same, a room full of smiling faces and new friends.

Plato knew right away this night was vastly different from any other Orientation he had ever been to. There were screams, real screams, and a menacing growl. He ran a quick search through his core mainframe engine to find any known matches to the howl. He quickly found a match with the recorded noises of the Beast of Bladenboro. Plato knew his signal wasn't coming to make a grand entrance. Something was really wrong. Without hesitation, he burst through the hidden trapdoor underneath the stage; the very same trapdoor they had constructed for his grand surprise entrance.

The crowd was in complete panic mode, already stricken with fear, once they caught sight of the mighty robot bursting from beneath the stage, it only added to the chaos. Of course, the new children had no idea Plato was there to help, and for them, the sight was horrific. Plato took a second to survey his surroundings. He zoomed in on the Beast of Bladenboro as it tore into Joe, who lay lifeless on the cold wooden floor of the stage.

"Master Joseph?" Plato's monotone spoke aloud.

The beast suddenly looked back at the automaton's immense body overshadowing. Plato swung its mighty arm, striking the beast away like a mere fly. The vile beast flew across the stage as if it were weightless. Its body crashed with a sickening thud into the far cement wall at the other end of the stage, leaving a large crater shaped indentation, it yelped loudly as it hit. Hunter and Elly ducked to avoid getting hit by the airborne creature.

Their eyes were red with tears, the children turned around to make their way over to their uncle in hopes of dragging him to safety.

"Please, we have to run!" Liv pleaded, grabbing Hunter's hand, forcing him away from their uncle.

"She's right," Alistair added, doing the same with Elly.

"Please evacuate." Plato looked back at the children, who were still fearful of his presence. "Master Joseph is a friend. I will protect him. He shall not fall to any more harm."

Plato reached down with his mighty metal arm and lifted Joe's motionless body with ease. "Weak pulse. Alive, yet unstable," Plato said, hoping to give Hunter and Elly some relief. It didn't. Both stood frozen in fear for their uncle's wellbeing. They couldn't find the strength to move on their own. Both Alistair and Liv pushed them towards safety.

The beast had regained its composure. It stood up-right now, snarling at the massive automaton that had its meal clutched in its protective arms. It circled Plato cautiously, ignoring everything around it. It stalked, waiting for the right moment to strike, not showing any fear of Plato's size or strength. Plato in turn stood steadfast, waiting for the beast to strike. Plato tapped into his core mainframe, running calculations and algorithms, attempting to figure out the beast's next move.

It was, in a sense, a stalemate. The auditorium had now been evacuated. All the children were broken up into groups and taken to the safety of their rooms.

The beast wouldn't surrender, nor would Plato surrender Joe's body to the vile creature. Suddenly, it pounced at Joe's unconscious body, which was held up and out of harm's way by Plato's awesome strength. The fierce cat-like beast was smart enough not to try and stand toe to toe with Plato. Instead, it jumped on Plato's left leg, crawling its way up and around the robot's large frame, swiping at Joe's body every chance it got.

Plato swung its two-ton arms in a fury to knock the beast off, but couldn't manage to free himself of the beast's mighty claws. Joe's body fell to the floor, landing hard on his right shoulder. He made a loud, sickening thump when he landed, yet he made no noise or movement. It was like a lifeless doll had fallen to the ground in a broken heap.

The beast quickly jumped off Plato and grabbed Joe by his tattered shirt, trying to drag him off stage. Plato closed in on the beast, but he didn't strike for fear of hitting Joe. Plato was a massive robot, powerful beyond any human, but he was slow and not very agile.

"Release him!" Plato demanded.

The beast snarled back, pulling Joe's body closer towards the exit.

A large dart struck the beast in its hindquarters. It yelped and turned quickly towards the direction of the strike. Across the large auditorium stood Dominick holding a large rifle with a scope, and his partner, Agent Roberts beside him. Dominick had a wicked smile on his face, hidden behind the weapon.

"Got you!" He grinned.

"Nice shot, boss," Roberts added. "That cat should be asleep any minute."

Chapter 12
Disaster

"Children!" Margot yelled. She had burst through the door in a frenzy. Her chest heaved with every breath. Behind her was Sebastian, who was obviously upset by the current state of affairs. His normally chiseled smile was gone, along with his perfectly parted blonde locks, which were now a hot mess, his bangs were wet with sweat, clung to his forehead.

"Margot, please calm down," Sebastian uttered, gasping for air.

"I'm so glad to see you. I lost track of you when the commotion happened." She ignored her fiancé and spoke to the children.

Elly, Hunter, Alistair, Liv, and a few others were crammed in a small storage room outside the auditorium's main hall. A tall, frail man, who looked more frightened than the children, was with them.

"A beast!" the man yelled, practically pushing the children out of his way as he approached Sebastian and Margot.

"Sir?" Margot looked up to see the tall man frantically barreling towards her.

"A monster! Running wild!" he yelled.

The children could feel the tension. They were already fearful, and now the one adult they had hidden with was losing it, scaring them even more.

"That thing will hunt us down! Eat us!" the man cried. He pushed Margot out of his way, grabbing Sebastian by the collar shoving him violently up against the wall.

"Y-You gotta save us, man!" the tall man begged. He was an older gentleman, with a few thin strings of hair combed over his bald spot.

He wore a green sweater vest that was now soaked in sweat.

Sebastian froze. He spent his days digging up excavation sites, mingling with ancient tribes, dusting off ancient pottery bowls. This sort of thing wasn't Sebastian's forte. He swallowed hard, unable to think of anything to say.

"Sir" Margot yelled. She pulled the man forward, spinning him around, forcing him to face her. She slapped the fool with all her might. The slap loudly in the small room. "Get a hold of yourself, there are children here!"

"But I-" The man stopped for a second, took a deep breath and exhaled loudly. His cheek swollen from Margot's slap, "I'm sorry, you're right..."

"How long have you worked here? You know this could happen at any time!" Margot yelled.

"I'm just a janitor though; I don't know much of anything," he argued.

"You know our drills. These children depend on your leadership. You're an adult, so act like one!" She shot a dirty look at Sebastian, who still looked a bit shook up.

"Hunter, Elly," Margot beckoned, her eyes darting around the room, looking for their faces. She found them both sitting in the corner, crying softly with Alistair and Liv attempting to console them. "Children, what's wrong?"

"That thing took Uncle Joey," Elly muttered through her sobs.

"What?" Margot's jaw dropped.

"It killed him!" Hunter yelled in anger, fists shaking violently.

"No... I... I saw him hold you two back. Then I lost track-" Margot tried to remember the events...

"Margot..." Sebastian put his hand on her shoulder. "I saw it... It's true."

"What?" her mouth quivered. "...and you did nothing?"

"I was across the room," he replied. "What on earth could I have done?"

"Something!" she yelled, pulling away from his hand.

"Plato grabbed him before we got pushed off stage," Alistair interrupted.

"Yeah, I'm sure he saved him," Liv added.

"What's your name?" Margot said to the tall man.

"Bobby," he held his jaw, attempting to rub the soreness away.

"Watch the kids, do *not* have another meltdown. Do you understand me?"

"No, I'm fine now. I will watch them."

"What are you doing?" Elly asked, sniffling through her tears.

"Yes, what exactly are you planning on doing?" Sebastian frowned.

"Going out there to help, of course." She grabbed a hammer from a nearby toolbox.

"And do what exactly, fight off that beast with a bloody hammer?" Sebastian mocked her.

"To help, Sebastian. To *help*!" She turned from Sebastian holding back the urge to slap her fiancé as well.

"Really?" Sebastian added with disbelief. He grabbed her shoulder, preventing her from leaving. "I will not allow my future wife to run out of this room towards some crazy monster," he said with determination.

"Then come with me." She pulled away from his grip, opened the door and left Sebastian standing in the room with the kids and Bobby.

"Bloody hell!" Sebastian muttered as he quickly followed.

Margot sprinted down the hallway and back towards the auditorium. Her hands shook uncontrollably with every stride she took.

"Margot!" Sebastian yelled, trying to keep pace.

Margot ignored him, she didn't care to converse with him anymore. Her blood boiled with anger. She didn't understand how anyone could sit back and watch a man get attacked by that thing without trying to help. The thought of watching Sebastian sit idly by while that beast clawed away at Joe, made her sick to her stomach. She made her way to the double doors and threw them open. There in front of her stood Dominick and Agent Roberts, Dominick with his rifle aimed at the beast.

"Stay back!" Dominick yelled.

"Oh, my lord..." Margot dropped the metal hammer, causing a loud thud on the floor. There in the beast's mouth was Joe's mauled body. He was motionless, his clothes ripped, his flesh torn, blood pooled beneath him.

"We hit the beast... calm down. Let him fall," Agent Roberts whispered.

The beast dropped Joe from its jaws. It shook its body violently attempting to shake the dart loose. It succeeded, the dart flew from its hindquarters, landing on the stage. The beast leaped violently into the air spreading its huge wings. Margot watched in horror at how fast the beast could move. It flew across the entire auditorium in seconds. Too fast for Dominick to reload his rifle and line up a second shot.

"That thing should be out!" agent Roberts yelled in disbelief.

The creature soared swiftly to the high arch of the dome. It tore apart one of the vents and disappeared, into the mansion's ventilation system.

"Damn it!" Dominick cursed. "It got away again!"

"Medic, we need a medic!" Margot ran towards Joe's lifeless body.

Plato knelt down beside Joe's bleeding body. The robot's hulking frame had blocked out the light from the chandelier preventing Margot from seeing the damage that had been done.

"Master Margot," Plato said plainly, "it is imperative you stand aside."

"Let me see him!" Plato held out his long solid arm preventing her from rushing to Joe's aid.

"I am sorry, it is unwise to move Master Joe's body until proper medical attention is distributed. He has multiple unknown injuries, potentially but not limited to: spinal damage, multiple open wounds, concussion..."

"Over here!" yelled Abram, who had brought a team of three medics with him. They brought with them a large supply of medical equipment, including a portable stretcher to move Joe's body without further damaging any potential at-risk areas, most importantly his spine.

"Give him air, now," one of the medics said as a terrified Margot looked on in disbelief.

"Clear this area! We need room, we need room, now!" another yelled.

Plato carefully backed away from Joe's body. Now Margot was able to see the extent of the injuries. She fell to her knees, bursting into tears at the horrific sight. She had never seen so much blood; his body was completely covered, his clothes almost totally shredded.

"Is he going to be okay?" Sebastian put his hand on her shoulder.

"His injuries are severe," Plato said.

They watched the medical team surround Joe, doing everything in their power to save his life. "Systems indicate a faint heartbeat. Tapping into portable medical operation machine's mainframe, now." Plato paused for a brief second, collecting data. "Signs of low oxygen level registering, probability of recovery low…" Plato paused again as if to come to terms with the sudden turn of events. "Personal emotional converter suggests a mixture of sadness and anger."

The mighty automaton always spoke his thoughts aloud. He couldn't think consciously like humans, his thoughts were expressed through speech alone…His simulated feelings got the better of his judgment, his mighty fists tensed with anger. Plato angrily swung a fist at the ground, crashing it forcefully through the floor board through.

"We have to transfer this guy to the med bay posthaste. Move, move!" Another medic yelled securing Joe on a stretcher and carried him off.

"Honey, we need to get out of here." Sebastian wiped the tears from Margot's cheek. "They have him now; he's in good hands."

Margot didn't move; she dropped her head into Sebastian's arms, sobbing. Plato stood before her not knowing how to react. He had his core mainframe synced up with the world's largest database of information, freely connecting to any and all secure nodes throughout the internet at his disposal. Although he could give you information on any topic, answer any question imaginable in mere nanoseconds, when it came to the human condition, Plato had nothing more than his own experiences to work from. He bent down on one knee, offering his gigantic steel hand for Margot to hold. She did so, squeezing his cold steel fingers as tightly as possible.

"Mistress Margot," Plato said, lowering the pitch in his voice to add a sense of ease, "I will stay by your side as well."

"Thank you," Margot whispered back. "Thank you for trying to save him."

Chapter 13
The Medical Bay

Hunter and Elly sat in the waiting room for over six hours. It was, indeed, the longest and most painful six hours of their lives. They sat amidst the smell of stale coffee and the mundane sound of the ticking wall clock that sat directly above their heads. With them sat Margot and Sebastian, who wouldn't dare leave the children's side. Margot sat rocking in her chair, stirring the same cup of coffee she had poured six hours before and hadn't taken a sip of yet. Sebastian, on the other hand, had fallen asleep rather quickly, stretched out across one of the waiting room's small couches, snoring lightly. Margot wasn't pleased with this and had left his side rather early in the night to sit closer to the children.

Hunter was surprised by how similar the medical wing in the mansion was to the hospital waiting rooms back at home. He didn't have many memories of infirmaries, with the exception of the night his grandfather had passed away from a heart attack. He was pretty young when it happened, Elly hadn't even been born yet. He didn't know his grandfather very well, but he remembered his mother's reaction. He had never seen her cry so much. He thought often of the pain on her face, even though she tried so desperately to hide it from him.

"Your granddad is in a better place," his mother kept saying to him over and over again that night through sobs and tears. He never really understood why she said it. If it was such a great place, why was she so sad? People told him and his sister the same thing about their parents. "They're in a wonderful place looking down on you."

Hunter cringed whenever someone told him them that. He felt no comfort in those words. If anything, it made him angrier.

Neither of the children could sleep that night. There is little comfort trying to sleep in a waiting room while awaiting news of a loved one's life-threatening condition, with the exception of Sebastian of course, who seemed a natural at it.

"Children," Margot's voice was tired, hoarse. "I know it's hard, but please do not fight off sleeping. Sleeping will make the time go by faster."

"Every time I close my eyes, I see that monster jumping on him," Elly's face was pale, dark circles set in under her young eyes.

"Thankfully, Plato was there," Margot replied, more to herself than anyone in particular. She stood up and tossed her now cold coffee into a trashcan. She unzipped her sweater, and sat down between the children. "It's getting cold. Cuddle up with me, we can use my sweater as a blanket."

The children welcomed the suggestion, snuggling up with Margot to keep warm but mostly to feel a connection to someone who cared for them. It didn't take long for both of them to fall into a light sleep.

It was early in the morning. The sun slowly rose, bringing with it welcoming natural warmth through the windows. A couple of hours passed before the entrance door swung open. The noise startled the children, they both jumped awake. Professor Calenstine, followed by Liv, Alistair, and his father, Ben, walked in. Ben and the children brought a couple of trays of freshly made toast, biscuits, and pastries. Hunter was shocked to see Professor Calenstine follow them in.

"Hey, guys, we brought some food," Ben said, offering the children their choice. They both declined, as neither felt like they could stomach much at the moment.

"Have you heard anything?" Alistair asked, taking a seat next to Hunter.

"What time is it?" Sebastian interrupted. The commotion had woken him from his deep slumber. He'd slept like a rock.

"Welcome back," Margot bit her tongue. She had never been so upset with anyone in her life.

"Breakfast?" Sebastian was completely oblivious to her response. He grabbed some toast and a couple of single-serve jelly packets. "Honey," he held out a piece of jellied toast to Margot, "you need to eat."

She ignored him.

"I spoke with the surgeon, Dr. Wong." Professor Calenstine broke the tension with a very serious tone. "Your uncle has been in surgery for eight hours. They just now finished with him."

"Can we see him?" Margot blurted out.

"I'm afraid not. He needs rest now. He is not conscious, the next few days are going to be crucial to see if he pulls through," the professor explained.

"Pulls through?" Hunter quizzed.

"I'm afraid so…" Professor Calenstine added. "There was severe damage to his body. He lost a lot of blood, many broken bones, some head trauma… He *is* stable now, and his vitals are good."

"I'm sorry." Liv gave Elly a heartfelt hug. "It's so terrible."

"Is that good news?" Elly asked through her tears. "He's stable means he is going to be fine, right?"

"For now, yes; it is good news," Professor Calenstine noted. "I wanted to come down here and talk to you kids personally. I know your uncle from his previous stay with us. I want you to know that he is our family too. I wanted to assure you that I will personally do everything in my power to help him get better. Do you understand?"

"Yes," Hunter frowned. He wanted to believe Professor Calenstine. He wanted to think his uncle would wake up and be back to his normal jovial self, he couldn't find the faith to do so. He knew, deep down, he would probably never talk to his uncle ever again. Everyone he loved seemed to die; he thought he was cursed.

"Don't underestimate what it is we can do in our little mansion," Professor Calenstine explained. He rolled his wheelchair to where the children sat. "Look into my eyes and know that I mean this."

Elly stared at the old man's soft blue eyes. She felt, for a brief second, a moment of clarity.

"*We* are the creators of miracles," Professor Calenstine continued in a serious tone. "There is nowhere in the world your uncle would find better treatment. We are at the forefront of the medical world, when the top hospitals and colleges out 'there'…" the old professor pointed out the large bay window, "… fail, they come to us to save the day."

"Really?" Elly asked, feeling a small ray of hope.

"I do not lie, my dear. I never have, nor will I ever." The professor winked.

"Now, it is early in the morning, none of you got much sleep. I urge you to return to your rooms and rest."

The children nodded. Physically, they looked ill from all the stress and lack of sleep. Margot looked equally as bad.

"I have made the decision to shut down all current activities concerning the Orientation until further notice. Once we can assure the safety of the mansion grounds, we will continue with the festivities. Please take this time to rest." Professor Calenstine smiled, shaking both Hunter's and Elly's hand. "When the dust settles, I promise to speak with you, personally, about your parents' wishes." The professor spun his wheelchair around towards Alistair and Liv. "Children, thank you for being here and showing your support for the Jakobs family. I know you have just met, but these are the conditions that cement lifelong friendships. They will need your help and understanding through these troubling times."

"Thank you, Professor." Margot kissed his wrinkly check.

"Yes, my dear, that goes for you as well. I have told Ms. Ellingbee you are on a day's bed rest. Sebastian," he now turned his attention to her fiancé, "I expect you to take care of Margot for us. See that she is well."

"Of course, sir. She has had quite an emotional day."

"Shall I escort you back?" Benjamin asked.

"No, I'm fine on my own. Please, spend the time here, help settle the children into their rooms."

"Of course," Ben answered.

It was a long trip back through the mansion's winding halls. Liv hung by Elly's side; she didn't say much to her new friend, but words weren't as important as the comfort the children received by having them at their side. Neither Hunter nor Elly had much to say anyway and preferred the silence as they each tried to deal with their overwhelming emotions. Margot and Sebastian didn't walk with them; they separated from the group and returned to their own room.

"I spoke to your father already, Liv," Ben walked with the group down the winding hall towards their room. "He said if you'd like you, can stay with Hunter and Elly for the day. I've already decided Alistair and I will hang out with them as well."

"Really?" Liv replied. She smiled brightly at Elly. "Do you want me to stay?"

"Yeah," Elly replied.

"You're staying too?" Hunter turned to Alistair.

"Yeah, my dad asked if we would. Might as well be locked down together, right?"

"Right." Hunter forced a smiled.

Never before were the children happier to see their beds, which had been fixed and reset from the earlier incident with Trayer. Although it was early in the morning, no one had managed much sleep that night. Ben instructed the children to get cozy and that everyone needed to get as much sleep as possible. Ben he'd brought sleeping bags for the kids and he stretched out on the children's small couch. Trayer, who had been locked up all day, was ecstatic to see his friends. He made his way quickly on to Elly's bed, curling up next to her as she swiftly fell asleep.

"You awake?" Hunter waited about ten minutes Alistair's dad began snoring.

"Sort of," Alistair said through a yawn.

"Do you think my uncle will be okay?"

"I think so."

"I don't know," Hunter replied. "Everything bad happens to my family."

"Professor Calenstine said he is in the best place possible to take care of him, though."

"Yeah." Hunter wasn't as impressed with the professor's words.

He had heard the whole 'everything will work out' spiel on numerous occasions.

"How long do you think it will take for them to get that creature?" Alistair whispered back.

"Who knows? They should have gotten it a long time ago. None of this would have happened if they did their jobs right."

"I guess that's true," Alistair's eyes grew heavier and heavier with every word.

"Alistair…?" Hunter questioned, but his friend had fallen asleep, along with everyone else in the room.

Hunter stayed awake, staring blankly at the ceiling. A million thoughts rushed through his brain. He wished he could fall asleep like the rest of them. He wished he could shut off his brain even for an hour. Yet, there he was, wide-awake, thinking of his uncle, his parents, and that horrific creature that was the cause of all his heartache.

Chapter 14
Isolation

The children spent three days nervously anticipating any sort of update on their uncle's condition. It never came. Instead, they awoke every morning with hope that he would miraculously recover and storm into their room with a bright and inviting smile.

During this time, Uncle Joe was kept under constant watch in the medical wing's intensive care unit. Margot and Patricia didn't have the heart to tell the children how serious the situation was. His condition had worsened, he was no longer able to breathe on his own; needing the aid of a respirator. It was a grim sight to see the young man in such a frail condition, hooked up to a series of machines that manipulated his body stopping him from succumbing to his life-threatening injuries. Although no one would ever utter the words to the children, it was an absolute miracle that he hadn't already passed on.

Margot and Patricia spoke to the children the most during this troublesome time. They brought them their meals every morning and night. They both made time in their busy schedules to spend large portions of their day playing board games with them in hopes of keeping their spirits up. Hunter and Elly were thankful for that. It was when they were left alone that they found it the most difficult to cope. Their young minds wandered into deep and dark places.

Elly found solace by diving into one of her many books. She had spent the last few days researching the Cusith breed. She even found a specific training manual for the breed that was published through Belmonte Publishing, which she found a bit weird. Everything she learned from the book she implemented quickly into Trayer's daily regimen. Elly found it easier to train the large pup with the book's help. She was ecstatic about how quickly Trayer had learned everything; it only took one morning to teach the mammoth canine how to roll over and play dead.

Hunter spent most of his time staring out the large bay window, dreaming about how great his life was before his parents' accident. He often found himself staring at the family photo Margot had given him, fighting off tears. He hardly slept at night, tossing and turning, he rarely ever got any decent sleep, finding it very difficult to focus during the day because he was so exhausted. His little sister had almost given up on talking to him altogether due to his newfound quick temper. He knew he was snapping at his sister, through no fault of her own, he always felt terrible about it once he calmed down, but the bitterness and anger that stewed in him often got the better of him.

The children were also thankful for Alistair and Liv, who were allowed to spend a few hours a day with them under the guidance of Alistair's father, Ben. Professor Calenstine ordered that no children were allowed to walk the mansion's premises unless under the strict guidance of an accompanying guardian. Liv and Alistair were granted special privilege from Professor Calenstine and were allowed to leave under Ben's guidance for longer periods of time to help their friends during their time of need. No other children in the mansion were allowed to leave their rooms for more than an hour a day until the monster had been captured.

"We're really glad we get to come to your room and hang out," Alistair concentrated on the card game he and Elly played.

"Yeah, we're crammed up in our rooms with our fathers all day. My dad drives me crazy going on about how Uncle Dominick can't do his job right. Who's winning?" Liv asked, taking a seat next to them at the dining table.

"Elly always wins," Alistair admitted. "I can't believe they haven't found that creature yet."

"Doesn't surprise me," Hunter scoffed, hopping off his bed with a book in his hand.

"You've been reading?" Liv asked. "I thought that was Elly's thing." She laughed a little.

"I've been pretty bored" Hunter answered, a little embarrassed. "While Elly was reading about training Trayer, I found out as much as I could about the Beast of Bladenboro." He pulled a chair up alongside Alistair and the girls. "I couldn't find much out at first. This book tells about its first sighting back in 1953 in North Carolina. It attacked dogs and cattle, it only lasted for like a year. It says people think it was a rare sighting of a Carolina black panther."

"I read about that too," Elly added. "The town made it into a big deal."

"Well, I have this other book…" Hunter walked back over to his bed and pulled a very large manuscript from underneath it. He dropped it on the table, purposely making a loud thud. "Look who wrote this one." He pointed at the book with pride.

The children glanced at the cover. It read in bold print, "Mysteries Explored: a Journal of Wonders" by Professor Claudio Calenstine. Elly's eyes grew wide with excitement.

"Professor Calenstine wrote it?" Liv asked. She began thumbing through the pages of the seemingly ancient manuscript. "Some of this is written in weird languages," she noted.

"Yeah, I couldn't read all of it. I did find an entire chapter dedicated to the Beast of Bladenboro though. Professor Calenstine was actually there hunting the beast during that year," Hunter explained. "There's even this old picture of him, look." Hunter flipped through the yellowed pages until he found a black and white photo of three men standing in front of a city limits sign that read "Welcome to Bladenboro." It looked like the mayor, who was a round, pear-shaped man with a large beard, was in the middle of the photo. A younger man they didn't recognize stood to his right, smiling brightly with a gun slung across his shoulder. Hunter explained that this was Michael Roland, who was there working with Professor Calenstine as an understudy. To the left was Professor Calenstine. One would expect the professor to look younger, knowing that the photo was taken back in the 1950s. Yet, to the children's surprise, the professor was the spitting image of the man they had met in the mansion, old and scrawny with a well-trimmed white beard. The only difference between the professor then and now was that he was standing with the aid of a staff and not confined to a wheelchair.

"How old *is* he anyway?" Elly peered over Liv's shoulder.

"He looks like he has to be a hundred in this photo," Alistair chuckled.

"That would make him like a hundred-and-sixty-two!" Liv laughed.

"Well, he writes about how once the word spread things got a little crazy in town. The city started getting overrun with people trying to hunt it and collect the thousand-dollar reward. The professor writes that he first thought the mayor was making it all up, an ill attempt to get tourists to come to the town and spend money. Then, once he couldn't control the hype, he thinks the mayor claimed to have shot and killed a panther, ending the hunt, explaining that the large panther was the beast, and sparing the hassle of paying anyone the money."

"Okay, so it was a hoax?" Liv quizzed, wondering where Hunter was going with the story.

"Well, Professor Calenstine said he stayed for a few months to keep investigating. There were three reports of attacks afterwards, spanning a four-week period. He says the mayor kept it quiet, but the town was still bustling with sightings. The professor continued to explore with a group of people and spotted the beast in the wild. See, read..." Hunter pointed to a paragraph. "He describes it as a large winged panther!"

"So, it's the same creature?" Alistair asked.

"I dunno," Hunter said. "He said they were never able to capture it, but that when they tracked it, they found some sort of tag left in one of its nesting areas."

"A tag?" Elly asked.

"Yeah, he said he thinks someone had released it into the forest near the city and kept tabs on it in the wilderness. Collecting data or something."

"They do that with sharks in the ocean." Alistair got excited. "The tags have sensors so they can collect data from anywhere in the world. They sync with satellites, sending the information back to their labs. It's really cool. They can plot swim patterns, depths the sharks stay in, all kinds of stuff from one little tag," Alistair added. Elly gave Alistair a funny look. "What? I watch a lot of wilderness shows."

"How does that help us though?" Liv asked.

"Maybe someone is still tracking it," Elly suggested. "The same people from back then?"

"Well, these tags are a fairly new kind of technology; I doubt they had it back in the fifties, that's ancient times. They didn't even have laptops back then," Alistair noted.

"I don't know," Hunter said with a shrug. "I want to help find this thing. I hate being stuck up here like a prisoner. That thing is the reason Uncle Joe isn't with us anymore."

"Then let's do something about it." Alistair spoke up.

"What do you mean?" Elly stacked the deck of cards and put them away. She never liked this sort of 'rebellious' talk.

"I mean let's get out of here, like you and Hunter did before we came to the mansion. We can sneak out tomorrow night!" Alistair got excited.

"Really?" Liv couldn't help but show her excitement as well.

"How did you sneak out last time?" asked Alistair.

"It was easy." Hunter went on to explain how he stuffed the threshold of the lock with paper and waited to sneak out after everyone had gone to sleep.

"You guys aren't serious, are you?" Elly was a bit upset. "Do you *remember* what happened to me last time we snuck out?"

"There'll be four of us this time, and we'll be extra careful," Alistair explained.

"Yeah, Elly." Liv smiled. "We'll be fine if we stick together."

"And what if we do find the thing? Are we supposed to beat it up?" she added, now even more frustrated.

"No, we rush back and tell the adults where they can find it. This is a great idea!" Hunter added.

"No!" Elly walked away from the table taking a seat on her bed.

"Then don't go," Hunter mocked his little sister. "I told you not to come the first time. It's your fault you got hurt."

"It's okay if you want to stay here, Elly," Alistair spoke up, trying to ease the tension. "We need a game plan though."

"Yeah, we can't walk around the mansion, in the dark, searching for the thing." Liv responded.

"What about Trayer?"

The pup's head shot up at the mention of his name, his enormous tail started wagging, making a loud thumping noise on the wall. Hunter smiled. He remembered something his sister had mentioned about Cusiths a few days earlier.

"What about him?" Liv tapped her leg, motioning for Trayer's attention. The pup set its large head on her lap while she scratched behind his big floppy ears.

"Elly, you said Cusiths are great trackers, right?"

"Yeah so..." Elly added. "Dogs can't track something unless they catch its scent, stupid."

"Alistair, help me up." Hunter pointed to the large ventilation system that sat high on the children's wall.

Alistair boosted Hunter up, and Hunter peered into the vent and smiled.

"Yes!" He reached his fingers into the grate and pulled out a small clump of thick, coarse, purple hair. "It must have rubbed up against the vent too hard that night." He hopped back down. "Check it out?" He held out his hand, showing the group the matted hair.

"Will Trayer be able to pick up its scent with that?" Liv asked.

We'll find out tomorrow night." Hunter tucked the hair into his jeans pocket for safekeeping.

"Let's talk about the game plan." Hunter smiled for the first time in days.

Chapter 15
The Second Escape

Hunter prepped the lock once again with a wadded-up sheet of paper. Margot had come up at the usual time to say goodnight to the kids and take Alistair and Liv back to their respective rooms. She looked tired and sickly. The kids knew she was struggling with everything that had happened in the last few days. A lot of the mansion's staff wore the stress on their faces. Margot had deep, dark bags under her eyes and a sickly yellowish tint to her skin. She tried to hide it from the kids, promising that their uncle would get better soon, filling their ears with as much hope as anyone could muster.

Hunter felt bad for taking advantage of her kindness. Distracting Margot was easy; she was too tired to stay alert. Alistair and Liv bombarded her with questions about the beast while Hunter snuck over and stuffed the lock with the crumpled paper. Phase one of the plan was complete.

"I'm so sorry, children. There has been no news about the beast being caught." Margot collapsed tiredly onto Ely's bed.

"You look terrible, are you sick?" Elly asked.

"So much is going on right now. Nothing is right, I'm just overwhelmed," she answered.

"I'm sure Sebastian helps make things better. He's so nice," Elly said.

"Normally," Margot couldn't hide her frown.

"Are you two okay?" Liv asked.

"Since the attack… let's say we have not really seen eye to eye." Margot played with her engagement ring, spinning it around her finger.

"I'm sorry." Elly and Liv both hugged Margot.

"It's okay," Margot stood up from the bed and yawned. "It's getting late; let me take you children back to your parents. You and Hunter should get some sleep tonight. Hopefully something happens soon and they get that damned creature so we can get back to some normalcy here in the mansion."

"Okay, goodnight," Hunter stated with a mischievous smile that Margot was oblivious too.

Margot escorted Hunter and Elly's friends out of their room and locked their door. Hunter jumped into his bed with excitement.

"You should feel terrible. She's hurting just like us, except you act like nothing's wrong," Elly scolded.

"Shut up!" Hunter frowned. "Just because you're too scared to help doesn't mean…"

"I'm not scared!" Elly argued.

"Whatever, go to bed." Hunter turned his back. He reached under his bed, pulling out his backpack. He checked his supplies: water bottle, two granola bars, a large flashlight, and a Swiss army knife his father had gotten for him on his tenth birthday.

The knife his favorite gift from his father. He remembered the day fondly.

"I've had that Swiss army knife since I was ten. It's been in our family for generations," his dad said to him as he cut his birthday cake. "It's saved my life before… it's sort of an heirloom."

"Saved your life?" Hunter swapped out the different utensils in the knife. He was amazed at what the knife could do; it had a spoon, fork, corkscrew, a small knife, bottle opener, compass, ruler… the list went on. Hunter thought it had everything anyone could ever need at any given moment.

"More than once." His dad smiled. "Look here." He flipped the knife over in his son's hands. "There's your 'great-great-great' grandfather's initials." The letters L.G.J. were inscribed at the knife's base in dark gold lettering.

"L.G.J.?" Hunter asked.

"Laurence Glenn Jakobs," his dad said, smiling proudly. "I have a picture of him here." His father pulled out a bursting wallet that looked like it was about to fall apart at the seams. He unfolded it pulling out an old photo. There in front of a large mansion stood a young and masculine Laurence Glen Jakobs. He stood next to a scrawny old man, smiling, with his arm around his shoulders. Hunter remembered thinking the two seemed like best friends, despite the age difference. His memory was foggy now, and he wished he could remember the photo in his head; it was nothing but a blur

"Who's that with him?" Hunter remembered asking.

"Well, that's an old family friend," his dad answered.

The memory had escaped Hunter until now fiddling with the knife in his hands. The knife made him feel closer to his father. He wasn't quite sure why or how, but he felt comfort holding it.

He and his sister didn't speak for the rest of the evening. They lay in their beds with their backs to one another until the clock struck midnight. Hunter sprung out of bed swinging his backpack across his shoulders. He turned, startled to see his sister waiting by the door with her pack ready to go.

"What are you doing?" Hunter asked, annoyed. "Get back to bed."

"I'm not staying here alone."

"You're not coming with us." Hunter signaled for Trayer, who sat patiently next to Elly. "C'mon, boy," said Hunter.

"He won't move until I give him permission. He's my dog, I trained him."

"Whatever, I bet I can get him to come." Hunter challenged his little sister.

"Bet you can't," she protested.

Hunter opened his backpack, unwrapping one his granola snacks. "C'mon, boy, treat." He waved the food in the air. "I said treat, you stupid dog, treat!". Trayer waged his tail a little, his mouth drooled at the sight of the tasty treat. The large pup let out a small whine, as if asking Elly if it was okay to accept the treat.

"No," Elly said plainly, and Trayer immediately settled down.

"See, I told you. He listens to me. Now, if you want him to track that thing, then you need me to go along too," she explained.

"You said you were too scared to go."

"I changed my mind. If something goes bad, I want to be there to make sure my friends are safe."

"Fine!" Hunter frowned. "Shut up and follow me."

Hunter had memorized how to get to both Alistair's and Liv's rooms based on their directions. He recited it over and over in his head: Move down the hallway, fourth room on the left past the elevator. Hunter and Elly waited at the door impatiently. The hallways were lit up, unlike their first escape. They assumed they were left on to steer the beast away from roaming the halls. The door slowly creaked open, Alistair stuck his head out, signaling Hunter and Elly to keep quiet.

"It worked!" Alistair whispered.

"Your dad sleeping?" Elly whispered back.

"Like a rock, c'mon, let's go get Liv."

"Follow me." Hunter moved on down the hall.

Back to the elevator, hang a second right, down the hall past the storage closet, third room on the right, Hunter thought to himself as he led the way.

"I think this is it." He pointed to room 312. "Where's Liv?"

Alistair looked around.

"Behind you." Liv poked Hunter on the shoulder, startling him.

"Quiet!" Elly scolded, shooting her older brother a look of disgust.

"Sorry." Liv laughed. "I got bored waiting for you, so I took a walk down the hall."

"Is your dad sleeping too?" Alistair asked.

"No, he's out searching for the monster. So, we have to be careful we don't get caught. A group of parents are out patrolling."

"Great," Elly whined.

"How's Trayer?" Liv knelt down to pet the pup. "Is he already leading us?"

"Not yet," Elly answered. "He needs the scent first."

"Here." Hunter pulled the clump of hair out of his pocket and handed it to Elly. She took the hair, holding it to Trayer's nose so he could get a good smell. She then put the hair on the ground and pointed to it. "Trayer, find," she said with a strict tone. Trayer's tail started wagging, his nose centimeters from the floor, sniffing very loudly in a circle trying to pick up its scent.

"I don't think he's picking it up," Hunter frowned.

"Give him a second." Elly gave her brother a dirty look.

Then Trayer was off. The large green-haired pup began moving down the hall at a brisk pace, his nose to the floor, hot on a trail. The children rushed off, following behind. He stopped a few halls down at a window looking out over the back courtyard. It was blocked off with bright yellow caution tape. Where the windowpane had been there was now a thick layer of plastic to keep the heat in the building. The windowpane was scratched with deep claw marks that had stripped the paint off the walls.

"What do you think happened here?" Liv pointed to a few small shards of glass still in the carpet beneath the window.

"I think, maybe, it went outside through the window." Alistair answered.

"Let's check it out," Hunter suggested.

"Wait!" Elly protested. "No one said anything about going out of the mansion. Hunter, don't you remember how big and scary the forest was?"

"No one said we *wouldn't* go out of the mansion either," Hunter shot back.

"C'mon, Elly, we won't stay out long, we'll just check out around the mansion grounds. Maybe Trayer won't pick up the scent outside," Alistair interjected.

"Fine!" Elly wasn't happy but she went along with them anyway.

The group made their way to the elevator so that they could get to the main level of the mansion as quickly as possible. The elevator door opened and the children once again found themselves setting foot into the main foyer. Voices came from below them.

"Quiet," Alistair whispered, peering over the edge of the balcony and down onto the main floor. There he saw Margot and Sebastian arguing by the entrance. He waved the group over to listen.

"Frankly, I am a little confused as to why you're so upset over this Joe character," Sebastian's vice was stern, cruel. He tried to keep his composure, but he was failing miserably. His normally cool demeanor was gone, his red with anger.

"What's that supposed to mean?" Margot replied, her eyes swollen and puffy from the tears.

"You tell me," he scoffed, almost mocking Margot's ignorance of the matter.

"He's a friend who tried to save his niece and nephew, now he's on his deathbed!" Margot's words turned to anger.

"Is that it?" Sebastian slung his bag over his shoulder.

"You're leaving like this?"

"You know I have a plane to catch," he said hotly.

"In the morning, there's no need to storm out at this hour. You know that beast is out there."

"I'm not afraid of that *thing*." Sebastian laughed, insulted at the claim.

"You know it attacked Agent Roberts last night, drug him out of the fourth-floor window. No one has seen or heard from him yet. It's dangerous. Don't go out there; at least wait for me to get Ben or Abram to escort you out."

"Do not act like you're worried for me. Save your worries for your new friend," Sebastian turned to walk away.

"Sebastian…" Margot grabbed his shoulder. "Please stay and talk to me," she begged.

"We'll talk when I come back from my trip," he said coldly.

"I didn't mean it…" Margot cried.

"So, you *accidently* called me a coward?" He unlocked the front door, storming off into the cold night air. Margot sobbed loudly, making her way up the eastern side of the stairs that led to the elevator.

"Quick, down the other side, now!" Hunter pointed the group down the opposite side of the balcony.

"That was close…" Alistair whispered.

The children were now on the main level foyer. It was here Hunter had first set eyes on Liv. He remembered the brunch, how he had felt so awkward standing next to her for the first time. A lot had happened in such a short time. Now he stood beside her again, despite her beauty and his unfamiliar feelings for her, there was a comfort in her presence…

They stood underneath the mounted monster heads that had caught Hunter's attention when they first arrived. He knew, now, that they could very well be real. The thought struck a little fear into him, the confusion of not being able to tell truth from fiction. They had spent their entire lives being told monsters were not real. Now, one of those very creatures could have taken their uncle's life, and they were out hunting for its lair.

"They scared me too, when I first saw them." Liv stood next to Hunter, staring at the giant saber-toothed tiger's head.

"Oh," Hunter replied. "They don't scare me…"

"It's okay if they do. It's kind of a lot to take in. I wonder what really exists out there… you know? What we don't know about," she added. "This one's my favorite… the saber-toothed tiger."

"I think it's exciting," Alistair pushed in between the two, "…so much to discover."

Hunter gave Alistair a dirty look for butting in. He knew Alistair didn't realize he had broken up what Hunter thought was a shared moment between him and Liv, but alas he had.

"What?" Alistair shrugged his brow.

"Nothing, let's go." Hunter turned away towards the front entrance.

"We can't get out that way," Elly said, standing next to a window. "We don't have the key. It locks from both sides. Don't you remember?"

"What kind of door locks people in and as well as out?" Alistair whined.

"Probably the kind that doesn't want kids likes us outside in the woods after dark," Elly added. "Guess we should head back to our rooms now, since we can't get out."

"We can use the window," Alistair suggested.

"Yeah, c'mon, help me open it." Hunter grunted, trying to pry the window open. "It's stuck."

Alistair helped, together the boys pulled the window open, but not before the window let out a loud cracking noise, as if the children had broken some ancient seal.

Liv frowned. "Oh no, it's screened…"

"We'll punch it out," Alistair smiled.

"It's not that type of screen, look." She pointed to the screen, it was a thick wire mesh, not easy to get through like a common household screen.

"I knew this would come in handy!" Hunter pulled out his family's Swiss army knife. He flipped out a small pair of scissors, clipping the wire mesh until the window was free from any constraints.

"There we are," Hunter squeezed his way through the window dropping down onto the frozen grass. "It's a bit of a drop, so be careful," he said as Liv made her way through the window.

"Catch me if I fall." She jumped down.

Alistair came next. "C'mon, Elly, you coming?" he asked.

Elly sighed, she signaled to the window for Trayer to jump through. He did so, Elly followed.

"Okay we have to let Trayer read to the scent outside," Elly explained, once again allowing Trayer to sniff the clump of purple hair.

"Wait!" Hunter whispered loudly.

"What?" Elly shot back.

Hunter pointed towards the main entrance, where Sebastian still stood. He was talking to someone on the phone. The children backed up against the wall trying to stay hidden while he walked down the long winding path towards the mansion's locked gates.

"Wonder who he's talking to?" Hunter whispered.

The children could tell Sebastian was still angry. At one point, he threw up his hands in protest, yelling.

"I told you to meet me at one a.m., you're late!" he barked. He began walking in circles, pacing non-stop. He closed his phone, kicking up the gravel in frustration. A loud noise came from the forest, reminiscent of something large burrowing through the foliage.

"Hello?" Sebastian turned towards the noise off in the distance.

There was nothing but silence.

"Anybody out there?" he yelled into the woods.

Then it struck from the shadows, the wicked purple beast pounced from a large shrub. It moved so fast the children could barely make out what they were seeing. It was nothing more than a large purple blur that swept across the yard, tackling Sebastian hard, pummeling him to the ground in a heap. He screamed, but the growls of the monster were louder. It only took a few seconds for the creature to overcome the struggling Sebastian.

Hunter started towards the struggle, but Liv pulled him back.

"Where are you going?" She held his hand tightly.

"To help…"

"You can't! What can you do to save him?" she asked.

"Hunter," Elly added, "Didn't you read about how the monster eats?"

"What?" Hunter watched helplessly as the beast picked up Sebastian's body in its mouth.

"It's a bloodsucker. All the animals were taken alive and drained of blood," she explained.

"We have to follow it to its nest, then we can rescue him," Alistair added. "It makes sense. It kept trying to escape with your uncle, but Plato wouldn't let it."

The beast dragged Sebastian's body into the darkness of the forest with ease.

The children could hear Sebastian's faint voice mustering all his remaining strength to cry for help. It was an awful sound that would haunt Hunter's ears for years to come. The sudden attack brought back the dark imagery of their uncle's struggle with the beast. The hatred in Hunter grew to new levels, he clenched his fists tightly, his face red with anger.

"Hunter, are you okay? Look at me." Liv took Hunter's face in her kind hands, turning it away from the scene, directing his gaze to her soft blue eyes.

"We are going to kill that thing…" Hunter's eyes burned with rage.

Chapter 16
The Hunt

Elly had given the scent to Trayer, he sped off into the forest, hot on the beast's trail. The beast drug Sebastian deep into the western side of forest, away from the small winding road the children had traveled to the mansion on. They had no idea how far back the mansion's property line stretched, but they were in the midst of a thick forest that seemed to never end.

The children hiked through the rough terrain. Trayer had no problem weaving in and out of the bushes and foliage; the children however, were getting scratched and bruised with every step they took. There was no trail to follow, only the lush foliage that had been padded down from where the beast had crashed. The treetops were so thick that the canopy of trees blocked out the little moonlight that would have aided them. Now the four pressed on in the eerie forest with only their flashlights and Trayer's nose to guide them along the way.

"These are the creepiest woods I have ever seen," Alistair felt his heart racing.

"Yeah, who knows what lives out here?" Liv added.

"Look." Hunter pointed to a plant with a smear of red blood on it.

"Sebastian's," Elly said sadly.

"It's not much, so he's still okay. We're on the right track," Alistair added.

The deeper they traveled, the creepier the forest became. There were strange noises, foreign, completely terrifying to their young ears. Branches broke around them continuously, they thought at one point that the beast had turned around and begun stalking them. They pressed on though, unwavering in the darkened night.

"Are we going to be able to find our way back?" Alistair second guessed their decision to follow the beast. They had been hiking through the forest for what seemed like hours.

"We can use Trayer's nose to get us back," Elly answered.

"I'm tired… I need to rest," Liv stated. "Just for a second…" she wiped the cold sweat from her brown.

"My legs burn," Alistair took a seat on a large smooth rock.

"Okay, not for long though," Hunter took a seat next to his friend. "We don't know how long Sebastian has before the beast kills him."

"Agreed," Liv replied. She opened her backpack pulling out a bag full of grapes. "I'm starving."

"Do you hear that?" Elly frowned, a low-pitched ringing noise echoed through the foliage.

"Is that a phone," Liv asked.

"It's over here." Hunter shined his flashlight onto a nearby bush. Sebastian's cell phone was lit up playing an obnoxious ringtone.

"Answer it," said Elly. "Maybe they can help?"

"Hunter flipped the phone open and the name "Declan" appeared on the screen. Hunter hit the "answer" key, but the phone suddenly died.

"Battery died…" Hunter frowned. "Someone named 'Declan' was calling. Do we know a Declan?"

"Not that I know of…" Alistair took a long chug of water from his thermos.

"C'mon, he must be close," Liv stood back up, ready to move on.

The group collected their bearings and pressed deeper into the forest. Trayer led them into a small clearing that gave way to the darkest and dreariest cave they had ever seen. The clearing allowed the bright light of the moon to shine down, but this made the cave even scarier.

"Are you serious?" Elly asked. "No way am I going into that thing, you're crazy."

"We have no choice. Look," Hunter pointed, "Trayer knows the scent goes right into that thing."

"He's right," Liv added. "I don't want to go in there either, but we have to."

"We have Trayer to protect us, he's huge." Alistair started walking towards the cave's entrance.

"He's a puppy," Elly reminded the group.

Elly thought the entrance to the cave looked like a giant's mouth, it's teeth sharp, jagged, waiting to swallow the group whole, never to be seen again. They entered it cautiously to find it sloped downwards deep into the earth. It was damp, cold, and beyond dark inside. Luckily, the children's flashlights had plenty of battery left to guide them.

"I watch shows all the time about spelunking," Alistair broke the eerie silence. He wasn't afraid of the cave, he was enjoying the turn of events.

"Spe-whoing?" Elly made her away around a large rock formation that looked like an icicle growing from the ground up.

"—Spelunking," he explained. "That's what it's called when people explore caves. That big thing you moved around is called a 'stalagmite.' This cave must be made of limestone."

"How do you know so much about caves?" Hunter was impressed.

"Like I said before, I watch a lot of television. My favorite show is 'Myth Hunters.' My dad and I watch it every Tuesday night."

"What's that about?" inquired Liv.

"A group of people go exploring in crazy out-of-this-world places looking for mythical creatures and treasures. They spend a lot of time in caves. The team is led by Jonathon Gates, he's awesome," explained Alistair. "I guess it's a lot like what our families do, except they do it on television."

"It's getting cold," Elly said. "Do they ever find anything?"

"Not usually. Once they found a big footprint in the Himalayas, it made national news too. That was cool, claimed it was from the Yeti."

"Look!" Elly pointed.

The cave opened up to a large underground lake. It sat deep

inside, far away from the hands of man, undisturbed, it's surface calm looking, like a sheet of glass. Alistair had seen underground lakes like these on TV, but he never imagined how breathtaking the real thing was.

"It's gorgeous!" Liv eyes were wide with wonder.

"How deep do you think it is?" Elly asked. "I don't see a way across."

"Let's find out." Hunter took a step into the lake. It was freezing cold. He waded about halfway out before stopping. "It gets deep quick, going to have to swim across," the water reached his chest.

"I can't swim!" Elly yelled back.

"No problem," Alistair answered. "I have an idea…"

Liv and Alistair joined Hunter in the peaceful lake. Elly held onto Trayer's large collar while the pup paddled his way across the lake in record time.

"Look at him go!" Alistair smiled through the burning cold of the lake.

The children were more than exhausted by the time they made it to the other side. Worse than that, their clothes were soaked with freezing water. They didn't have much time to think though because Trayer was still hot on the beast's trail. They followed quickly behind, pushing through the numbing cold that burned their fingertips and toes.

Trayer sat and let out a small whimper, having lead them once again to a small clearing of the cave.

"This must be the place." Hunter signaled for the group to quiet down, he hide behind a large rock.

"Do you see it?" Liv whispered.

"The place is huge. I don't see anything," Elly answered.

"Look," Hunter pointed his flashlight towards the center of the clearing, there they saw a large clump of what looked like clothes.

"What is it?" Liv squinted trying to make it out, but she couldn't see anything.

"Let me sneak over there and find out." Hunter crawled over to the pile, taking his time so as to not make any sudden movements or noises. He felt his heart drop into his stomach once he reached his destination. It was tattered clothing stained in blood, underneath the clothes was a large rifle. Hunter had seen this same rifle before. Dominick had used a similar one the day he and Elly were attacked by the beast. He dug around the clothes a bit more finding a piece of the clothing that read "Agent Roberts" on it. Hunter dropped the clothes and shuddered in revulsion. He turned, running back to his friends, foregoing any sort of stealth.

"Hunter, stop running, be quiet!" Elly whispered his way.

"What's wrong? What was it?" Alistair asked.

Hunter ran back behind the large rock, trembling in fear. It took him a minute to catch his breath… "Err…I think it was Agent Roberts' clothes." He paused, letting the weight of his words sink in. "They were all torn up and stained with blood."

"Oh no…" Liv frowned. "Did you see him anywhere out there?"

"No, only his clothes and gun," Hunter frowned.

"Look over by those stones." Elly pointed. "It looks like a nest."

About 10 yards away from the bloody clothes was a large pile of rubbish, broken sticks, leaves, and anything else the creature could push together to create a nesting area.

"It's not here yet…" Liv added. "We must have beaten it here somehow."

The children made their way out of their hiding spot towards the center of the cave.

"What do we do now?" Hunter asked. "Wait for it?"

"You get the hell out of here," a raspy voice echoed from the far side of the clearing. The strange voice startled the children, causing Elly let out a small scream.

"Shut your mouths!" Dominick shined his flashlight on them. "You wanna scare the beast off before it gets here?"

"Uncle Dominick?" Liv smiled. "Thank God you're here!"

"What in the hell are you kids doing here?" he cursed, his mouth pulled in anger.

"We were trying to help find…" Hunter tried to explain.

"—Exactly!" Dominick interrupted. "You were disobeying orders again, putting yourselves in danger. You know how easy it would be to get killed down here?" His anger was boiling.

"We're sorry. We were trying to help." Alistair mumbled his words.

"I have been camped out in this cave for two nights, waiting for that thing to come back. Now you kids have probably mucked it all up."

"Is Agent Roberts okay?" Alistair pointed to the clothes.

"No." Dominick hid a frown. "He didn't make it."

"Oh," Elly gasped... she had hoped...

"Shut up!" Dominick barked, his head shot towards the entrance of the large opening. "Did you hear that?"

"No," Hunter replied.

"Quick, hide, don't make a noise!" Dominick pushed the kids behind a series of rocks. "I have one shot, I have to make it count."

Chapter 17
In the Belly of the Beast

The vile creature known as the Beast of Bladenboro snarled menacingly making its way into the opening of the cavern. Sebastian looked in rough shape, his clothes tattered from being dragged through the thick forest, and the rocky flooring of the cave probably wasn't easy on him either. He seemed to slip in and out of consciousness, groaning in pain while the creature carried him effortlessly.

Dominick looked toward the children, signaling for them not to move. He steadied his rifle on top of the large rock. The creature dropped Sebastian from its powerful jaws near its nest and stretched out its muscular back. The small laser dot rested on the beast's neck, Dominick smirked as he pulled the trigger. The dart whizzed out of the rifle, striking the beast dead on. The creature jolted backwards, pawing at its neck, knocking off the dart. The beast stumbled a bit before finally falling violently on its side, crashing hard onto the cavern floor.

"Got you, you bastard!" Dominick stood up. He motioned for the children to stay back as he cautiously approached the beast. He stood over it, poking it with his rifle, it didn't make a move. "It's safe," he said. "Quick, check and make sure this guy's okay."

"Are you sure? Last time that dart didn't do anything," Hunter stepping out from behind the large boulder cautiously.

"Tripled its dose," Dominick explained. "Quick, he needs help, use this." He unclipped a small medical supply kit from his belt and tossed it on the floor next to Sebastian. "I need to stand guard and radio this in."

"I can help, my dad taught me some stuff..." Alistair rushed over to Sebastian fumbling to open up the medical supply bag, digging through its contents. "—Any open scratches we need to sterilize with these." He handed Liv and Elly disinfectant pads. "Hunter, if anything is deeper, you need to stop the bleeding. Use these..." Alistair handed Hunter some large medical gauze and tape. "Anywhere there is a deep puncture, put pressure on it, and tape it down with as much pressure you can," he noted.

"Hurry up and get the bleeding stopped. We don't want him to die before help gets here." Dominick turned back towards the beast, unclipping his radio from his belt. "I'm calling in some reinforcements to get this thing out of here, and to get you stupid kids home safely. Your dad owes me for saving you, Liv," he snarled.

The beast awakened, swiping viciously at Dominick's legs. The sheer strength of the animal sent Dominick falling hard on his back, knocking the wind out of his chest. The beast was groggy but still able to jump on Dominick, sinking its razor-sharp teeth deep into his shoulder, he screamed in pain.

"No!" Elly yelled. Her eyes filled with terror.

Trayer heard the scream and quickly ran to Dominick's aid.

"Trayer!" Elly screamed, fearful for the pup's life. Trayer sprinted with all his might tackling the beast head on. The two monstrous animals hit so hard a deafening thunderclap echoed throughout the cave. The animals snarled and growled as they tore into one another's flesh with their mighty jaws. Trayer, still a pup, was slightly smaller and less muscular than the vile and bloodthirsty Beast of Bladenboro, but he fought with all his might to protect the children.

Tears streamed down Elly's cheeks as Trayer fell prey to the larger animal. The Beast of Bladenboro gained the advantage now moving over the pup, ready for its fatal strike.

"Save him!" Liv yelled.

Hunter saw the pile of Agent Roberts' clothes a few feet away, remembering the rifle.

"Get its attention!" Hunter yelled, handing Alistair a large rock.

"Throw it at him!"

"What?" Alistair frowned.

"Just do it!" Hunter yelled.

Alistair threw the large rock as hard as he could, hitting the beast square on the nose. It snarled loudly, showing its razor-sharp teeth.

"I don't think it liked that..." Alistair grabbed another rock, readying to throw it. "Elly, Liv, slowly move away from me..."

Hunter ran over to the pile of tattered clothes and grabbed the rifle. He had never shot one before, but he had seen Dominick do it earlier. He checked the chamber; there was a dart ready and loaded. The beast eyed Alistair while holding down Trayer, who whimpered beneath the creature's weight.

"You have to manually load it," Dominick whispered to Hunter, motioning how to cock the rifle. Hunter nodded, following the directions. "Point and shoot," he whispered again.

Hunter aimed the rifle; he was so nervous his hands shook, making it difficult to aim. Timing was critical, he had to ready the shot before the beast was able to attack Alistair or mortally wound Trayer. He lined up the sights the best he could, h took a deep breath and squeezed the trigger with all his might. The force of the weapon kicked back so hard that Hunter collapsed onto the ground in pain grabbing his shoulder. He hadn't held the butt of the rifle firmly enough against his shoulder, causing it to dislocate, he winced in pain as he watched the dart strike the beast on its hindquarters. This time, the beast had no fight left in it, it let out a weakened snarl before falling over once again.

"Good shot, kid," Dominick winced in pain.

"Trayer!" Elly and Liv ran over to the young pup. "Are you okay?"

Trayer whimpered licking his wounds. He sat upright, wagging its tail as the girls showered him with attention.

"Only a few cuts," Liv said.

"Are you okay, Hunter?" Alistair helped his friend up from the cold stony ground.

"Yeah," Hunter grimaced. "That rifle really hurt my shoulder..."

"I think it's dislocated," Alistair noted. He pointed out the weird lump on Hunter's shoulder.

"Quick, get in my bag," Dominick ordered, he tossed his backpack to the children. "There are industrial strength steel cables in there. Tie the beast's feet up in case it wakes up again."

"Is it safe now?" Elly unzipped the bag pulling out the steel cables. They were surprisingly heavy for being so thin.

"I sure in hell hope so," Dominick added. "I'd do it, but I can't move my right shoulder. Could you patch me?" He nodded to Alistair. "You seem to know a thing or two."

"Yeah, a bit." Alistair smiled.

"How's the other guy?"

"We got the bleeding stopped. Lots of scrapes and bruises," Alistair noted.

"Those rifles have a wicked kick back to them. How's your shoulder?" Dominick took a deep breath, swallowing down the dull pain.

"I can't move it," Hunter answered, trying to hide his tears.

"Tie that bastard up good," Dominick managed to unclip his radio with his good arm. He flipped its switch on pressing down the talk button. "HQ, report, suspect is controlled, injuries on site, need medics and cleanup crew."

"You got it?" Patricia's familiar voice chimed in over the radio.

"Confirmed, immediate medical attention required. One man down, three injured, ranging minor to severe. We need a team out at Cerberus Cave. Repeat, we need a fully operational team at Cerberus Cave, stat."

"Copy, who is with you?" Patricia answered.

"Young male, mid-twenties, was brought in by the beast. I have four kids with me, you will not be happy."

"Kids? Way out by the caves? What kids?" Patricia's voice grew stern.

"The Jakobs kids and their friends, again."

"What?" Patricia yelled over the radio. "Please, Dominick, keep them safe..."

"Get me my team, have our helicopter ready to fly out of here, with the creature in our possession as promised, and you've got a deal."

"We always honor our commitments, Dominick," Patricia answered. "The team has already left. Do *not* let harm come to those kids. I repeat, keep them safe."

"You hear that, kids? Tie that beast up good. That's the best way to keep us safe until the team arrives to get us out of here."

"How long's that gonna take?" Hunter grimaced attempting to straighten out his arm. He had to sit down due to feeling lightheaded from the pain.

"Stop moving it!" Dominick ordered. "—Only gonna cause yourself pain. Sit tight and get as comfortable as you guys can; it may take a while for them to get here."

The children huddled up together to keep warm in the dreary cave. Liv had found a small blanket in Dominick's supplies and used it to cover up Sebastian. The group was banged up, bruised, and tired. Hunter's shoulder was swelling, the discomfort was becoming unbearable. He was embarrassed sitting next to Liv, as he failed to keep back the tears of pain streaming down his red cheeks. Sebastian drifted in and out of consciousness, rambling incoherently.

"Hunter, it's okay that you're hurt..." Liv sat close to him, whispering.

"It's not that bad," Hunter tried to save face.

"That was very brave of you," she smiled.

"Err...Oh?" Hunter's face now flushed with embarrassment.

"And, Alistair, I never knew you knew so much about medical stuff," she said.

"My dad taught me a lot," Alistair smiled.

"Kids," Dominick sighed. He popped open a bottle of pain pills swallowing a mouthful of pills. "Quiet, please... my head is throbbing. Sit there and wait. Okay?"

The children nodded. Then they waited.

Chapter 18
Unsung Heroes

The children waited another hour in the freezing cave before Abram's group of adults showed up to escort them back to the estate. It was quite a show; Hunter thought it looked like a small army had come to their rescue, including the mansion's very own helicopter, which was hovering over the cave entrance waiting for the team to bring out the injured. A second helicopter with bright yellow lettering with 'MFPA' written on its tail end, hovered in the distance.

The entire trip back Abram was shaking with anger, yelling at Liv in front of everyone. Despite the loud noise from the rotor blades, the children could still make out his words perfectly. Hunter felt terrible, knowing he was somewhat responsible for the situation, as Liv fought back the tears of embarrassment.

"—Sneaking out, in the middle of the night, looking for a cryptid!" Abram yelled. "Do you have a death wish?"

For Hunter, the night had been bittersweet. Because of him and his friends' help, the beast had been caught. Yet, it seemed that none of the adults cared about their help in capturing the villainous beast and focused more on the simple fact that they had snuck out for a second time.

Patricia waited eagerly at the mansion's main door for the helicopters to arrive and drop the children off at the safety of the estate. She paced nervously around the large stone porch, going over and over in her head how she was going to yell at the children for their selfish actions. Patricia's hands started shaking in anger the moment the children stepped foot back on the ground.

"You kids have really done it this time!" her voice shrieked.

No amount of apologies or excuses would work, the children knew this. It was hard, but they swallowed their pride and took the verbal lashings. Meanwhile, the injured Dominick took all the credit for capturing the beast.

"Next thing I know these idiot kids show up, potentially ruining my shot at getting the bastard," Dominick explained to the large group of people that were now crowded in the mansion's foyer. Hunter was shocked to see all the people who had heard the beast was captured; there were easily a few dozen parents and their children listening with curiosity. "I had camped out for over a day waiting for the beast to return. By the time I got there, it was too late for Roberts," Dominick frowned. "It got hairy, especially trying to make sure those damn kids didn't screw everything up."

The crowd was glued to every word Dominick said. He sat upright on a small chair while medical assistants checked his vitals and cleaned up his wounds a she spoke.

"We need to stitch you up, it's pretty deep," said one of the EMT's.

"So, what are you waiting for?" Dominick grinned. "Don't interrupt my story again…" He went on to elaborate in greater detail how he single-handedly captured the creature.

"Pretty sure you're the one who got the final shot," Alistair mumbled as Dominick continued soaking in the praise. "You would think he'd give us some credit."

But Dominick didn't. In fact, Dominick's demeanor toward the children went ice cold. He never spoke of Hunter saving his life, nor the children's part in the capturing of the Beast of Bladenboro. He took it upon himself to take credit for saving *their* lives for the second time.

"Liar," Alistair moaned.

"Alistair," Ben hid a faint smile. "What have I told you about sneaking out?"

"Not to get caught?" Alistair smiled in return.

"Exactly," Ben whispered so that Patricia couldn't hear. "Don't worry, Patty. I'll make sure Alistair here is punished for his part in this."

"I am sure you will," Patricia gave Ben a dirty look. "This is a serious offense, Benjamin."

"You're lucky *I'm* your father, buddy." Ben pointed to the staircase, and Alistair slowly walked up towards his room.

"Yes, parents, please get your children back to their rooms. It's early in the morning, I am sure Professor Calenstine will be scheduling a meeting for first thing in the morning."

"You march right up to your room and don't even think about getting out of bed!" Abram yelled so loud his voice echoed throughout the main foyer.

"But dad…" Liv's face reddened.

"No buts!" he barked. "I am so ashamed of you; I can't even look at you right now!" He escorted his daughter up to her room.

"Children-" Patricia shook her head with disgust.

"Sorry," Elly uttered.

"Hunter, you need medical attention. As soon as Margot gets here, she will make sure you get treated." Patricia couldn't even look the kids in their eyes when she spoke.

"Yes, ma'am." His shoulder still throbbed with pain.

"It looks like it may be dislocated. See what happens when you defy authority?" Patricia quizzed with no time for Hunter to answer. "You get hurt. Luckily, you kids didn't get killed out in those woods. If you only knew the things that called the forest home, I promise you, you would never think twice of setting foot out there ever again."

"Elly, follow me back to your room. You and Trayer will be on lockdown until further notice, do you understand?"

"Yes." Elly hung her head down as she walked behind Ms. Ellingbee.

Margot came shortly thereafter. She had heard about the news of her fiancé's run in with the beast and was quite hysterical at the sight of him. Sebastian had sustained heavy injuries, but he was awake and coherent by the time he made it back to the mansion.

"Oh no!" Margot ran to his side. "Are you okay?" she sobbed.

"Yes, love." Sebastian smiled. "A bit banged up… don't remember much but…"

"The kid is on heavy pain meds," Dominick interrupted; his fan base had now left him. "He's a bit out of it. He's going to be in a lot of pain once they run out."

"Poor baby…" Margot eyes were red with tears. "I am so sorry; I hate it when we fight," she added, carefully touching his wounds with her finger. "You could have died…"

"I know, darling, I know," Sebastian replied.

"Margot," Patricia interrupted. "He needs medical assistance, as does Hunter."

"Yes, I'm so sorry, of course…"

"Dominick, I know you got patched up down here, but you should really head up to the medical bay as well for further treatment. Margot can show you the way when she heads up with the other two."

"Thanks, but no thanks." Dominick stood up from his chair. "I have a helicopter out there with a pretty gnarly beast in it. I need to fly that bird back to my company. The quicker I'm out of this hell hole the better," he frowned.

"Fair enough," Patricia said. "We are truly sorry for the loss of your friend."

"Save it," he snapped back. "We know the dangers of our work."

"Even so," she added, "…thank you."

Dominick ignored the friendly gesture making his way out through the main door. He paused for a second and turned back to Patricia. "If that ignorant boss of yours has a problem with me taking my prize back home with me, tell him to shove it." He bent over, grabbing his large bag, swinging it across his good shoulder, he slammed the front door behind him.

Chapter 19
The New Beginning

Hunter woke early the next morning in a stark white hospital room. For a moment, he forgot how he had gotten there. He sat up, the sudden dull pain from his shoulder sent a flood of memories from the night before into his head. It took him a second to catch his bearings, he realized there was a bed alongside his. There, Uncle Joe lay motionless on a white sheet. His skin was pale, so pale that it took a second for Hunter to recognize him. He was hooked up to many different machines, all beeping and blinking causing Hunter's head to hurt.

"You're awake?" Margot half smiled.

"Margot," Hunter asked, "…did you stay the night with me?"

"I spent my night moving from this room to the one across the hall where Sebastian is. He's recovering very well."

"Oh," Hunter replied. "That's good." Hunter found himself staring at his uncle.

"I want you to know I have spent every night up here next to your uncle since he got hurt."

Hunter replied. "Is he doing any better?"

"He's stable, which is good news." She stood up and stretched. "How's your shoulder?"

"It's sore," Hunter's mouth pursed in pain as he tried to move it.

"Feel good enough to make it down to the auditorium? Professor Calenstine wants to address everyone about the current state of affairs. A lot of craziness has happened in the last few days."

Hunter nodded; he wanted to be anywhere other than staring at his uncle. The two made their way down to the auditorium, where they met up with Patricia and Elly. The room was filled with people sitting, waiting patiently for Professor Calenstine to appear on stage.

"Patricia is really mad at us," Elly whispered.

"I saw Uncle Joe," Hunter answered, still a bit stricken by the sight of his uncle in the hospital.

"You did? Is he better yet?" Elly asked.

Hunter shook his head.

"Have you heard from Alistair or Liv?" he asked.

"There's Alistair with his dad." She pointed out Alistair and Ben across the room. Alistair had already spotted Hunter and was waving with a smile. This made Hunter feel better. He was glad to see Alistair hadn't gotten into too much trouble and seemed to be fairly happy. It was a good feeling to see a friendly face.

"Look, there's Liv." Elly spotted her a few rows behind Alistair. She sat as still as a stone next to her father.

"...She doesn't look too happy," Hunter noted.

Elly waved to her from across the room. Liv looked up briefly and smiled. She went to wave, but her father, Abram, said something with a very stern look on his face and she quickly put her hand back down.

"I don't think her dad likes us much." Elly frowned.

"Children, take your seats," Patricia ordered. The usual friendliness of her voice was absent due. They dared not defy her, quickly taking their seats.

"Excuse me," Professor Calenstine rolled his wheelchair onto the large stage, "...can everyone hear me all right? I'm afraid we have had some acoustic issues in the auditorium due to the damages caused by the attack during the orientation." He waited for the audience to nod their heads. The attack had left the room almost completely destroyed. They had done a decent job cleaning the place up, but the damage was still quite evident. "Wonderful," he added with a bright smile.

"Elly," Hunter whispered. "Did you get into a lot of trouble last night?"

"Ms. Ellingbee didn't say a word to me, not even good night," she replied.

"I must apologize," the professor went on. "Never before in our estate's history has anything like this happened. We have had to endure many tragedies in the last week. Even more troubling is that it happened to fall during the sacred celebration of our new generation's Enlightenment," despite everything, Professor Calenstine's voice was still as youthful and as jubilant as ever.

"—The last time we were here, we welcomed our next bloodline on to this very stage, our potential future Seekers. I understand how scary and confusing this may seem to our new guests. I assure you, however, that the Beast has been apprehended, removed from the premises, and the grounds are once again safe. Starting tomorrow, we will continue with the ceremonies. Ms. Ellingbee and our lovely young Margot will start the morning off with a tour of the mansion and a meet and greet with some of our professors."

"I would like to remind our parents in the auditorium that both scholastic studies and the 'Enlightenment' winter courses begin the first of November, less than a month away. Take this time to prepare your children and familiarize them with our wonderful estate. School uniforms have been dropped off to each family's lodgings along with guidelines on proper dress codes for your children during their stay here at the Belmonte Estate. As usual, colors are khaki pants, white button-down shirt, and our royal blue vests for our regular students. Those of you who follow in your parents' footsteps and are enrolled into the Enlightenment courses will each have a similar wardrobe with our society's crest stitched onto the left breast. Girls, as always, have the option of wearing royal blue skirts as well." Professor Calenstine sipped his bottled water.

"We are a large family here at the mansion. There are many people here with many different roles, together we all work as a machine to make the world a better place to live. We have our Seekers, sworn to secrecy, our professors spreading knowledge, doctors keeping us healthy, scientists, who study and research the findings that the Seekers learn in the field. And of course, we have our house staff who keep the whole thing running smoothly. We welcome the families here with open arms, and I expect that we will all treat one another with respect and dignity."

"Respect?" a loud voice interjected. The auditorium door flew open, causing a loud thud as it hit the side of the wall. There stood a smirking Dominick. "That's a joke; we all know you love your Seekers far more than anyone else." He stood alongside a very well-dressed man who leaned on a glossy black cane. The man had wavy, shoulder-length black hair with a hint of grey at its roots. The very sight of the man sent shivers down Elly's spine. He stood a few inches taller than Dominick and appeared to be in good shape for a middle-aged man. He stood silently, staring up at Professor Calenstine.

"Dominick," Professor Calenstine replied, unaffected by his sudden appearance. "I was under the impression you made off with the Beast of Bladenboro and had no interest in returning to our humble home." The professor tipped his glasses down his nose. "…I see you've brought a friend."

"You have not aged well," the mysterious man stated with a wicked grin across his face. "If I knew better, I would say you were knocking on death's door."

"I see you have not lost your sly humor," Calenstine shot back.

Abram shot from his seat, pulling a small silver pistol from under his jacket, pointing it at the middle-aged man. "You have ten seconds to leave," he threatened.

The audience gasped at the sight of the firearm.

"Now, now, Abram, please take a seat. After all, Dominick is family, no need for such drastic measures. Am I right, Professor Aten?"

"For now, yes," the middle-aged man replied with a cocky smile.

"I heard rumors that Dominick here had found support for his Monsters and Fiends Protection Agency under the mysterious Aten Corporation." Calenstine frowned.

"And yet you still hired him to clean up your mess?" Professor Aten mocked.

"I was hoping to talk my friend out of such stupidity. Unfortunately, I was unable too."

"I see," Aten took in a deep breath. "I find it strange standing here, looking at the weathered and brittle old man you've become. It's hard not to think that without my ambition, I would be staring into my own mirrored image."

"You call it ambition now?" Calenstine laughed at the thought. "I call it a rather large God complex issue. I do not know how it is you defy our natural progression, my old friend, but I know the evil that flows through your veins. I am sure it is something dark, something inconceivable to most men's standards."

"There is the difference, is it not? Claud, old pal?" the man mocked.

"I'm sorry, I guess I don't follow," Calenstine answered.

"Well, I am not most men. I have reached vastly greater heights than *most* men could even dream of."

"Oh, Deckie." Now the professor mocked the man in return. "As cocky and self-indulged as ever, I see."

"You know I hate that name, old man," Professor Aten's fists clenched tightly.

"What's going on?" Hunter whispered to Patricia, who had turned as pale as a ghost.

"Who's that creepy man with Dominick?" Elly asked.

"Quiet, children," Patricia whispered.

"Enough with such witty banter," Aten replied. "I am not here to rekindle our friendship. I came here for business."

"And what business do you have with me?" Calenstine added.

"Now who's the cocky one? My business is not with a stupid old fool. My business is with your people. You see, I spent a lifetime trying to locate your precious little *estate*. Trying to hunt you down so I could finish the job I started, oh so many years ago."

"Is that so?" Professor Calenstine's cool demeanor wasn't fading.

"Please, old man, do not interrupt me." Aten smiled, evidence that he was enjoying the exchange between the two. "It wasn't until I found Dominick here, who had been shunned and shamed out of living his dream. He was more than eager to share your little society's secrets with me, including the location of this lovely little place.

"Dominick, you bastard!" Abram yelled.

"Abram, I presume?" Aten replied. "I would also ask that you refrain from such rude interruptions while a man of my stature is speaking."

"Are you kidding me?" Abram blurted out.

"—Abram!" Calenstine yelled. "Now is not the time."

"Yes, foolish brute, sit down and show some respect to your elders," Aten ordered. "I come with nothing more than an opportunity. I offer my hand in a mutual partnership for anyone who finds themselves employed here under Claudio's care. I offer so much more than the professor here can give you. Wealth, fortune, fame, you name it, the Aten Corporation makes dreams come true. Isn't that right, Professor?"

"The dreams of few I'm sure," Calenstine replied hotly. "I ask that you do not listen to the venom that pours from this man's mouth. He is deceitful, evil, vile as any wicked cryptid we have ever caught."

"Is that so?" Aten smirked. "Dominick here was told he wasn't welcome in this little secret society. He wasn't *good* enough, not of *pure* enough blood to be welcomed as a member. Instead, he was told he could sit back and take orders from his cousin, Abram. Is this fair? No, I think not. Instead, I took Dominick's shattered dreams, gave him complete control of his own team, funded his goals, and now he stands leader of the MFPA. Isn't that right, Dominick?"

"It's true. Professor Aten believed in me when Professor Calenstine pushed me aside like trash. I know a lot of you, called you friends at one time. I was nothing here, a lackey to a stubborn fool. Now I am living my dream, I have my own team, I paid nothing for it. Don't let Calenstine make this decision for you; make up your own minds. It's true, the Aten Corporation and the Belmonte Estate have vastly different ideas on just about everything. I don't go home to a stale old apartment in a dusty old mansion, I have my own mansion. I live in luxury. Aten gave this to me."

"You see?" Aten smiled. "Aten Corporation is a business model, and a rather wealthy one at that. I invest in my people and their happiness. I have at my disposal the top science labs and medical stations in the world. I can offer you everything this pathetic estate can and much more. I need the greatest minds in order to pursue my own goals, and in exchange for those talents, I can offer you anything your heart desires."

"Spoken like the devil himself," Calenstine interrupted. "You expect to waltz into our home and recruit the very people who have dedicated their lives to our cause? I'm sorry, but I am confident in my people to know a false prophet when they see one. I would suggest if you're done slandering my good name that you leave before I do allow my team to forcefully remove you from the premises."

"Is that a threat, old man?" Aten exposed a crooked smile.

"No, just a promise to an old friend."

"I see," Aten replied. "Do not worry about contacting us. I promise I shall be in contact with you about any potential recruitment processes."

"Deckie," Calenstine said hotly as Aten and Dominick turned.

"That's 'Professor' to you, old fool."

"Neither you or Dominick are welcome back to this estate. If you ever set foot on our grounds again, there will be repercussions."

"No need, Claud, old pal." Aten laughed. "I have a feeling your people will seek me out." Aten turned back to Professor Calenstine, bowing down to him in one final mocking gesture. "The next time we meet, Claudio, you will be dead at my feet. Let's go, Dominick. We have work to do…"

The two men left the auditorium of their own free will, leaving in their wake the murmurs and whispers of curiosity.

"What happened?" Hunter asked.

"That man," Patricia whispered, "has haunted Professor Calenstine for many years. I fear we are heading into dark times."

"Do you really think people will leave and go work for him? He seems so scary," Elly frowned.

"I hope not. We have many dedicated people who have been with us for years, who have family ties with us dating back generations. I fear that Professor Aten strikes at a greedier chord though. What he says is true. He can give anyone nearly anything they desire."

"Who is this guy?" Hunter wondered aloud.

"To be blunt," Patricia added, "he is the exact opposite of Professor Calenstine. All that man cares about is money and power."

"People, people, please calm down," Professor Calenstine attempted to regain control. "I do apologize. Such an interruption was uncalled for. I ask anyone who may have been poisoned by this man words, please, before you do anything rash, speak to me in private. Let us not dwell on this subject though. Let us rejoice and relax. Children, remember tomorrow is an early day with a tour and meet and greet. Thank you all once again. You have the rest of the night off to mingle and get to know one another."

"Children," Patricia noted bluntly. "I am acting guardian until further notice. I don't have time to sit here and mingle with the others. I will be seeing you to your rooms for the rest of the night."

"What?" Elly and Hunter protested.

"Children!" Patricia barked. "You do realize that last night you snuck out of the mansion."

The children fell silent.

"This is only part of your punishment. To your room, now!"

Defeated, Hunter and Elly made it up to their room, where their good friend Trayer waited patiently for their return. A lot had happened in the last twenty-four hours, they both had plenty to think about. Surprisingly, they were much more tired than they had even realized. It didn't take long for them to doze off into a peaceful sleep.

Chapter 20
Answers and Questions

"Children!" Margot poked her head through the children's bedroom doorway with excitement spread across her youthful face. She turned their light on and off like she was sounding some sort of silent alarm.

Hunter rolled over onto his side and stretched out yawning loudly; his bedside clock read six a.m. He wanted nothing more than to hide his head under his cozy comforter and return to his peaceful sleep. Hunter hadn't gotten a 'peaceful' night's rest in over a month, and now, the first time he was able to do so, he was unfairly awakened before the sun was even up.

"Why so early?" The sudden bright light burned Hunter's eyes.

"Elly, wake up! Time to rise and shine!" Margot nudged Elly's shoulder until she finally rolled over wiping the sleepiness away from her eyes.

"You kids slept like rocks. I came up to see you last night and you were both fast asleep."

"Yeah," Hunter replied. "I guess we were pretty tired from everything. You should let us sleep in..."

"Afraid not, I'm here to take you to Professor Calenstine's office. He wants a word with you both before the day starts."

"He does?" Elly jolted upright with curiosity. They had been waiting for forever to meet their godfather one on one. With everything that had happened since their visit, Dr. Calenstine had never made the time to sit down with the children.

"Is it news about Uncle Joe?" Hunter sat up in his bed.

"I'm afraid not. However, I came from visiting your uncle. He's still in stable condition."

"Is he ever going to get better?" Elly frowned.

"Of course, dear… of course he will." Margot tossed the children their new school uniforms she had brought in with her. "Get ready and meet me outside your door. They should fit."

"Okay," they said in unison. Hunter unfolded his royal blue vest and inspected the symbol stitched on the left breast. It was the same symbol he had seen on the computer screen in the room beneath the library. It had the serpent shaped in the letter "S" sitting over an oval crest.

"Look," He pointed it out to Elly. "That logo must be the Seekers' emblem."

"Duh," Elly said, "…obviously."

"Don't act like you knew that," Hunter slipped his vest on over his white shirt. "These outfits suck." He frowned. "Why can't we wear jeans and a T-shirt like normal kids?"

"I like my skirt!" Elly peered into the full-length mirror.

"C'mon, hurry!" She ran to the door. "We finally get to meet Professor Calenstine in person!"

Margot waited patiently for the children to come out of their room. She was as excited as the children that they were getting to meet Dr. Calenstine. She knew they had wanted to get to know their godfather more personally since the minute they entered the estate. She secretly hoped it would help them find closure over the loss of their parents, help them open up more to this new life.

When the children finally made their way out of their room, she led them down the hall and into the elevator. Elly thought Margot looked prettier than ever with her dark black hair curled up. She wore a black skirt much like the blue one Elly was wearing.

"How's Sebastian doing?" Elly asked waiting for the elevator doors to close.

"He's still healing, lots of cuts and scrapes. He's in good spirits though."

Between the goings on with her fiancé, the condition of her newfound friend Joe, and caring for the children, Margot's life had been turned upside down. She would never speak of the pressures to anyone, but privately she was feeling herself giving in to the stress. Even though Elly thought she looked as pretty as ever, behind the makeup and cute outfit, Margot's eyes were tired and her heart was heavy. What made it worse was that every time she looked at Hunter and Elly, she felt the guilt swell up in her chest. In her eyes, the problems that kept arising in her life paled in comparison to what they were dealing with. She found encouragement in their youthful smiles.

"Where's Professor Calenstine's room?" Hunter asked.

"It's in the sub-basement of the mansion, underneath the Ocelot Room," Margot answered.

"The *what* room?" Elly questioned.

"The big computer room you guys met Plato in. Remember? During first time you snuck out," she added a bit more sternly.

"Oh, yeah." Elly's cheeks flushed red with embarrassment.

"You know that Dominick took all the credit, but we helped out a lot getting that monster captured," Hunter added with his own sense of sternness. He knew sneaking out was going to catch them a lot of heat with the adults, but if they would only listen to their story, maybe they would realize they did more to help Dominick than hinder.

"You did, did you?" Margot was only half listening.

"No seriously, it's true!" Elly interjected. "The creature had Dominick pinned down. Hunter took a rifle and took the last shot. He saved his life! And Alistair knows a lot about medicine and stuff, so he helped everyone out too."

"I see." Margot led the children through the library largely unimpressed. "Either way, I don't think you two realize the amount of danger you were in. You could have died."

"We know," they both said defeated, realizing no matter how much help they were, it would forever pale in comparison to the fact that they were just kids.

"Do you remember where the hidden lever is?" Margot stopped near where Hunter had originally found the entrance into the top-secret Ocelot Room.

"Yeah," Hunter ran over to the stone gargoyle. He turned the beastly head around clockwise until the gears could be heard turning in the wall.

"All right," Margot smiled, "...after you." The large bookshelf opened, revealing the winding stairwell leading deep into the depths of the mansion. The children made their way down the steep staircase and into the large computer chamber, the Ocelot Room. In the far corner stood the towering automaton, Plato, who was working on a giant touch-screen computer that was the size of the entire eastern wall. Regular computers weren't fit for a mighty android with mega-sized mechanical hands.

"Plato?" Hunter smiled. It was because of this lovable robot that their uncle wasn't one of the Beast of Bladenboro's meals.

"I don't think the three of you have been properly introduced," Margot interjected.

"Children: welcome to the central intelligence hub of the Belmonte Estate, codenamed: Ocelot Room." Plato turned his dome-shaped head from the large computer screen, his eyes glolwing a bright blue. He towered over the children to the point Hunter felt a kink in his neck from staring up at him too long. "Apologies: it was apparent upon our first meeting that I somehow managed to alarm you."

"Err... we didn't know what you were." Hunter laughed.

"Understood: my human emotion registry system suggested the act of chasing you only supplemented your anxiety levels. I have saved the events in my memory core and have added variables for future meetings to refrain from such a repeat outcome. Note: will speak before pursuing."

"We wanted to thank you for helping out our uncle," Elly had never spoken to a giant robot, finding it hard to verbalize her gratitude.

"Master Joseph is an honorable friend. My memory core had a significant lapse in any form of communication with him for approximately three thousand eight hundred seventy-nine days, sixteen hours and thirty-four minutes. If my simulated social/emotional data link is functional, I surmise I was excited to see him again. He made many people smile while he lived amongst us. I have not been able to link into the medical wings network. How is he doing?"

"He is doing well actually," Margot said. "We came on business, however. Could you be a dear and open up the energy field to the lower catacombs please?"

"The energy field?" Hunter asked.

"Yes, the energy field. It's a high-tech security force field that prevents anyone from going any farther into the Ocelot Room. We have a system of catacombs deep beneath the Ocelot Room that are highly classified. Plato here is the gatekeeper to the only entry point."

"Catacombs?" Elly questioned.

"Yep, the catacombs are the name given for what lies beneath the mansion. It is all quite secretive, even I don't know everything that the catacombs contain. See there," Margot pointed through the transparent energy field towards two large steel elevator doors on the opposite side, "those are the elevators and the only entrances to the Ocelot Room. I don't even have high enough security clearance to clear the main lift; I'm only able to open the one that leads to Professor Calenstine's private chambers."

Plato walked over to the buzzing energy field placing his large mechanical hand on the screen beside it. He keyed something in, his large metallic fingers banging loudly as he entered his pin number. Shortly thereafter, the energy field dissipated, allowing entrance to the elevators.

"Quickly, it only stays down for ten seconds." Margot rushed the children through the threshold. "Thank you, Plato." She smiled at the robot. "A gentleman and a scholar, as always."

"Be safe," the said the robot.

"We're going to the elevator on the right," Margot pointed.

"So, what does Plato do down here?" Elly asked. "You know, besides letting people through that energy thing."

"Plato has many jobs, including being our librarian. The Ocelot Room is also where he charges his battery to keep himself working;

it's kind of like a giant computerized bedroom for him."

"Oh." Elly was a bit surprised by the answer; a computerized bedroom was fascinating to her young mind.

They stepped into the elevator taking a long trip down to the sublevels of the mansion. Professor Calenstine's office must have been miles underground because Hunter felt like it took ages for the lift to finally get to its destination. Once the lift settled and the metal doors slowly opened, they unveiled a giant elongated hallway filled with all sorts of mysterious décor. The long walls stretched out, showcasing a bunch of fascinating things that one wouldn't believe unless they were there staring at them in the flesh.

Elly peered down towards the opposite end of the hallway where it opened up into a large study. There was a large half-circle mahogany desk with a busy Professor Calenstine hard at work. There he sat sifting through stacks of papers and smoking from a long cob pipe while he hummed a peculiar tune that Elly could make out. The minute she heard it, she knew it was the same song her mother would hum when she was hard at work, whether it was getting the kids breakfast or balancing her checkbook. Warm memories of her mother surfaced, she couldn't help but wonder how odd it was that they hummed the same song.

Hunter was easily distracted, he hadn't noticed any of the peculiar decorations that adorned the long halls, nor did he take notice of the professor humming away at his desk. It was what sat behind the professor that caught Hunter's eye: a giant flat-screen monitor that covered the entire wall. Currently it was broadcasting a live video feed of what looked like some sort of jungle. It was larger and clearer than any movie theater screen Hunter had ever seen, including those special high-definition ones only found in bigger cities.

"I love his office," Margot smiled. "Look at the walls as we make our way towards his desk. They're littered with treasure's he's experienced during his life. See that?" Margot pointed to a large framed picture. It was black and white, appearing to be quite old. "That was when the professor was still an active Seeker, check it out."

Hunter inspected the photo from a bit closer. There was an older man standing next to a tribe of aboriginals smiling brightly. Upon closer inspection, Hunter realized it was a younger Professor Calenstine. Although Hunter thought the word *young* wasn't quite the right term. He looked as old as he had the night of the Orientation, except he was able to stand and wasn't confined to the wheelchair. He also carried a bit more weight with him, but Hunter could recognize the youthful smile anywhere. That was not the first picture Hunter has seen of the professor, he immediately remembered back to the old photo from the book he read about the Beast of Bladenboro.

"What's behind him?" Elly pointed out a large creature that coiled up behind the men like a snake.

"The largest Anaconda the world has ever seen, over sixty feet long." Margot pointed out its head in the picture. It was so big Elly thought it could have easily swallowed an adult whole with little to no effort.

"Wow, really? I wish Alistair was here to see this." Hunter's mouth gaped at the size of the serpent's head.

"Over here," Margot pointed to the other wall, "…this is Professor Calenstine with President Carter outside of the White House. Here is one with President Clinton at a rally…"

"Who's this one?" Elly pointed to an old grandiose oil painting. This time it was Professor Calenstine standing next to a rather scary looking man with a balding head and bushy white hair that stuck out on its sides.

"Oh," Margot answered. "Well, that's President Van Buren," she answered.

"Who?" Hunter asked. He had never been taught about President Van Buren in school.

"When was he, President?" Elly asked.

"Well…" Margot paused for a second not quite sure how to answer, "…let's not worry so much about that photograph," she dodged the question. "What do you think of the room?"

"Is that a big television on the back wall?" Hunter pointed.

"Sort of," she led them down the long walk to his desk. "It's more like a security system. He can switch to any of the camera feeds we have set up around the estate. He always says the Demeter Station feed is his favorite, which is what it's on right now."

"The *what*, station," asked Elly?

"Demeter," Margot corrected. "The eastern conservatory, it's a giant bio dome where we have created a unique ecosystem that resembles a rainforest. I think it's the sound of the wild birds and the constant rain that puts him at ease."

Hunter paused for a second, he could hear the faint chirping of birds, croaking of toads, and all sorts of other wildlife noises throughout the large room. Finally, they approached the friendly old professor sitting comfortably at his desk.

"Welcome, children," Professor Calenstine looked up from his studies with a wide smile. He puffed out a dark cloud of smoke from his cob pipe. On his lap sat a small scruffy dog that wagged its tail anxiously at the sight of the children. It was a scrawny old thing with hair as white as snow. They seemed a fitting pair, dog and owner, both looking as old as old as the earth itself.

"You have a puppy?" Elly loved animals.

"This here is Monte, and I'm afraid to say a puppy he is not." Professor Calenstine pet his furry companion. "He's been my best friend for longer than I can remember."

"How old is he?" Elly asked.

"Older than you and Hunter's age combined my dear, and then some." Calenstine chuckled. "He doesn't get around much these days. His age has crept up on his body as it did with mine. He spends most of his time resting on my lap. He's a lot like me, you know? Nor man or beast can escape time, I suppose. Age has eaten away at our physical bodies, but not our minds, we are as sharp as ever, isn't that right, boy?"

The old dog let out a small bark in agreement.

"Please, have a seat," Calenstine waved his old wrinkly hand towards two comfy leather chairs sitting in front of his desk. "I implore you, make yourselves at home. You are guests here, special guests. It's very rare for anyone to be summoned, or even see, my personal chambers."

The children shot quizzical looks at one another.

"Why so secretive? It's only a big old room, isn't it?" Elly replied.

"Only a room?" Calenstine chuckled again. He opened a drawer in the oak desk pulling out a small remote. He clicked something that turned the giant monitor from channel to channel. It started at the live feed from the Demeter Station, then there was a feed from the main foyer looking down towards the giant wall of stuffed monster heads, then another feed outside the estate overseeing the large gargoyle covered gates, finally a feed that looked like it was streaming from Antarctica, nothing but snow and the star-lit sky. "I am the central hub of all things the Belmonte Estate is privy to. I have eyes everywhere, you see."

"That's awesome," Hunter practically drooled at the large screen. "Do you get cable in here?"

"Cable? Oh no, no time for such things. I am a very busy man, my young boy. No time for television." He set the remote down on the desk. He lit a match and put it to the cob pipe in his mouth, puffing gently.

"Tea, anyone?" The professor lifted a hot teakettle pouring himself a fresh cup.

"No, thanks." Hunter hated yea, he thought it tasted like dirty water.

"I asked you children down here to have a heart to heart. To open up and allow you to ask any questions you may have, and I promise I will answer as truthfully as I can. You have been through a lot-more than any children your age should ever have to deal with. We kept many secrets from you when you first arrived in hopes of keeping you safe and away from harm's reach. Please know, your safety was our main concern…"

"Now is your chance," Margot added. "No running around in the middle of the night trying to find secrets, here is your chance for an honest conversation with your godfather."

"Err…I have a question," Elly raised her hand.

"Please go ahead, anything, and everything, don't be shy."

"How did you know our parents? Why are you our godfather and not our Uncle Joe? We don't even know who you are."

"Yes… a fine question. Your mother comes from a long line of Seekers, your grandfather, great grandfather, so on and so forth," explained the professor. "Your father married into the bloodline and was inducted into the tradition through the sacred bonds of marriage. They were both beautiful people, it saddens me to have lost them so young," Calenstine's lips pursed tightly as he spoke of his friends. He took a long sip from his hot tea, cleared his throat and continued on, "…as for why they chose me to be your guardian, I believe it is because I shared a very strong bond with them both. We had been working on some very secretive plans. They knew the dangers, I believe they knew the best way to keep you kids safe if anything were to happen with them, was to have you under my guidance."

"Oh," Elly bit her lip. She thought asking the question would bring forth some sort of closure to her parents' death, but it didn't. She hoped it would fill a bit of what was missing inside her, but she still felt the emptiness burn every time she thought of her parents.

"I was reading a book on the Beast of Bladenboro that you had written," Hunter interjected, "There was an old photo of you in it, and you looked the same," Hunter added.

"So, there was." Calenstine pushed his glasses onto the tip of his nose. "You two are quite the pair of sleuths I see; most students don't start wondering about my age until their third or fourth years."

"Oh?" Hunter didn't quite know how to reply.

"Let me answer by telling you I am beyond old. I have seen many things in my lifetime, a great many things. I promise you though, as I sit before you a wrinkled old man, bound to this chair, I do age. I feel it in my bones every morning."

"What about the Seekers, and the secret society thing?" Hunter blurted out. He had spent weeks thinking of questions he wanted to ask his godfather, he didn't want to forget a thing.

"The Secret Seekers Society," Calenstine cleared his throat, "—is something you will learn about in much more detail during your Enlightenment classes. That is if you decide to stay with us. However, I suppose it wouldn't hurt if I briefly explain. The society has ties dating back to the early 1700s, the first Seekers were born from my bloodline; we searched and recruited others like us, brave souls who shared the same passions of the unknown, fearless men and women wanting to better the world. The Society was created to be the frontiersmen of the unknown; we would go where no one else dared. We traveled the world seeking out the truth, sifting through myths and legends, focusing on seeking out cryptids, relics, hauntings... you name it, and we have dealt with it."

"What are cryptids?" Elly asked, completely lost in Calenstine's words.

"Modern times have shown a rebirth in interest in these monsters. The word 'cryptid' is a shortened term used to describe an unexplained creature or legendary beast, derived from Cryptozoology, which in turn is the study of such creatures."

"Like Big Foot?" Elly chimed in.

"Correct." Calenstine clicked the remote one more time. Now the large screen behind him showed the giant version of the Seekers' logo, the "S" shaped snake sitting in front of the circular emblem. "This is our insignia; you wear it on your vests. The double-headed serpent shaped like an "S" represents our Seekers' name, and the duality of our lives. We hide our true selves from the world, sworn to secrecy about our findings. You notice the large ape behind it?"

"Yeah, Big Foot, right?" Elly asked, as if it was a stupid question.

"Or Sasquatch, Yeti, the Skunk Ape, all named depending on where the sighting takes place; the most famous of all cryptids in modern culture. Now to the right of it," Calenstine pointed to the large stone with a thick broadsword stuck in it, "...any idea what that symbol represents?"

"Well, it's no animal," Hunter said.

"Correct, we don't only hunt and investigate cryptids, we also explore relics as well. What you are looking at is the fabled Excalibur sword. King Arthur pulled this mighty blade from a stone to prove his lineage to the throne. If one were to wield its blade in battle, it is said to have magical powers that grant the user the ability to never be wounded."

"Wow... really? Is it real?" Elly wondered.

"Perhaps." Calenstine couldn't hide his smile. "Below Excalibur we see another famous cryptid. Any takers on our long-necked friend?"

"Loch Ness Monster?" Elly answered. "I read about that in one of the books. That one is not real, right? It was a hoax."

"Well, perhaps you will find out once you begin your courses," Calenstine winked. "Finally, on the bottom left we have the six-sided star. This one is a little tricky, not as popular as the other three."

"That's Solomon's ring!" Elly was quite proud of herself for knowing.

"Show off," Hunter mumbled.

"Impressive, young Elly. I didn't think you would have known such a peculiar item."

"I read a lot," her cheeks flushed red.

"And can you explain its significance?" Calenstine asked.

"Um..." Elly thought for a second. "It has magical powers, right?"

"It is said to possess the power to speak to spirits, demons, and animals as well."

"Demons?" Hunter was baffled. "Why would anyone want to do that?"

"Well," Calenstine stroked the white hairs on his chin. "Demons are not quite what you would expect. Needless to say, its powers have been sought after for ages." Calenstine flipped the channel back to the Demeter Station. "Now, anyone who wears this badge of ours is sworn to a lifetime of secrecy. We have upheld this notion over a millennium, and unlike many other societies, we have managed to keep ours out of the modern world's eyes. We are virtually unknown, with the exception of a few partners on the outside world. One might say we are completely off the grid."

"So, Mom and Dad were Seekers. That's where they went on all those work trips all the time," Hunter said aloud to no one in particular.

"There weren't any old Seekers... your parents were the best. They understood *why* we do what we do. They dedicated their lives to making this world a better place."

"Why do we *do what we do*?" Hunter asked.

"That's an easy answer," said the Professor. "Like I said, we want to make the world a better place. Understanding our world, discovering its many mysteries only opens new doors to be explored. Did you know we found a living Mongolian death worm that excretes fluid that has healing properties when treated correctly? It's true. We also want to provide misrepresented creatures with protection from the outside world. For example, your new friend Trayer is widely feared and would be hunted down, or worse, tied up in some laboratory somewhere. We rescued a small den and have tried to keep them safe here, giving them an area to grow and be stable. Not all cryptids are evil, bloodthirsty monsters."

"So, that's what we do then," Hunter added. "We hunt these things down, find out if they're real, if their nice, we save them."

"A part of what we do, yes. These creatures are endangered; this is why they are so rare and so called 'legendary.'"

"What about the scary man that interrupted the meeting yesterday?" Elly added.

"Professor Aten," Calenstine sighed. "A terrible, wicked man. I fear he has no soul; he would kill anyone to see his goals achieved. He is rich, powerful beyond your imagination; it wasn't a good sign seeing him within our walls."

"He seems to hate you," Hunter stated.

"He is angry because I have what he thinks is rightfully his. He even tried to kill me once, foolish man. Ever since then, he has been hunting me down."

"What's that?" asked Elly.

"Destroy everything that I love and believe in. The Seekers, the estate, everything and anything I hold dear. All you really need to know is that Aten is evil and to not fall for his slick tongue. Understood?"

The children nodded.

"Can I ask…?" Elly hesitated for a second, thinking better of it.

"My actual age?" Calenstine chuckled.

"Well, I was curious."

"Yes, I did purposely beat around that bush. Let's say that I am by far the oldest person you will ever meet and probably the wisest as well." He laughed. "Don't let my body fool you; it is a physical misconception, as I said before, my mind is as sharp as can be."

"Okay," Elly agreed, still a bit unsure about what he meant.

"If you have no more questions, I have one of my own for you."

"Oh?" the children replied, taken a little off guard.

"You now know what it is the mansion has to offer. I must ask you both now; will you join your family's decorated heritage and follow in the footsteps of your parents?"

"What about Uncle Joey? What if he doesn't get better? Who will take care of us?" Hunter asked, a bit uneasy about the question. He still wasn't sure about all this secret society and monster hunting nonsense.

"I have asked Margot to take on the honors of raising you kids and to be your guardian during your Enlightenment until your uncle is fully fit to make a decision."

"Margot, really?" Elly smiled.

"You would do that for us?" asked Hunter.

"Of course, I would." Margot took both the kids hands.

"I want to stay," Elly answered.

"But…" Hunter was a bit more hesitant.

Suddenly the large screen behind Professor Calenstine's desk beeped. The words "Incoming Call: Patricia Ellingbee" flashed on the screen. The professor turned and answered the call. A large window of Patricia popped up on the screen. She looked tired, large bags showing under her eyes. Yet she seemed excited.

"Good!" Patricia beamed. "I was hoping the children were still with you."

"They are, yes," Calenstine added.

"Joe woke up!" Patricia yelled. "About a half-hour ago, he opened his eyes, and was asking for the kids. He's awake now!"

"Uncle Joey!" Elly literally jumped in place.

"Can we see him?" Hunter asked.

"Of course, of course, go now!" Calenstine ordered.

Chapter 21
The Awakening

"How do you feel, dear?" Patricia asked, "–don't overdo it now."

"I feel like I was hit by a truck," Joe's voice was no more than a raspy whisper. It hurt for him to move anything, let alone speak. "…I thought I was on pain meds?" he mused.

"I assure you, you are pretty well dosed up." Patricia smiled. "Your niece and nephew have been worried sick; they thought they had lost their uncle, you know."

"Well, I can't blame them, look at me." Both of Joe's eyes were swollen, bruised and black as the night itself. His body was wrapped up in numerous gauzes covering up his stitches that covered the majority of his body.

"What do you remember about that night?" Patricia filled up a glass of cold water.

"Hurts to swallow anything," Joe waved the water away. "I don't remember much, strange as it sounds. I don't remember pain… or terror… I only remember the thing attacking me and the kids crying."

"I see. Best for you not to remember, I suppose. I have summoned Hunter and Elly up to see you, they should be here shortly. You have missed out on a lot since you've been unconscious."

Patricia went on to explain how Hunter, Elly and their friends, Alistair and Liv, snuck out once again, this time venturing off into the forest. She also explained to him the curious events regarding the mysterious Professor Aten and his relationship with Calenstine. Although Joe was very curious about all that he had missed, it was almost too much to take in, and his head throbbed with pain.

"Professor Calenstine spoke with the children for the first time since all this craziness happened. They should get some answers."

"Good. I hated keeping them in the dark," Joe coughed, clearing his throat.

A light knock came from the door. Margot entered pushing Professor Calenstine into the room followed by the rambunctious Elly and Hunter.

"Uncle Joey, you're okay!" Elly ran up to her uncle for a hug stopping dead seeing the poor state her Uncle was in, "…can I hug you?" she asked with a frown.

"Only if you never frown like that again." Uncle Joe smiled. "And be careful, I am tender."

Elly gave Uncle Joe the warmest, softest hug she could muster.

"Hi, Uncle Joe." Hunter half smiled. He didn't like the sight of his uncle bandaged up, he stood beside him awkwardly.

"Hunter, don't be shy, I'm okay, I promise," Joe reached out and placed his hand on Hunter's shoulder.

"It is very good to see you awake and smiling," Professor Calenstine nodded. "Your actions on that night prove why you were always such a great Seeker. I have never seen such an act of love and valor in my life."

"It was a no-brainer really. I'm no hero, anyone would have done the same for these kids," Joe made light of the situation.

"You're so modest… You are a hero, and don't forget it." Margot reached over and kissed Joe on the forehead.

"I understand now why you decided to leave our family in search of your true self. I admire your honesty," Calenstine added.

"What do you mean?" Joe asked.

"When you came to me that day, a decade ago, and told me you wanted to live your life away from the mansion, I knew why. After your sister had Hunter, something in you changed. You may not have known it at the time, but it is because of the love you have for these children. You were the one who stayed behind and raised them while they were off doing Seeker business."

"I suppose," Joe replied, a bit embarrassed.

"You have a long road to recovery before you are going to be back to your old self," Patricia told him. "Rehabilitation is going to be hard. Lucky for you we have Margot here with her degree in physical therapy."

"Oh?" Joe smiled.

"Well, yes…" Margot blushed. "Before I came here to the estate, it was what I went to school for."

"I guess there is some sort of light at the end of the tunnel then, huh?" Joe chuckled. Margot's face reddened, she brushed her bangs off her face.

"We're really happy you're getting better." Elly hadn't stopped holding her uncle's hand since they had arrived.

"I hear you kids got into some trouble while I was out," Joe added.

"Just a little," Hunter looked down to the floor, averting his eyes.

"They are very much like you and Ben were, at that age," Calenstine interjected. "They have their fingers in a lot of different pots. Their curiosity is going to make for some grand Seekers." The Professor grinned.

"Have they taken the oath?" Joe asked, "Did I miss that too?"

"Well, we were getting to that…" Calenstine said.

"Well?" Joe asked, looking at the kids, who were a bit stumped at his notion.

"What?" Elly asked.

"Are you kids going to commit to the Enlightenment and stay here in the mansion to follow in your parent's footsteps?"

"I want to!" Elly beamed. "The professor said Margot could be our guardian!"

"Oh?" Uncle Joe frowned.

"Well," the professor interjected. "—One of their guardians, if that is okay with you. Of course, you will always be their primary guardian."

"I am?" Joe's frown now turned into a smile.

"You did come to me the night before the attack and ask for me to forfeit my personal guardianship of them to you, did you not?"

"You did that?" Hunter's smile grew ear to ear.

"I did ask," Joe added. "I was hoping that Professor Calenstine would allow me to stay here with you kids, be your guardian, rejoin the Seekers."

"I told him I wasn't sure. You see, there has never been a Seeker who has left and been welcomed back in. It's a bit of a rule we have," the Professor added.

"That's not fair." Hunter frowned. "He's the only family we have left."

"Well," Calenstine went on. "I understand that. I thought long and hard about it. After seeing your uncle's dedication and the love he harbors for the both of you, I would be an evil man to allow some silly old rule to prevent you from being happy."

"Really?" Elly squeezed her uncle's hand with all her might.

"Now, one rule I cannot bend is that there must be two guardians to aide in the Enlightenment duties. This is why I chose Margot as your second. That is, of course, if Joe will accept her help."

"Oh…" Joe was caught a bit off guard. "I think there would be no one better. The kids love you."

"I am honored," Margot replied, fighting off small tears of joy. "I think we'll make great guardians."

"Well then, it is settled. Patricia dear," Calenstine pointed to the door, "…please close the door."

Patricia closed and locked the door.

"Normally, we have a ritual where each family meets at our Chamber of Secrets, but with our recent set of events, I think this room will do."

"Chamber of Secrets?" Hunter asked.

"Our society's secret meeting place. We let each family have their own ceremony, inducting their next bloodline into their new home with us in the mansion."

"Cool," Hunter replied.

"Shall we begin? Please hand me the sacred Grimoire, Patricia."

"Sacred Grim-*who*?" Hunter repeated.

"Grimoire," corrected Patricia. She walked across the room to where near Uncle Joe's bed where a large canvas bag sat. She pulled from it a thick and ancient book.

"Children, this is the Grimoire, a magical and powerful tome."

Patricia handed the children the book. Hunter flipped through the pages while Elly looked over his shoulder. To their dismay, the book was empty of words pages upon pages of blank, yellowed paper.

"Nothing is in it," Elly frowned. "What's so magical about that?"

"That *is* the magic, young one." The professor smiled widely as if sharing an inside joke that only he got. "Come, put the book on my lap, open it to any page you wish."

"Okay." Hunter laid the book down face open onto the professor's lap. "Children, each of you place one hand on a page. Now, Margot put your hand atop of Elly's, and Joe, let's move close so you can put your hand on top of Hunter's."

"This seems silly," Hunter stated.

"Do you believe in magic?" the professor asked bluntly.

"Well, I don't know anymore. I didn't before," Hunter didn't know what was real any more…

"You didn't believe in monsters either, yet you stared down an evil cryptid and lived to tell about it. I ask that you have faith, let the Seekers guide you to the truth."

"Okay," Hunter nodded.

"Now, before we go on. Are the four of you willing to take the first oath, to dedicate yourselves to fulfilling the Enlightenment?"

"We are," the kids answered.

"Then repeat," Calenstine cleared his throat:

"We, true of self, righteous and noble
Seekers of knowledge and Enlightenment
Hereby, give our oath to thee, great Grimoire.
To follow the path of virtue
And honor those we supersede
Through steadfast gallantry
And concrete morality.
To conquer those wicked and cruel
And save those who're pure and true."

As the group repeated the ritual word for word, the book warmed to the touch. Hunter could feel his palms begin to sweat from the raw energy surging within the pages. As they continued on with the recital, words began to eerily appear within the pages, first forming in weird, foreign characters that looked much like ancient scribed hieroglyphs, slowly finally morphing into modern English.

"There we have it!" The professor removed the book from beneath their hands and slapped it shut.

"What happened?" Elly's hand was red from the heat of the book.

"Well, you are now officially a Seeker. Your essence has been added to the sacred Grimoire, and it now knows your essence personally."

"It knows our *essence* personally?" asked Elly.

"It's a sacred book that has ties to those who swear the Seekers' creed. Your very soul now has its own page dedicated in its bindings. It has seen into your heart, it knows your true self. In time, it may open itself up to you in a period of need, to bestow answers or words of wisdom if it so chooses."

"If it chooses, so it's sort of alive?" Hunter asked.

"In a way, yes..." explained the Professor. "It has documented every Seeker's oath, following them through their journeys, transcribing their lives into its very own pages. Some people it has befriended, offered advice too in times of need, while others it has ridiculed and mocked. It has its own agenda and goals rooted in the Seekers' tradition."

"How does it show itself to someone?" asked Elly.

"Let me answer that one," Joe chimed in. "Before I left and had my page erased from the book, it came to me in the middle of the night. I was struggling with my courses, doubting myself like every teenager does. One day I woke up from a wicked dream, there it was on my desk. I opened it, and there was a story for me to read. I can't get into much detail... it was meant for only my eyes..." Uncle Joe spoke slowly as to not overdo himself. "But it changed my life in a positive way."

"Trust in its guidance. It has been with the Seekers since day one."

Calenstine nodded.

"That's so cool." Elly was mesmerized by the concept.

"So, we are Seekers now? Like Mom and Dad were?" Hunter asked his uncle.

"Like I was too," he answered.

"Children, let's leave your uncle to rest. He is still weak and needs to conserve his energy. Please report back to your rooms and let the events of this morning settle on our souls." Calenstine placed the grimoire back into the sack and tied it shut.

The children followed the professor's request. Much had rested on their souls, their minds heavy with wonderment. However, for the first time since coming to the estate, they had gotten many answers.

Elly spent the rest of the afternoon with Trayer, trying to teach the eager pup how to properly play fetch. He was great at retrieving the toy, even returning it to her but he lacked the ability to give up his prized possession. Instead, the mighty pup (who had already grown another foot taller since they first got him) pranced around proudly with it in his slobbery mouth while Elly begged him to drop it.

Hunter sat at the window looking out into the large western forest. So much had happened since they arrived at the mansion. He wondered how it was so easy for his sister to return back to normal, playing with Trayer as if nothing strange had really happened in the last month of their lives.

In the end, he did feel a small ray of hope. They had gotten their uncle back; he and Margot had sworn to take care of them during their time at the mansion. For the first time since his parents' demise, he felt like he had a family once again. No matter how strange and bizarre his journey into the mansion had been, there was no other place in the world where he would rather be at the moment. It was for the first time that he peered out his bedroom window not longing to escape and run away.

He thought of his new friends, Alistair, and the ever-so-gorgeous Liv. His heart beat uncontrollably in his chest as he found himself daydreaming about her beautiful blue eyes. He had made friends, close friends, people who he had already learned to trust and rely on.

Perhaps, he thought, this mansion wasn't as dark and mysterious as it seemed.

"Hunter," Elly broke his concentration. She stood behind him with a bright smile on her face, her hands hiding something behind her back.

"What?" Hunter tried not to act too annoyed.

His little sister dropped a large dusty book on his lap.

"What's this dirty old thing?" his nose twitched from its musty smell.

"I found it on the bookshelf, 'A Seekers Study Guide, A Compilation of First Year Notes.' Excited?" she asked wide smiled.

"You're kidding me, right? You're going to start studying for something we haven't even started?" Hunter shook his head in disbelief.

"It's less than a month away!" she grabbed the book from his lap, jumping back on her bed, happy as could be. "I'll make sure to tell you about everything I learn. That way you can do as good as I do."

"Right," Hunter peered back out the window, hiding a faint smile.

Hunter felt a little apprehension stirring in his stomach. Less than a month away... A whole new school year, with new kids, new teachers, and this thing called the "Enlightenment."

What on earth had they gotten themselves into...

To be continued in:

The
Secret Seekers Society
and
SOLOMON'S SEAL

View other Black Rose Writing titles at www.blackrosewriting.com/books and
use promo code **PRINT** to receive a **20% discount** when purchasing.

BLACK ROSE
writing™